# ANOTHER LOOSE END

"If you are seen here, everyone will be certain you are guilty," said Neville from behind Priscilla.

She rose. "Where is the constable?"

"On his way back to his office, thoroughly chastised, I add, by your comments."

"He is grasping for straws to speak with the children."

Neville held up his hands and chuckled. "Don't lash out at me, Pris. I am in agreement with you on this matter."

"And on this?" She opened her fingers.

He took the button and examined it. "Odd that we did not see this before."

"It was twilight and dawn when we were here. In the bright sunshine, it sparkled like an earthbound star. It could not have been the duke's."

"And it does not belong to anyone in your household?"

"No."

"Then it must belong to the murderer."

She nodded. "Exactly what I deduced, but there is only one problem with that assumption, Neville. There are no military men in Stonehall-on-Sea at this time. The closest garrison is probably in Rye, a day's ride from here."

"So the murderer may not have been from the village."

"That button throws out every theory we or the constable have. If we believe that belongs to the murderer, we are more in the dark than ever." She sighed. "I cannot imagine how this situation could become any worse.

# A RATHER
# NECESSARY END

*Jo Ann Ferguson*

## ZEBRA BOOKS
### Kensington Publishing Corp.
http://www.kensingtonbooks.com

*For Pam Johnson,*
*a dear friend.*
*Thanks for all the laughs we've shared*

# One

The first scream came from the kitchen.

Lady Priscilla Flanders frowned. "Gilbert, will you see what is amiss?"

Her butler hurried out of the room, his gray coattails flapping behind him.

She looked around the table. How could adolescent Daphne and Leah and young Isaac appear so innocent and unsettled at the same time? They had been subdued during the year of mourning for their father and the six months for their grandfather. She would not be surprised if, now that first mourning was over, they intended to set off one prank after another.

"Daphne," Priscilla began, focusing her attention on her eldest, "I have told you—"

Another scream, this one more shrill than the first, burst around the door that opened onto the steps leading down to the kitchen.

Priscilla scowled. The evening meal was, without question, the one time she demanded proper behavior from everyone in her household. This was the time to discuss the day's events and participate in quiet conversation. The children often were busy elsewhere during the day, but the evening meal brought the family back together. This dining room at Mermaid Cottage with its light blue paint offered a serenity she relished.

Usually.

Beginning anew, Priscilla said, "Daphne, if you have let another rat loose in the stillroom—"

Her oldest daughter, who had inherited her guinea-gold locks and blue eyes, shook her head. "Mama, I would not do such a thing now. I did that when I was Isaac's age."

"Isaac?" She looked at her wide-eyed son, who had inherited from her father the title of Lord Emberson, Fifth Earl. At nine years of age, he seemed to grow an inch more each time she looked at him. He already was following in the steps of his trickster sisters.

"Do you think *I* did something to Mrs. Dunham?" he asked with a credulity that might be genuine.

Leah, as always the peacemaker, hurried to add, "I vow, Mama, that we have done nothing to set off Mrs. Dunham. We know how difficult it would be to find another good cook in Stonehall-on-Sea."

A woman screamed. Then another. Then a third.

Mrs. Moore burst into the dining room. The door to the kitchen stairs slammed back against the rosewood sideboard, something that the housekeeper would have chastised one of the maids for. Mrs. Moore ran to the table. She tried to speak, but her breaths came out in furious pants as she pressed her hand to her gray bodice.

"What is it?" Priscilla asked, rising.

"An intruder! In the kitchen!" gasped the housekeeper.

"Really?" Isaac jumped to his feet.

"Sit down, Isaac," Priscilla ordered. "Calm heads are needed just now."

"You must send for the authorities!" cried Mrs. Moore.

"Calm heads, Mrs. Moore."

The housekeeper nodded reluctantly, then shrieked

as someone else did in the kitchen. "He is killing some-one! I know he is. Send for help."

"Constable Forshaw is likely at his supper," Priscilla replied, frowning when she heard scurrying feet through the open door. "Surely one of the footmen can toss this intruder out."

"They tried! He fought them off. He's a madman! You must do something, Lady Priscilla!"

Grabbing his dinner knife, Isaac asked, "Do you want me to deal with him, Mama?"

Priscilla grasped her son by the sleeve before he could race into the melee. If this was not one of the children's pranks . . . Putting her hand over her heart, which was beating at a pace as fierce as Mrs. Moore's panting, she said, "I sent Gilbert to find out what was wrong. He should be able to deal with this."

"Gilbert may be dead. When I fled the kitchen, the blackguard had him pinned against the wall with a sword."

"No longer!" crowed a triumphant voice. The door crashed back against the sideboard again. Every dish rattled. A tall form, cloaked in black, leaped through the doorway, brandishing a bare rapier with a master's skill.

"Mama!" Daphne and Leah screamed and jumped to their feet, reaching for her.

Isaac dove under the table, his knife in hand. He pulled the tablecloth down to cover him, and his plate and silverware clattered to the carpet. A vase with flowers toppled atop them.

The intruder's dark eyes slitted above the dusty ker-chief concealing his lower face as he turned to Mrs. Moore and raised the sword. "I have dealt with the butler's assumption that he could halt me, and now I shall take great pleasure in dealing with you, my lovely."

Mrs. Moore screamed and collapsed in a faint. Priscilla pushed past her daughters to catch her, then looked up. Exasperated, she said, "Really, Neville!"

"How did you recognize me?" he asked, sounding rather vexed. "This disguise was good enough to baffle everyone at Lady Arlington's masked ball last week."

"They must not have noticed your voice. Few highwaymen speak with the education and elegance of the *ton.*"

"But if I had spoken so, I would have frightened you clear away from your senses as well. I didn't want to do that." He chuckled. "But I did frighten you, didn't I?"

"Of course not." She leaned the housekeeper back on the paisley rug and reached for her napkin. Wafting it in the woman's face, she did not look up as her daughters rushed to greet Sir Neville Hathaway. She did not want him to guess how his bizarre arrival had unnerved her, for he would never allow her to forget it. "I have become accustomed to your odd ways. But can't you, just once, knock on the front door like the rest of my callers?"

He pulled the kerchief off to reveal the even features that drew the eyes of marriage-minded misses before their attentive mamas warned them to heed the rumors surrounding Sir Neville Hathaway. He was dashed wealthy, and he treated everyone he met with the same charm, whether a duke at a card table or a girl in a shop; but he was, without question, a black sheep in a family infamous for having more than a full herd of black sheep already.

Born in genteel obscurity, if Priscilla were to believe the stories about him, Neville was said to have worked with Bow Street as a thief-taker and then spent some time on the stage until all his male ancestors died through reckless behavior, when he found himself with a title and enough money to do as he pleased. And what he pleased was to have a grand time with the Polite World and the demi-monde and beyond, for he had not set aside his old friends when he, his title, and his fortune were welcomed into the *ton*.

Sliding the sword back into its sheath, Neville chuckled as he draped his arm over Leah's shoulders. He mussed Isaac's hair as the boy popped out from under the disheveled table and crawled across the sodden spot on the carpet, crushing the flowers.

"I didn't want to disappoint you and your household, Pris," Neville said, chuckling, "with such an ordinary beginning to my call."

"I think they would be far less disappointed if you did something out of the ordinary for *you.*"

"Such as?"

"Not racing harum-scarum through my house might be a start."

"That was funny, Uncle Neville," Isaac said.

Neville picked a carrot out of her son's light brown curls. "Is this the latest style in Stonehall-on-Sea?"

As the children laughed, Priscilla bent to check her prone housekeeper. Neville was not the children's real uncle, but they had called him that since they were babes. Priscilla's late husband had introduced her to this outrageous man shortly before they were married. There were those who considered Sir Neville Hathaway an improper comrade for a vicar, but neither Priscilla nor her husband, the late Reverend Dr. Lazarus Flanders, had ever judged a person by gossip. The two men had been dear friends, and Neville had become Priscilla's friend as well. She appreciated his wit and his sense of humor . . . *usually.*

"You're looking good, Pris." Neville grinned as he came around the table. "Can I believe you have a lover stashed somewhere in the house?"

"Neville, will you watch what you are saying? The children are listening."

"Ah, they know all about lovers and such." He winked at her daughters, who giggled. "After all, Daphne is about ready to be fired off into the Season."

"That's right," Daphne hurried to say as she rushed to stand beside him. "Tell Mama that she should let me go before this year's Season is finished."

Priscilla gave Neville a scowl that halted even his teasing.

Quickly he said, "I trust—as you should—your mother to decide what is best."

"Thank you," Priscilla replied as she wondered how long it would take for Mrs. Moore to regain her senses.

"So why are you looking so well, Pris?" he persisted, much to the children's delight, if she was to judge by their wide smiles. "Do you have a lover in mind? I do hope it is not that humdrum Mr. Tiddles whom I met on my last call to Stonehall-on-Sea. By all that's blue, how can you receive a caller whose name sounds like a pet cat's?"

"Neville, please curb your perpetual prying into my personal life. My thoughts are solely on reviving Mrs. Moore, who has had a fit of the vapors at the very sight of you."

"Not the most complimentary thing you have ever said to me."

"But certainly one of the most honest."

"Lady Priscilla!" Gilbert bolted into the dining room, holding the torn sleeve of his coat to his arm.

"Over here, Gilbert." She was amused to see that, even now, when he must believe he had been attacked by an interloper, her butler wore an expression of no more than mild disquiet.

"I fear I must report there is an intruder somewhere in the house. He attacked——" He halted when Neville turned and bowed. "Oh, Sir Neville, it is only you. I should have guessed as much."

"'Twas a good fight you put up to defend the house and persons of Lady Priscilla and her children," Neville replied, tipping his black cap to the butler, then tossing it to a footman who was staring, wide-eyed and wide-mouthed. "Most exemplary, indeed, if you thought you were fighting a true trespasser. But rest assured that I have not yet gone on account as a land pirate." Glancing down at the senseless house-keeper, he said, "I do believe Lady Priscilla would appreciate it greatly if you have *sal volatile* brought for Mrs. Moore."

In quick order, aided by the smelling salts, Mrs. Moore was brought to her senses, received Neville's apology, and retired to her rooms to rest. With his long face even more dolorous than usual, Gilbert sent the gawking maids to bring food and two clean place settings—one for Neville and one for Isaac whose food was scattered across the rug.

The children chattered like a flock of birds as the girls demanded to know the news from Town and Isaac pestered Neville for the gift that he always brought for the boy. Neville calmed them with some interesting gossip that was—Priscilla noted—appropriate for their young ears. Then he presented Isaac with a tin soldier to match the one he had brought last time he had called . . . shortly after her husband's death.

Priscilla toyed with her roast beef as Neville ate with enthusiasm. Without his ebony cloak, he was dressed as befitted a gentleman spending the day and night at his club. His hair was as dark as his well-made coat and his eyes nearly the same shade as the overturned earth in her garden. Tall and broad-shouldered, he drew the maids' eyes.

"Why are you smiling, Pris?" he asked as he paused between bites.

"When did you last dine?"

"What day is this?"

She arched a single brow. "Your streak of good fortune must have been a long one."

"It was." He gave her a boastful smile.

"Then it will not damage your pockets greatly to buy gifts to soothe my household."

He wagged his fork at her. "You are a dashed hard woman, Pris." He chuckled. "And a dashed smart one as well. Only you would take note of my *voice* to unmask me. What small gifts do you suggest?"

She counted off the staff on her fingers and the largess that would be most appropriate. Lace for handkerchiefs for the kitchen maids and the tweener who assisted Mrs. Moore as well as Mrs. Dunham. A book of poetry for Mrs. Dunham, who fancied it. Two bottles of an excellent vintage for the housekeeper and the butler. Two more bottles of a lesser quality for the pair of footmen who were Gilbert's responsibility.

"And for you?" he asked when she finished the list, which brought a groan from him and laughter from the children as she cited each item.

She smiled coolly. "A sincere apology will be sufficient."

"I am sorry that I unsettled your household."

"Good."

"Which obviously needed some shaking up."

"Is that why you decided to call after all this time?"

He grinned. "I was traveling this way, so I thought I would stop by and see you and the children tonight."

"Can't you stay longer, Uncle Neville?" asked Leah. "You haven't been to visit us for so long."

"I shall try to stop by again another time soon," he said, his smile fading.

He had disrupted her house simply to get some food after a marathon of gambling? She should have had Gilbert toss him out. Neville was a dear friend, albeit an *intolerable,* dear friend, so she must make him feel welcome at Mermaid Cottage.

Priscilla pushed back her chair and said to the maid who was picking up the broken flowers, "I will take that, June. If you will excuse me . . ."

"Where are you off to?" asked Neville.

"To pick some flowers to replace the ruined ones."

"In the middle of a meal? If I said something to distress you—"

"Don't be absurd. 'Tis the middle of *your* meal. As you can see, I have finished. I shall return before dessert is served in the parlor."

Leaving him chatting with the children, Priscilla went down the stairs to the kitchen. She did not pause to appease Mrs. Dunham. That would be Neville's task, and he would be wise to do so, judging by how loudly Mrs. Dunham was clattering the pots.

Priscilla hurried into the garden when she heard Mrs. Dunham snarl a curse. Muriel, the younger maid, followed, offering to help. Priscilla suspected the girl, who was Daphne's age, had a good reason to want to escape.

The garden was peaceful, without even a sound drifting from the houses on either side of the garden wall. The cottage's stable was between the back wall of the garden and the chalk cliffs that led down to the shore. Its stone walls were dark from decades of salt air. Her garden was her refuge. Here, she did not have to mediate between Isaac and Leah who seemed to disagree about everything. Nor did she have to tell Daphne—yet again—that waiting another year to go to London for the Season was a good idea.

"Gather some lily of the valley from by the well," Priscilla ordered. "I shall collect other flowers from the beds."

"Yes, my lady." The girl skipped toward the well where the flowers were blooming.

Priscilla went toward the back wall. The flowers there had not yet closed for the night, so she decided to gather some of the crocuses and hyacinths blooming around the fritillaria. The white crocuses with purple hyacinths and red fritillaria would be lovely.

A shadow stretched across the flower bed. Not a shadow, she realized. A person was lying with outstretched arms in the very center of her flowers. A man. Had someone in a drunken stupor wandered from the Dog and Crown public house into her garden?

"Wot be wrong with 'im?" asked Muriel, her hands filled with flowers.

"I am not sure." She reached down to shake the man's shoulder. With a gasp, she pulled back her hand, but it was too late. It was already stained with the blood that was soaking into the ground, as scarlet as the fritillaria blossoms drooping toward the dead man.

Behind her, Muriel screamed.

# Two

Neville frowned as he came to his feet in Priscilla's pretty green parlor. Who was screaming now and why? No other intruder would be coming through the kitchen tonight. Stonehall-on-Sea was not Blackheath with criminals waiting to ambush the unwary.

"Stay here," he ordered when the children began throwing questions in his direction.

Walking out of the parlor, he motioned to Gilbert who was rushing toward him and said, "Watch the children."

"Lady Priscilla will not be pleased to have another jest played on her tonight."

"If it is a jest, it is not mine. Stay here and watch over the children."

Another scream erupted through the house.

"Very well, sir," Gilbert said, taking his place by the parlor door. The butler was clearly relieved to take on this duty. One incident an evening was enough for the staid man.

Neville took the steps down to the kitchen three at a time. As he bounced through the kitchen door, he saw a slender brunette holding her apron over her eyes. Two girls, their hair falling from beneath their caps, stood beside the door that led outside. One was shrieking like an off-key banshee.

He pushed past an immobile footman. When the

screeching maid refused to move, he picked her up by the elbows and shifted her aside. She gave another scream, then folded to the floor.

"Mrs. Dunham, get the *sal volatile*. It is upstairs in the dining room." He grimaced. It had not been his intention to witness so many of Priscilla's staff fainting.

He did not wait to see if she obeyed. He took a lantern hanging near the kitchen hearth and lit it. He started to walk out but stopped when a hand gripped his sleeve. In astonishment, he turned to find the other maid holding onto him.

"Don't go out there, Sir Neville. There be something awful out there," groaned the girl. "Muriel . . . She saw it. She started 'owlin' and ran back in 'ere. I asked 'er 'ow she could leave Lady Priscilla—"

He pushed past the maid and into the garden. In the lowering twilight, nothing appeared out of the ordinary. Flowers were bobbing on the gentle breeze. Hoping he was not stepping on anything irreplaceable, for Priscilla would have his head if he ruined her plantings, he ran toward a silhouette near the back wall.

Priscilla's silhouette, he realized, for the last of the day's light played off her blonde hair. It was an appealing silhouette, for although she must have seen more than thirty-five years, she retained her youthful figure and visage. Her somber black gown accented the golden wealth of her hair which was, as always, in a prim twist at her nape. She seemed intent on something in a flower bed. His stomach cramped when he saw what was in front of her.

"Are you all right?" he asked.

"As well as can be expected when I have found that." She pointed toward the ground.

Holding the lantern high, he looked at the man lying in the flowers. The man's coat was of an excellent cut and, when not soaked with blood, must have been a dark green. His silver hair was matted with drying blood, but it could not hide that his head was dented in a manner that suggested a cudgel had been swung against his skull.

Neville looked at Priscilla. Her usually pink cheeks were ashen. "Do you recognize him?"

"Yes, he is—was the Duke of Meresden."

"What is he doing in the middle of your flower bed?"

"I think it is obvious," she said with a shudder. "He is dead."

Neville squatted. "I can see that quite readily, Pris. My question should have been: What is he doing in the middle of your flower bed instead of being dead somewhere else?"

"I doubt if he had much choice in the matter."

"Was he a regular caller on you?"

She shook her head. "The duke has never called here. I have seen him about the village, of course. His estate is east of here along the shore."

Taking the lantern, she walked away. The gate between her garden and the one belonging to the Muir brothers next door was open.

"What are you checking for?" Neville asked.

"How he got in my garden. This gate is open." She crossed the space between the walls in less than a dozen steps. "The other gate is open as well."

"Is that customary?"

"No," she said coming back to where he still squatted beside the corpse.

"So he could have come from either direction."

"He is facing the Ackerley house, and the blow was to the back of his head. Assuming that his assailant was behind him, then it is likely whoever attacked him must have come in through the gate that connects this garden and the Muir brothers'."

"Unless he was turning to face his attacker." He pointed to the man's skull. "The blow is not directly to the back, but closer to the ear." He reached to turn the body over.

Priscilla seized his arm. "Neville, do you think you should be disturbing him?"

"I doubt if he will mind."

"But the constable might. He is certain to want to see this exactly as I discovered it."

"True." He stood, pulled out a handkerchief, and handed it to her.

"Thank you." She wiped both palms as she called, "Muriel, will you—"

"Muriel has taken leave of her senses."

"I need to send someone for Gilbert."

"Gilbert is standing guard on the children." He gave her a lopsided smile. *"Now* I understand why you demanded such an expensive apology. When I heard the screeches, I wanted to make sure they remained safe."

She put her hand on his shoulder. "Thank you."

Priscilla took a step toward the kitchen, then looked back at Neville who was once again crouching by the body. Could she trust him to leave the corpse face-down? He was as curious as Isaac, but Neville would know the importance of allowing the constable to see the duke as she had found him. She hurried inside and sent a footman to take Gilbert's place, so the butler could come to the garden.

Mrs. Dunham was helping Muriel to her feet and to a chair by the inglenook. The cook asked, "Is it true? Is there a dead man in the garden?"

"Yes. Did you see or hear anything?" Priscilla asked.

She shook her head, her face nearly the shade of

her red hair. "I was so angry at Sir Neville for playin' 'is pranks on us that I was stormin' 'bout the kitchen. Didn't see anythin' either."

"What of the girls or the footmen?"

"I asked them, but they saw nothin'."

Priscilla nodded. Interrogating witnesses was a task best left to Constable Forshaw. Telling Mrs. Dunham to have plenty of hot water for tea and to have someone bring some brandy to the parlor—for Priscilla suspected they would need something stronger than wine—she dipped her hands in the bucket by the door. Mrs. Dunham moaned as Priscilla tried to scrub the blood from her palm.

"You sent for me, my lady?" asked Gilbert. His face was a bit paler than usual, but he remained imperturbable.

"Gilbert, please send for Constable Forshaw."

Her butler nodded, and she noted a tic by one eye. "I shall send young Juster at once. He is swifter of foot than Layden."

"Thank you. When the constable arrives, please send him to the garden."

"Of course, my lady." He paused, then added, "Miss Daphne is not happy about being kept in the parlor when she is curious about what has happened."

"Send Juster for the constable. I will placate her."

Priscilla followed the butler up the stairs and into the dining room. Stepping around the wet spot where the vase had fallen, she went to the parlor. Lamps were lit, blinding her eyes that had become accustomed to the dusk.

"Mama!" cried Daphne as she ran to the door. "Gilbert said Uncle Neville told him that we were not to set a foot outside this parlor."

"An order I would have given myself." She cupped her daughter's cheek, then pulled back her hand when she saw the bloodstains on it. "Daphne, stay here. Keep your brother and sister here."

"But what is happening, Mama? I heard Gilbert tell Juster to go for the constable."

"I will explain later, but, for now, you must remain here."

Leah inched forward. "Are we in any danger?"

Clasping her hands behind her back so that the children did not catch sight of the dried blood, she said, "I will know more after Constable Forshaw arrives."

Isaac puffed up his thin chest. "*I* will watch over everyone."

"Thank you." She looked out the door and at Gilbert.

The butler nodded, although she had not spoken a word. Whoever had murdered the duke would not get past the butler while Gilbert still breathed.

She headed back to the garden, hoping that Gilbert's resolve to oversee this house and her family was not tested more tonight.


Constable Radley Forshaw could not hide his vexation at being dragged away from his dinner to call at Dr. Flanders's house on the road leading from the village and toward the shore. Tonight, his plate had held roast chicken, a rare luxury for a man who had to depend on the generosity of those in the shire to supplement his paltry income. He did not need Lady Priscilla's footman bursting in and ordering him to come and check what the man claimed was a murder.

Murder? In Stonehall-on-Sea? The only murder was that fine chicken growing cold on his plate. And it was most definitely a crime to leave it there in its coagulating gravy.

His irritation added to the thump of his fist against the door of the elegant house that stood between two much smaller cottages. This house was called Mermaid Cottage, but that was not an accurate name, for it was twice the size of its neighbors combined. Still, it was a simple house compared with the ones owned by the peerage who had flocked, along with the Prince Regent, to England's southern shore to partake of the sea air.

Why wasn't someone answering? He had his speech prepared for Lady Priscilla. He had practiced and refined it on every step from his small house on the far side of St. Elizabeth's Church. Although he had not considered Lady Priscilla likely to surrender to panic, for he had seen her composure when she had attended the memorial service for her late husband, she had to be told—lady though she might be—that disturbing a man who was about to savor a roast chicken dinner was something that must not be repeated.

The door opened just as he was about to knock again. He strode inside, expecting to see pandemonium. Instead Lady Priscilla's butler Gilbert stood there, impeccable from his gray coat to the shiny buckles at the knees of his breeches. The house was quiet, save for hushed voices from the parlor.

"Lady Priscilla asked that you attend her in the back garden, Constable Forshaw," the butler intoned so calmly that the constable would have sworn that he was announcing that tea was to be served.

Twice, Constable Forshaw had come to this house and been offered tea. The first time had been when the lady's younger two children had gotten themselves up a tree, unable to climb back down. On the other occasion, it had been because the lad had disappeared, only to be found next door with the Muir brothers. Lady Priscilla had invited him to stay for tea on both occasions so that her offspring could apologize to him.

"The back garden?" Constable Forshaw repeated.

"That is where the body was discovered. If you will follow June . . ." The butler gestured toward a maid who stepped out of the dining room.

The constable nodded but glanced back at Gilbert. The butler stood beside the parlor door, needing only the uniform and furry hat to be a Beefeater. There was no doubt the man was guarding something, but what?

Constable Forshaw craned his neck to see what was within the chamber but was rewarded only with a cramp in his shoulder. Once he saw what was in the back garden, he would come back here. His roast chicken was already ruined, so there was no reason for him to hurry.

"This way, Constable," murmured the dark-haired maid. One of the Bailey girls, if he was not mistaken. He noticed how her hand trembled as she reached for the latch on the door at the far side of the dining room.

He nodded to Lady Priscilla's cook and the other servants who were clustered by the kitchen hearth. They simply stared as he walked behind June to the back door. If their eyes had not moved, they could have been a life-size portrait. What was going on here?

"Thank you for coming so quickly," Lady Priscilla said as she stepped out of the shadows beyond the door.

"At last," mumbled a man who was stooped over a flower bed by the rear wall.

Priscilla fired a scowl at Neville. Wanting to tell him to have a more magnanimous attitude when the constable had risen from his supper, if the gravy spotting his waistcoat offered a hint to what he had been doing, she said, "We appreciate your quick arrival."

"I hope the children are not in an awkward situation again."

Under other circumstances, she might have found the constable's statement amusing. "Constable Forshaw, didn't Juster explain to you why I needed you here?"

"He muttered something about someone being killed, but he had few details."

"Then come and look for yourself," Neville ordered.

When the constable glanced at her, she said, "That is a friend of my late husband. Sir Neville Hathaway."

He nodded again, still wearing that perplexed expression. She walked with him toward where Neville was staring at the body that was almost lost in the shadows. Tapping Neville on the shoulder, she was not surprised that, although he edged aside, he did not stand.

The constable leaned forward. When Neville handed him the lantern, Constable Forshaw stiffened and choked, "He's dead!"

Priscilla put her hand on the constable's arm. He was a relative newcomer to Stonehall-on-Sea, and she appreciated the fact—tonight more than ever—that he had some education. His predecessor would have created a bumble-bath, destroying any chance of finding out what had happened in the moments before the duke died.

"That is what we have been trying to tell you, Constable Forshaw," she said quietly.

"But he is *dead!*"

"Would you like some brandy, Constable Forshaw? It might steady your nerves." She took the glass Layden was holding on a tray as if this were a pleasant gathering. No doubt, Gilbert had sent the footman. She must remember to thank her butler later.

Constable Forshaw took a gulp of the brandy, then coughed. With an embarrassed glance at Neville, he swallowed the rest.

"Want another?" Neville asked.

Looking as if he would like to down the whole bottle, the constable shook his head and knelt beside Neville. "A blow to the head, I would say."

"Tilt the lantern here, and you can see where the blow was struck."

"When did this happen?"

Before Priscilla could reply, she heard footfalls and a soft voice ask, "Lady Priscilla?"

The voice was hesitant, but Priscilla recognized it. Only two people spoke with an American accent here. Thomas Ackerley and his sister Martha who had been leasing the house next door for the past year. With the increasing hostility between England and her onetime colonies, the Ackerleys had found it wiser to remain here than to try to return across the sea. Thomas was providing for them by tutoring several youngsters in the village, including Isaac.

Priscilla went to where Martha stood at the gate separating the garden from the Ackerley cottage. Martha was a beauty, with fresh, pale skin and hair only a shade darker than Priscilla's. She could not have been more than a handful of years older than Daphne, but the two girls had not developed a friendship. Martha seldom left her house unless she was going to the village to get something for her brother.

"I think it would be better if you did not come in," Priscilla said.

"Thomas thought he saw the constable at your door."

"That is why you should not come in. There has

been a terrible . . . That is—" She forced a smile. "There has been an accident."

"Oh, my! I hope no one was seriously hurt."

The constable's voice reached through the twilight. "Lady Priscilla, if you please. I have some other questions."

Priscilla took Martha's hand and squeezed it. "I will give you a look-in tomorrow and tell you all about it."

"All right, but Thomas is sure to have questions."

"Tell him that I shall answer them when I bring Isaac for his Latin lesson."

Martha tried to look past her, but Priscilla pushed the gate closed and latched it. She started to turn, then reached up and dropped the bar. In all the years she had lived here, this was the first time she had locked either gate. She looked at her house. With rose vines climbing up its back wall and beneath the thatched roof, the stone house had become her home and her haven after Lazarus's death. She wondered what he would make of this. He always had been pragmatic about everything that happened. She must do her best to emulate him.

"Lady Priscilla!"

For a moment, she thought the impatient voice belonged to Constable Forshaw. Then she realized it was too deep. Peering through the dusk, she saw someone by the other gate. Walking past the constable who was coming to his feet, she went to where two elderly men were waiting.

"Good evening," Priscilla said, not knowing what else to say. But she did know that Constable Forshaw—and Neville who continued to examine the body without touching it—wanted to keep everyone out of the garden.

She closed her eyes when a lamp was held up. Blinking, she tried to see, even though she knew what her other neighbors looked like. The Muir brothers had lived in the cottage on this side when she had come here as a young bride. Twins, they were almost identical with their gray hair, hawkish noses, and perfectly pressed clothes. Only the quizzing glass that Irwin wore allowed her to tell him apart from his brother, Walden.

"What is going on?" asked Irwin, the elder by only a half-hour.

"We saw the constable arriving," added Walden.

"Nothing is wrong with the children, is there?"

"If you need us to help search for the young lad, we are willing."

"He is not at our house this time."

"We would have told you that straightaway."

Priscilla intruded to say, for the brothers could continue in this singsong dialogue for hours, "No, the problem is not with one of the children. Rather it is . . ." She gestured toward the ground.

Both Muir brothers stared at the body in the flowers. As always, Irwin spoke first. " 'Tis the duke," he said in his deep voice.

"What is he doing there?" asked Walden.

"Is he injured?"

Constable Forshaw clearly was losing patience. "Gentlemen, return to your house."

Irwin said, "Not until we find out what is amiss with the duke. He is a friend of many years."

"Many, many years," seconded Walden. "At least four decades."

"Almost five."

"Closer to four."

"Four and a half."

Walden nodded, placated at the compromise. "At least four and a half decades. So please tell us why you are letting the poor man lie here in Lady Priscilla's garden."

"The duke was attacked," the constable said in a clipped tone. "If you will return to your house, please, and let me handle this."

The two men went back into their own garden. As Priscilla closed that gate and barred it as well, she heard mutters of "presumptuous pup" and "young sprig." She hoped Constable Forshaw had not heard the disparaging words.

Priscilla was surprised when the constable asked her to sit on a bench not far from the duke's corpse. How long was the constable going to let it remain there?

The constable folded his hands behind his back. "I must ask you some questions, Lady Priscilla."

"Of course."

"Would you mind if I write down your answers?"

"No . . . No, I suppose not."

She was astonished when he opened a bag hooked to his belt. Taking out some folded paper, he set a bottle of ink and the lantern on the bench. Then he sat beside her and opening the bottle, asked, "Did anyone see you find the body?"

"Muriel was with me."

"Muriel?"

"Muriel Foster, who works in the kitchen. I came out here to get some flowers for the table."

He was trying to keep up with what she was saying. "She was with you when you found the body?"

"Yes."

"Right here?"

Priscilla shook her head. "No, she was by the well."

"So she did not see you find the body."

"No. I was planning to pick some crocuses, and I stumbled over the duke's body—almost quite literally."

Constable Forshaw glanced back, and she turned.

As she had expected, most of the servants had inched out into the garden to see and hear what was happening. Only Gilbert was not in sight. He would not abandon his post by the parlor door.

Her attention returned to the constable when he asked, "So no one can state if the duke was dead before you encountered him?"

"Someone can! The person who struck him."

"Which could be you."

"Me?" She saw every eye, but Neville's, turn toward her. Neville was still squatting next to the corpse as if he expected to discern some answers to this appalling puzzle simply by staring at it. She was glad he was not hovering over her. He respected her ability to handle herself in any situation—a trait a vicar's wife needed. However, she would have been glad to have him leap to her defense just now.

"He *is* in your garden, my lady. Do you deny that?"

"Of course not, but I did not do the heinous deed, Constable. I was with my children and Sir Neville in the dining room at the time the duke must have been attacked."

He frowned. "So you heard nothing?"

"There was a commotion within the house."

Neville came to his feet and brushed his hands against his breeches. "Constable, I was the cause of the commotion in Lady Priscilla's house. A jest with her children."

Constable Forshaw glanced from the gentleman's taut face to Lady Priscilla's pale one. One look would suggest that they were speaking the truth, but he had learned—through humiliating lessons upon his arrival in the village—that looks can be deceptive. He recalled muffled chuckles about how he had been a fool to believe someone hid in the church's steeple. Why shouldn't he have believed the upstanding and otherwise honest residents who had asked him to check? He would not be so gullible again.

He blew on the paper to dry the ink, then folded it and put it in his bag along with the stoppered bottle of ink. Standing, he said, "Lady Priscilla, I regret to inform you that I must consider you a suspect in this crime."

"Me?" she gasped. From behind her, where her household staff was eavesdropping openly, came soft moans of despair.

"Now see here," began Sir Neville.

Lady Priscilla rose and put her hand on the gentleman's arm. "I think it would be for the best if we listen to what Constable Forshaw has to say. I would like to know why he considers me the one who did this horrible thing."

"Until I speak to others and discern the truth of what happened here," he said, aware of how everyone in the garden thought he was silly to accuse the late vicar's wife, "I must be honest and say that you are a suspect."

"I must be honest and say that you are mistaken," Sir Neville retorted.

Constable Forshaw glanced at him and then back to Lady Priscilla who was not hysterical in the face of his accusations. He was unsure if that meant she was innocent and knew she would be proved so or that she was guilty and did not want to give him any additional cause to believe that.

"Do not leave Stonehall-on-Sea, my lady," he said quietly, "for that will look bad."

"I do not have any plans to do so." She looked at the man beside her. "What of Sir Neville?"

"He should remain in Stonehall-on-Sea, too, until we know what happened."

Sir Neville said, "I will stay here."

"But, Neville, you said you were only calling for the—" Her gaze slipped away. For a moment, Constable Forshaw thought she might be trying to protect the gentleman, but then she said, "Neville, you are welcome to stay in Mermaid Cottage as long as necessary."

"That is good," Constable Forshaw said, glad that this had been handled so easily. "I hope this will not disrupt your plans, Sir Neville."

"You may rest assured, Constable," Lady Priscilla said before the gentleman could reply, " that *my* plans will not be disrupted."

"Your plans?"

"I plan to find the real murderer so that I can clear my name."

Constable Forshaw cleared his throat and looked again to Sir Neville. Surely the gentleman would help him impress on Lady Priscilla that this was not a task for her. Swallowing bile in his throat, he did not want to add—even to himself—that it was not a chore he relished either.

The gentleman said nothing, so he replied, "That might not be wise, Lady Priscilla."

"Do you expect me to go to the gallows for a crime I did not commit?"

He shook his head, dismayed. "No, no, my lady. I meant only that you should leave the handling of this horrible crime to a professional."

"An excellent idea."

He smiled. He did not like the idea of her getting involved with a criminal . . . unless, of course, she was one. He did not want to believe that, but the previous constable, who had held the post since King George III was a young man, had told him that everyone must be considered a suspect in a crime until they were proved not guilty. Although Constable Forshaw had argued that English law dictated a man was innocent until proved guilty, the old constable had said that an investigation and a trial were very separate matters.

"I am glad you see that, my lady," he said. "It is best to leave this in skilled hands."

"I agree." She turned to the gentleman. "Neville, with your experience, I believe you are the very best one to help me with this."

Sir Neville smiled broadly, and Constable Forshaw, deciding he was the most unfortunate constable in all of England, simply groaned.

# Three

"Isaac, you cannot use the duke's tragic death as an excuse not to attend to your lessons with Mr. Ackerley." Priscilla tightened her hold on her squirming son and finished hooking the buttons at his knees.

"But he didn't die, Mama. He was"—his voice dropped to a whisper—"he was murdered."

Priscilla stood. "I realize that, Isaac. If you do not hurry, you shall be late for your lesson." As he started out of the parlor, she added, "Juster is waiting to escort you."

"Escort me? Next door? Is it that dangerous?"

She did not want to frighten him, but she would not lie. "I think it is best you don't go out without someone else."

He grimaced. "But, Mama, if someone sees Juster with me, I will be teased for being a baby."

"Would you prefer I walked with you? I told Miss Ackerley that I would call on her today."

"All right," he said after considering the idea. "Please spend a long time talking with her. Otherwise . . ."

"I am certain that I shall spend enough time to prevent anyone from thinking poorly of you." She smiled and put her hand on his shoulder. "However, Juster will escort you home."

"Mama—"

She held up her hand. "He will meet you at the Ackerleys' back door and bring you through the garden."

"Really?" His eyes twinkled with excitement.

"You must come directly into the house. Constable Forshaw intends to go out there after he finishes speaking with Mrs. Dunham and her staff. Nothing must be touched until he checks whatever he intends to."

"Nothing?" That twinkle brightened. "Do you mean the dead duke is still out there?"

Priscilla wondered what it was about young boys that gave them such a morbid turn of mind, for Isaac was always bringing home dead frogs, fish, and insects and talking about other distasteful objects he had chanced upon. Quietly she said, "Of course the duke is not still there. Someone from Meresden Court came last night to take the body away."

"Where?"

She gave him a gentle shove toward the door. If she allowed him to, he would keep this conversation going until it was too late for his lesson. As well, she did not want to discuss how ignobly the duke had been carted away in the back of a wagon. Such a lack of decency seemed a final indignity for the kind man.

Telling Isaac to wait by the front door, Priscilla went to get her bonnet. Once the constable finished his work, the Muir brothers could come and plant new flowers where hers had been crushed by the duke's corpse. No sign of the murder would be visible by nightfall.

*No sign outside of the house.* Within, it was too quiet. The servants were hush-footed and spoke no louder than a murmur. Her daughters had developed a sudden interest in embroidery that kept them seated in the solar, but they had flinched as one when she went in to check on them earlier.

Neville had left a message that he was going to

spend the day with Constable Forshaw. She hoped the rumor that Neville had served as a Bow Street Runner was true. Constable Forshaw had been successful in halting poachers and making sure any drunks got home, but she had seen his doubts about his ability to find the duke's murderer.

Her son was talking intently with Juster when she reached the door. The footman glanced in her direction, wearing such a guilty expression that one would believe he was the culprit the constable sought. Her son was grinning, and she surmised that Juster had been informing Isaac of every detail of what he had witnessed last night. When she returned home from taking Isaac to his lesson and completing her own errands, she would ask Gilbert and Mrs. Moore to remind the staff that some of what they had seen and heard was not appropriate for a nine-year-old boy with a vivid imagination.

The day was sunny with only a few clouds perched on the horizon where the sky and the sea merged into a hazy gray. With the breeze coming off the water, the air had a pleasant zest. It also carried voices from the Muir house, and she heard the familiar rhythm of the brothers' conversation.

"Is it true . . . ?" Isaac clamped his mouth closed when she frowned. He should know better than to speak on this public way of gossip the servants shared with him.

The Ackerleys' house was as much a twin to the Muirs' as the two brothers were to each other. Both were constructed of stone. Windows were few and narrow, and the upper story must have very low ceilings. A wall surrounded the front garden and connected to the one around Priscilla's garden. Lazarus had told her that a past owner of the house they had purchased before leaving Stonehall-on-Sea for London, had the two houses built for his two mothers-in-law, so he could keep them out of his home. It was as good an explanation as any.

Lazarus always seemed to know the history of Stonehall-on-Sea. It was not simply because he was responsible for the church records. He had liked the people here and cared about their well-being. That kind heart was what had first drawn her to him. During their marriage, she had learned that he would listen to his heart and follow it, even as he was being pragmatic. She admired that in him.

Priscilla knocked on the door, then said, "Isaac, you should not speak with either Miss Ackerley or Mr. Ackerley about anything you have seen or heard in our house since our meal last night."

"I know that, Mama." He frowned, clearly offended that she felt she must speak to him of this.

Martha Ackerley answered the door, as she always did. That familiarity offered Priscilla more solace than she had expected.

"Lady Priscilla!" Martha gasped.

"You look astounded to see us. It is time for Isaac's Latin lesson."

"I had thought . . . That is . . ." She gulped, then said, "My lord, Mr. Ackerley is waiting for you in his study."

As Isaac walked away with all the enthusiasm of a convict on his way to putting his head in a noose, Priscilla said, "Martha, you did not need to address my son so formally when he comes for his lessons. He does not need to think that his title gives him *carte blanche* to do as he pleases."

"But he is an earl."

"He has the title, that is true. However, he has much to learn before he is ready to take on the obligations that my father once handled with such ease."

Martha nodded and wrung her hands as she had

done in the garden last night. "May I ask you a question?"

"Of course."

"Is it true that Constable Forshaw is going to question all of us again?"

"I didn't realize that he had questioned you."

"Yes, both of us. This morning." She paced from the large hearth to the settee beneath the parlor's sole window. "Now I have heard that he has not finished interrogating us."

"I don't know his plans, but I collect that he will do all he must to capture the person who killed the duke."

She shivered. "He asks such personal questions, and he seems perturbed when I cannot answer them."

"What sort of questions?"

"He asked if I looked out the kitchen window when I was preparing supper last night. I am sure that I must have. I mean, I usually do. It's just that I cannot recall if I did last night. And if I did, then I cannot say when I did."

Priscilla grasped Martha by the shoulders. "You are fretting too much. No one expects you to remember every detail of what was an ordinary day until I found the duke."

"But I do not want to say or do the wrong thing."

"Just be as honest as you can, and you will have done the very best you can." She rubbed her hands together as Martha had.

"Do you think the constable can find this person he seeks?"

"I hope so." She glanced out the window that offered a view of her garden wall. "I truly hope so."


The Dog and Crown could have been any public house anywhere in England. At this early hour, it was deserted save for two old men playing chess in one corner where sunshine came through the window in the thick walls. The screen was pulled down over the bar, warning that the bartender was not serving.

Odd, Neville thought as he crossed the dusky room, edging around wobbly tables and benches that were worn smooth by the many people who had sat on them. He would have guessed there would be a crowd here to gossip about the duke's death.

Priscilla had apologized to him at breakfast for the delay in his travel. He smiled. This hiatus was as good an excuse as any to see how she and her children were faring a year after Lazarus's death. His smile disappeared. This had been the longest year he had ever lived. He had left Priscilla and her family to mourn the good man they had lost, because he had feared sharing his grief would only make their burden heavier. So he had kept it to himself, even as he wondered how they were doing.

"Pubkeeper?" Neville called to the men.

One hooked a thumb toward a door to the left of the bar.

"Thank you."

All he got in return was a grunt. He heard the click of chess pieces as he went to knock on the door.

It opened before the echo of his knock vanished. A bent man with white hair that looked as thick as the public house's thatched roof peered out, but he kept the door ajar only far enough for him to stick his head out. The apron he wore over his simple shirt and breeches identified him as the pubkeeper.

"Who be ye?" the old man asked.

"Neville Hathaway. May I speak with you?"

The old man eyed him up and down. "I don't know ye."

"I am visiting Lady Priscilla Flanders. Dr. Flanders was a friend."

As he had expected, the names eased the man's distrust. "Ask me wot ye want to know."

"Can we talk over some ale?"

The old man hesitated, then nodded. "Come along."

"Back there?" He pointed toward the room behind the door.

"M'boys are back there."

A voice called, "Let'm in, Kenyon. May'ap 'e can tell us more about what 'appened to 'Is Grace."

The pubkeeper, who must be Kenyon, hesitated, then threw the door open wide.

Neville was not surprised to see a dozen men, dressed in the rough clothing of farmers and laborers, sitting and leaning on kegs and wooden cases. When he saw the lettering on one case, he glanced at Kenyon, who lowered his eyes. Neville wanted to calm the man, for every public house in southern England had a few cases of smuggled French wine and brandy hidden in a back room.

"Good morning," Neville said as the men stared at him. He did not expect much welcome, especially now.

"Did ye see 'Is Grace dead in Lady Priscilla's garden?" asked a young man from the right side. His question earned him scowls from his mates.

Acting as if he had not seen the uneasy looks, Neville said, "I did."

"Said 'is 'ead was bashed in like a squash."

Knowing that they would be as interested in the details of the duke's murder as young Isaac was, Neville gave the men enough to prattle about. He kept anything to himself that might jeopardize the constable's investigation.

"And," he finished, "there seems to be no clue as to who did this horrible thing or why."

"Bein' said that Lady Priscilla put out 'Is Grace's lights with a whack to the nob," a tall, thin man said.

"What reason would she have to kill the duke?"

Kenyon, the pubkeeper, nodded. "There is that. She 'as been kind to each one of us, even after 'er 'usband was sent off to London to preach at St. Julian's."

There was a general rumble of agreement and something Neville guessed was disappointment. No man wanted to send Lady Priscilla to the gallows, but their fury and frustration at the Duke of Meresden's death needed a focus.

"Mr. Kenyon," Neville said as the other men talked among themselves, "I would like to speak with you, if I may."

"All right." The old man gave him a wary look, but went with him back into the main room of the public house. Leaning one elbow on the bar, he said, "Say wot ye need to, 'Athaway."

"Was there anyone in here last night who may have been drinking a bit more than usual?"

Kenyon scratched his side, then the top of his head. "Jes the regular lot. They 'ad a few pints. No more. I can check with Lenore who works servin' at night, but I don't remember seein' any strangers stoppin' in last night."

"Strangers?" Neville smiled coldly. "I am not speaking of strangers but of the residents of Stonehall-on-Sea."

"Ye think a local lad dealt the fatal knob to the duke?"

"Neither the Muirs nor the Ackerleys saw any strangers about yesterday."

Kenyon spat in the direction of a spittoon beside the bar. "Them Americans. They be a strange pair."

"I had been led to believe that Thomas and Martha Ackerley had lived here for more than a year."

"But they be strange."

"Being odd does not make one a murderer."

Kenyon's lips twisted in a wry smile. "That be true. Jes wish they'd be on their way across the sea. Ain't liked Americans since I was over there when they turned their backs on our good king. They be far too proud of themselves."

This was getting nowhere. Neville let the old man sputter on about his experiences in America before asking, "So no strangers were in here yesterday?"

"All day yesterday?"

"Do you remember someone?"

"A man who was travelin' through on 'is way to Brighton."

"From London?"

Kenyon paused, searching his mind before saying, "'E did say somethin' about London."

Neville frowned. "Going from London to Brighton by way of Stonehall-on-Sea would have added miles to his journey."

"May'ap 'e didn't come direct from London. 'E said somethin' about Rye, too. I'll 'ave to ask some of the lads. Their young brains may remember better than my old brain."

"Do that." He smiled. "If any of them recall anything, tell them that I am willing to buy a round for the house in exchange for good, honest information."

"Good, *'onest* information?" Kenyon laughed, the sound unexpectedly youthful. "Now there be the rub, eh? If one of the lads 'as somethin' to share, shall I send 'im to Lady Priscilla's 'ouse?"

"That would be the best course."

Kenyon lowered his voice. "Tell 'er ladyship that no matter wot rumors say, I don't believe she be guilty of whackin' the duke."

"I will tell her that." Neville clapped the old man on the shoulder. "And I know that she will be relieved to learn that not everyone believes she might be involved."

"Folks may talk 'bout it, but let 'er know not a body in the village believes she would do such a thin'."

With a nod, Neville went out into the bright sunshine. The only thing he had learned was that Priscilla was loved and respected in Stonehall-on-Sea. He hoped the constable had had better luck with his questions.

Neville strode from one side of Constable Forshaw's small office to the other in three steps. Where was the man? The constable had agreed to meet him after he questioned Priscilla's servants and neighbors. By this hour, he had had time to speak to half the residents in the village.

This office in a small house in the shadow of the church's steeple did not inspire any confidence. The constable's desk, which was the only piece of furniture other than a pair of rickety chairs set on either side of a small stove, was topped with the remnants of what must have been the man's supper. Not a single paper was in sight, so Neville suspected Forshaw never communicated beyond Stonehall-on-Sea.

*Talk to everyone; listen to everyone.* That had been one of the first lessons Neville had learned in the sordid side of London. He had not guessed that he would be teaching that to a constable in this small village.

Neville turned as the door opened. Forshaw came in, nearly staggering. The man was exhausted, Neville realized. He poured some coffee that must have been left over from the previous day and handed the cup to the constable.

With a nod, Forshaw took a sip. He grimaced and put the cup on the desk beside the plate.

"Damn fine meal that was," Forshaw grumbled.

"This might make you feel better." He set a bottle of wine next to the coffee cup. He did not want to send the constable to sleep in the middle of this discussion, but the man needed to stop lamenting about the meal that had gone uneaten.

Forshaw opened the door and tossed the coffee onto the grass. He held the cup up, and Neville filled it with wine.

When the constable took a sip and looked up in surprise, Neville said, "It is one of Priscilla's best bottles. Her late husband appreciated an excellent vintage." He leaned against the wall and put his boot on the desk. "Did you learn anything of value from those you have talked to?"

"No one seems to have seen or heard anything, although several mentioned that it was unusual for the garden gates to be left open. Mayhap the duke was killed somewhere else and brought to Lady Priscilla's garden."

"Dragging the body into the garden would make more noise than the actual murder. The duke was not a small man." He watched the constable drink the wine like a thirsty man who had been lost in the desert. "Will there be a coroner's inquest?"

Forshaw shook his head. "There is no need. It is quite obvious how His Grace was killed."

"But such an investigation might reveal some clue as to who murdered the duke."

"That is true."

"But you still will not have an inquest?"

"Lord Sherbourne . . . The new duke has requested that there be no public inquest."

Neville motioned for the constable to refill his cup. "Did he say why?"

"Respect for his late father."

"I would have guessed that respect would be better expressed in doing all that he could to discover the identity of his father's murderer."

The constable tilted back the mug and took another drink. Wiping his sleeve against an upper lip littered with whiskers, he sighed. "The coroner, Mr. Semple, has examined the body and spoken with Lady Priscilla."

"He has?" Blast Priscilla! She had not mentioned that. In the midst of all that had happened and her efforts to protect her children, she must have forgotten. He could understand her yearning to safeguard them. He was determined to do the same. 'Twas not just his duty as their father's friend, for this whole family had always had a special place in his life. Almost as if it were his.

Forshaw smiled coolly. "Just a short time ago. Mr. Semple would have spoken to you, but you were not present."

Neville silenced his sigh. It was not like him to be so excitable and assume the worst. Apparently the respectability that had come along with his title had eroded the edges off his cunning and perception. "If the coroner wishes to speak to me, I am available."

"No need. The inquest has been completed to the duke's satisfaction. But I'll be continuing my investigation."

"It may be time to get some help."

"Yours?"

"I am offering." He lowered his foot from the constable's desk. "I do have some experience."

"With murderers?"

Neville knew his smile was cold when the constable sat straighter. "One cannot be in London for long without encountering all sorts of people in every walk of life."

"But this is Stonehall-on-Sea." Pushing himself slowly to his feet, Constable Forshaw gave him an icy smile in return. "I will thank you, Sir Neville, to let me proceed with this as I have been trained to do."

"If you change your mind, you know where I am staying."

As Neville walked out, the constable said nothing. Neville had not expected him to.

# Four

Stonehall-on-Sea had not changed much in the past two centuries, save for the oaks lining the walkway between the houses and the road toward London. They had grown thick and majestic and gave an aura of serenity. The green was a triangle with a tiered fountain set above the spring at the point closest to the church. St. Elizabeth's had been built from stone taken out of the medieval monastery that had given the village its name before being ransacked during King Henry VIII's rule. Most of the houses along the green were as old. Their timbered fronts had darkened with smoke from the chimney pots and dust raised by the carriages.

The main street was edged with a row of buildings, each with a sign for the business within. An apothecary, a baker, a seamstress, the tobacconist, and several other shops served the residents. One sign, the apothecary's, had been recently painted a bright red and yellow, but the other signs were faded. Like the houses, the shops were made of stone but had slate roofs unlike the thatched ones on the houses.

As Priscilla strolled along the cobbled walkway, she doubted if anyone was fooled by her calm demeanor. Did her neighbors who paused to watch her walk past notice how stiff her smile was beneath her black bonnet and parasol? Everyone knew of the duke's death by now and where he had died and who may have been involved. If Napoleon and his generals had a means of communication even half as swift as the gossip in Stonehall-on-Sea, England would have been doomed years ago.

She could have stayed home and waited for Neville to return, but then she would have had to watch the servants pretend that everything was just as it should be. Leaving her children to read a book recently delivered from a bookseller in London, she hoped they would be able to lose themselves in the story. It was the latest novel by Walter Scott, *The Lady of the Lake*. She wanted to know what Neville had discovered, and she looked around the green, hoping to catch sight of him. It would serve her right if he was at Mermaid Cottage now.

Opening the bakery door, she heard, "La, I can't believe the old duke is gone. 'E was near 'is time, but to 'ave those few years taken from 'im . . . 'Tis a crime. A true crime. Don't understand why *she* would do such a thing. 'Er being quality and a clergyman's wife and all."

"'Appens all the time. Looks one way, lives another," came an answer. "Best thing would be for 'er to marry now that she's out of mourning for the vicar. 'Tain't right for a woman to be alone. Might make 'er mind not right, ye know?"

Priscilla closed the door and her parasol. Mrs. Crockett, the baker, stared, open-mouthed, while the two men in the corner pushed themselves to their feet.

Quietly, as if she had not heard anything out of the ordinary, Priscilla asked, "Do you have my order ready, Mrs. Crockett?"

"But yer cook usually picks it up." Mrs. Crockett's

face was alternating between a dangerous red and a white as deathly as the duke's features.

"She is busy just now."

Mr. Dunham, the older of the two men, tipped his cap, revealing his bald pate. "Beggin' yer pardon, my lady, but is she all right?"

"Mrs. Dunham is fine." She gave the man a comforting smile. Her cook was his daughter-in-law. "As is everyone else in Mermaid Cottage."

"I 'ear the constable was there again this morning."

"He was and he may return again, so I suspect we are the safest household in all of Stonehall-on-Sea at the moment."

The other old man, Mr. Lang, sniffed his disagreement, earning himself a scowl from Mrs. Crockett and Mr. Dunham.

"See 'ere, Lang," grumbled Mr. Dunham. "That is no way to sound when a lady is present."

"Mind yer manners, Mr. Lang," seconded Mrs. Crockett as she placed Isaac's favorite sugary rolls into a small box.

For the first time since she had discovered the duke's body, Priscilla had the urge to smile. Like the buildings, nothing changed with the residents here. She had been amazed by how closely related through marriage and experience everyone was, but she quickly learned that connection gave each one the right to comment on anyone else's foibles. Just as if they were, indeed, an extended family.

Mr. Dunham went on, "Why would the constable return to Mermaid Cottage, my lady? The body can't be there still."

"The constable wanted to ask everyone in the kitchen if they chanced to see or hear anything out of the ordinary last night," she replied.

"And you agreed to this?" Mrs. Crockett wrapped

string around the box. "Wot if one of them says something to condemn ye more, my lady?"

"I have insisted that everyone be honest. I have nothing to fear from honesty." She took the box and, thanking Mrs. Crockett, walked out of the shop.

The buzz of conversation began even before she had closed the door behind her. Were they discussing the murder or her possibilities of marriage? Marriage . . . She had not considered remarrying. She glanced toward the church across the green. She did so miss having someone who shared her life and to whom she could speak about anything. To be held again in a man's arms would be grand, but she had a good life now. She enjoyed Mermaid Cottage, and her children were a pleasure when they were not a trial.

Or, more accurately, she had had a good life until the duke was found in her garden. Again, she was grateful that Neville had called. Between him and Mr. Ackerley's classes, she was sure to find ways to keep the children from experiencing this odd sensation of guilt where there should be none. Never before had she had imagined how conscience-stricken one could become when everyone believed the worst.

"Lady Priscilla!"

Reverend Mr. Kenyon came toward her at his top speed. He tipped his hat. The clergyman from St. Elizabeth's, her husband's last parish before he went to London and St. Julian's Church, was an elf of a man, and she would not have been surprised to see him perched on a mushroom cap or a leaf. Like the Flanders family, he was a newcomer to Stonehall-on-Sea, for his family had been in the village for only two generations. With outrageously red hair sprouting in every direction and a mustache that refused to thicken beneath his nose, he usually wore a smile.

Today, he did not.

"Good morning, Vicar Kenyon," she replied.

"I am glad to see you, Lady Priscilla, looking so at ease."

She shifted the box to her other hand so he could walk beside her without being bumped by her parasol. "It is an illusion."

"I have heard the most frightful rumors."

"I am sure you have."

"You should know, Lady Priscilla, that I did not harbor, not for an instant, any thought that you might be involved in this tragedy."

"Thank you." She sighed. "I wish you could persuade Constable Forshaw to share your opinion."

"That young man wants to prove himself by arresting the murderer. He is like a dog with a small bone. He will not release it even when a bigger bone is offered to him. In this case, that bigger bone is the truth." He hesitated, then asked, "What do you think truly happened to His Grace?"

"I have no idea. We were at dinner, so we did not have a view of the garden."

"Your habits are something the murderer may have been familiar with."

"That would suggest that the person who killed the duke is someone we know well."

Vicar Kenyon sighed. "I suspect that is the case. Any stranger would have been noted."

"In the bakery, I heard it said that the duke's body had been sent to Meresden Court. I had thought it would be sent to St. Elizabeth's."

"So had I until Lord Sherbourne insisted that his father be returned to the estate, although he has informed me that he wishes to have a memorial service at the church."

"Lord Sherbourne? Is he here?" That was, indeed, a surprise, for the duke's heir seldom visited. Instead

Sidney Sherbourne preferred to spend his time in London or elsewhere with his comrades.

Vicar Kenyon nodded. "I have had the most uncomfortable thoughts at the coincidence of the son being here at the time of his father's death."

"I am sure you are not the only one."

"Lady Priscilla, please do not misconstrue what I am about to say."

"Go ahead." She suspected she knew what he was about to say. Even so, she steeled herself.

"Throughout the village, it is being repeated that you and your family did not hear anything amiss because you were receiving a caller. A caller who arrived within an hour of when the duke was discovered dead."

"Yes. Sir Neville Hathaway, who was my late husband's best friend."

The clergyman's shoulders sagged from their stiff pose. "Dr. Flanders's best friend? My, my, that puts a completely different complexion on the whole."

"I would appreciate you so informing anyone who speaks of Sir Neville's possible connection to the murder. We cannot jump to any conclusions. That, I am learning, is a most dangerous sport when the conclusions are false."

"You have weathered other storms, Lady Priscilla. I know you will weather this one." He smiled. "And I will pray that the storm passes quickly."

Priscilla took his comforting words with her as she continued on to Mermaid Cottage. She waved to the Muir brothers who were working, as usual in the spring, in their garden. It would be a showy delight by summer.

Closing her parasol, she reached for the door. Noise exploded outward as she opened it.

"Mama!" Leah ran to her and threw her arms around her.

"What is amiss?" Her mind rushed toward the most appalling thoughts. Where were her other children? Had something happened to them? She grasped Leah by the shoulders. "What is amiss?"

"Isaac has hidden my favorite ribbon, and he will not tell me where it is."

Priscilla released her breath. This commonplace situation was so precious today, even though she usually found the children's pranks on each other vexing. When she heard footsteps, she looked over Leah's head to see Neville walking toward her with Daphne following close behind.

His face was set in a frown, and she guessed his morning had been as unsatisfying as hers. She wanted to ask, but she refrained when the children were in earshot. He would be honest with her, for he never had watched his tongue in her presence. It was because he had seen how Lazarus spoke to her as an equal instead of as a wife who had nothing in her head but thoughts of fashion plates and invitations. She wanted that honesty now. Unlike Constable Forshaw who believed she might be a suspect and at the same time did not believe a vicar's widow could be capable of doing such a thing, Neville knew exactly how aware she was of the world beyond the pleasant surroundings of a vicarage.

In quick order, she sent Daphne to retrieve her brother and Leah's hair ribbon. She handed the box to a footman, asking him to ask Mrs. Moore to come to the foyer at her earliest convenience.

The housekeeper appeared so swiftly that Priscilla guessed she had been waiting in the dining room. Mrs. Moore's smile was nowhere in sight, and she was wringing her hands in her apron as Martha Ackerley had.

"Mrs. Moore," Priscilla said, "please have some trays brought into the parlor for luncheon. Some cold meats and fresh bread would be fine. Lemonade, if Mrs. Dunham has some."

"Yes, my lady." Mrs. Moore went to give the orders to the kitchen, seeming relieved to be busy.

Neville said quietly, "Priscilla, we should talk."

"After luncheon," she replied. If they spoke now, the children would find a way to be privy to all of it.

She heard him mutter something and suspected it was an oath that would be unfit for Leah's hearing. She did not chide him. She empathized with his aggravation that his visit had been made into a jumble by this murder.

But when she saw him glancing up the stairs with a hint of a smile, she wondered if Neville truly was annoyed by the extension of his visit. She had learned soon after she first met him that he enjoyed, as he had said last night, shaking things up a bit if they became too boring. Yet, even Neville would not shake things up this much. The question remained: Who had?

As Priscilla herded her children into the parlor and gave the ribbon that Isaac returned to a gleeful Leah, she wondered why Neville had called here at Mermaid Cottage. She had asked him at dinner last night, and he had evaded her answer as he was wont to do when anyone probed too closely. She had not had a chance to ask him again.

Daphne began to chatter about some small incident. Isaac and Leah seemed to be leaning on every word, and Priscilla guessed they were eager to avoid speaking about what had happened yesterday. The reality that a kindly old man had been killed so savagely must be reaching past the first burst of excitement.

She kept her arms around her daughters and noticed that Neville had draped an arm over Isaac's shoulders. Daphne did not pause while the trays were brought in and they began to eat. Whether the meat and bread and large glasses of lemonade had any flavor, Priscilla could not tell.

As he ate, Neville made the appropriate mumbling sounds that encouraged Daphne to continue with the tale that most certainly did not interest him. Daphne paused and turned to answer a question from her sister.

Neville leaned toward Priscilla and lowered his voice so the children would not hear. "So this is the punishment you will inflict on me for upsetting your household? Listening to your daughter's young miss tales?"

"Exactly." She was grateful for his teasing. Her smile wavered. "Neville, why are you here in Stonehall-on-Sea?"

"I thought I would give you a look-in now that you are out of first mourning for Lazarus."

Neither her husband nor Neville had ever spoken of where they had met. She suspected Lazarus had rescued Neville from some mishap, because Neville was not likely to have attended her husband's services. It no longer mattered, because Neville was as much a part of her life as Lazarus had been and the children were.

"That was unexpectedly kind of you," she said.

"I have been known to do something nice on occasion." He gave her a wry grin. "When it suited me." He became serious. "Why are you asking about why I am paying you a call?"

"You haven't called in so long and then . . ."

His lips curled in a feral grin. "Are you suggesting

my visit might have been the trigger for the duke's murder?"

"I am not, but there is gossip in the village that it may be." She looked at her children who were finished with their meal. "Why don't you go to the kitchen and see if Mrs. Dunham has any special treats for your dessert?"

Isaac and Leah jumped to their feet and ran out of the room at a pace that would have usually earned them a scold.

Daphne stood but hesitated. "Mama, I am not a child. You should not banish me while you and Uncle Neville speak of important matters."

"Right now," Priscilla said, "I am depending on you to help keep your brother and sister from intruding."

"Intruding? On what?"

Priscilla glanced at Neville, then back at her oldest. "I will not be false with you. I do not want the younger ones to interrupt my—" Again she looked at Neville. "*Our* attempt to find the person who murdered the Duke of Meresden, so our names might be cleared."

"Your names? Someone thinks that *you* are involved, Mama?" Tears filled her wide eyes.

"You know how gossip spreads at times like this. I do not want you to heed it, and I do not want your sister and brother to *hear* it."

Daphne nodded, her lips trembling. "I will do what I can to help, Mama." She hurried out of the room, and the distant sound of the door to the kitchen closing drifted back in.

Gilbert brought wine into the parlor. He set it on the table next to Neville. Without a comment, he left again.

Neville poured himself a glass. "A most efficient household you have here, Pris."

"Fortunately." She asked him what he had learned this morning. When he was finished with his tale of visiting the public house and the constable, she began to tell him what she had learned. Talking to him was so different from talking with Martha. He listened closely and without visible emotion.

"Kenyon?" he asked when she mentioned the clergyman. "Are the pastor and the pubkeeper related?"

"Mr. Kenyon is Vicar Kenyon's uncle." She smiled. "You soon come to see that the relationships are very close and very tangled here. Vicar Kenyon told me that the duke's heir has requested that the body be taken to Meresden Court instead of the church. What do you know of him?"

"Sherbourne?" He scowled and poured more wine into his glass. "A most disagreeable fellow."

"That I know. What else can you tell me about him?"

"How has he been disagreeable to you, Pris?"

She waved his concerns away. "Do not try to act as my dashing gallant. It is an uncomfortable and most unaccustomed role for you, and, to own the truth, it is beyond vexing. You know I do not need coddling. Rather, as I have never met the man, I would beg you to favor me with what you know of the next Duke of Meresden."

"He is appallingly high in the instep. Within seconds of meeting one, he remarks that he is first in line to ascend to his father's title. He is much favored with the ladies because he is tall and has hair the shade of yours, Pris."

"A Viking type?"

He laughed without humor. "You may be closer to the truth than you guess, for his reputation as a prime rake is well established. Conversation is something he disdains, for he prefers an endless monologue and a rapt audience."

"That is bothersome, especially when you enjoy jousting with words, Neville. I hope whatever business that you were bound for when you stopped here can wait."

He frowned at her. "Why are you asking about that? I thought you wished to learn more about Sherbourne."

"Forgive me. Continue." She smiled behind her glass of lemonade, but her smile faded when she realized that Neville must be quite upset if he had spoken so tautly to her.

Twirling the wine in his glass, he said, "He is a coward when it comes to making the big wager."

"Because he is short of funds?"

"I had considered that, although the duke himself has become—had become known for his generosity."

"Yes. He purchased a new bell for the tower at St. Elizabeth's. No widow or orphan anywhere in this shire will be without food or wood when the weather turns cold."

Neville arched a brow. "Such a saint, but he did not pass that generous heart to his son."

From the doorway, Gilbert cleared his throat. "My lady, Constable Forshaw is calling." He glanced over his shoulder. "Again."

"Show him in," she said, coming to her feet.

The constable entered, his mouth working. At first she thought he was distressed. Then, she realized that he was trying to smother a yawn.

"Good afternoon, Constable," she said. "Could we have the kitchen fix you a plate?"

"Thank you. That would be welcome." This time, when he tried to suppress a yawn, it escaped. "Excuse me."

"Nonsense. You have been working hard, and you should not be ashamed of that. How can we help you?"

He folded his hands behind his back. "Lady Priscilla, I would like to speak with your children."

"No."

He glanced at Neville. She wanted to tell the constable not to look to Neville for assistance, for he had no say in what the children did or did not do.

Neville held up the bottle. "Do you want something more bracing than lemonade, Constable Forshaw?"

"I fear it would knock me completely into the land of Nod." He took the glass Priscilla handed him. "Thank you, my lady. As for the children—"

"They are privy to nothing that has happened." She would not be budged, and the sooner he realized that, the better off they would be. "They were within the dining room with Sir Neville when I went to the garden. When I discovered the duke there, you can be assured that I did not allow them so much as peek out a window overlooking the back garden."

"But, Lady Priscilla—"

"If that is your only reason for calling, Constable, then you have wasted your time." As her hands clenched into fists, she said, "Please excuse me. I am in need of some fresh air. Good afternoon, Constable."

Priscilla left the parlor before she burst into tears. Sweet heavens! She would not have her children tormented more. Following her angry thoughts at how the household had been put on edge by this appalling situation, she was striding through her garden before she quite knew where she was headed.

She halted in midstep. What once had been a sanctuary was now defiled. She would go inside, gather the children, and walk along the shore. That would give them a chance to escape for a short time.

Turning back to the house, Priscilla saw, in the middle of the flower bed, something twinkling in the sunshine. She picked up the object and turned it over. A button! She had seen its like on military uniforms when her husband had been in London and garrisoned soldiers had attended Sunday services.

But the duke had been an old man, long past his prime. This button was as brightly polished as if it had been on a uniform on parade yesterday. Mayhap it had not belonged to the duke, but had been left by the murderer.

She knelt and ran her hands through the patch of bent and broken crocuses. She found nothing but pebbles and an acorn that must have been brought by some squirrel last fall.

"If you are seen here, everyone will be certain you are guilty," said Neville from behind her.

She rose. "Where is the constable?"

"On his way back to his office, thoroughly chastised, I must add, by your comments."

"He is grasping for straws to speak with the children."

He held up his hands and chuckled. "Don't lash out at me, Pris. I am in agreement with you on this matter."

"And on this?" She opened her fingers.

He took the button and examined it. "Odd that we did not see this before."

"It was twilight and dawn when we were here. In the bright sunshine, it sparkled like an earthbound star. It could not have been the duke's."

"And it does not belong to anyone in your household?"

"No."

"Then it must belong to the murderer."

She nodded. "Exactly what I deduced, but there is only one problem with that assumption, Neville. There are no military men in Stonehall-on-Sea at this time. The closest garrison is probably in Rye, a day's ride from here."

"So the murderer may not have been from the village."

"That button throws out every theory we or the constable have. If we believe that belongs to the murderer, we are more in the dark than ever." She sighed. "I cannot imagine how this situation could become any worse.

# Five

Priscilla had been wrong. Things *could* get worse, she discovered the next morning when Gilbert came to her study. His face was serene as always, but she would have wagered that she heard a quaver in his voice as he announced, "My lady, you have a caller."

"Who is calling?" She needed to know if she must gird herself for another conversation with Constable Forshaw. She was waiting here for Neville, so they could take the button to the constable. Discussion of it would be better in his office, rather than here where the children could overhear.

"Your aunt, Lady Cordelia, my lady."

"Please show her to the parlor." She kept her face serene until the butler closed the door behind him. Constable Forshaw would have been easier to deal with than her aunt.

She had never forgiven Priscilla for, in Aunt Cordelia's opinion, marrying beneath her. A clergyman in a small parish was not a proper match for an earl's daughter. The fact that Priscilla had loved Dr. Lazarus Flanders deeply, and he had returned that affection throughout their marriage, did nothing to change Aunt Cordelia's mind. Even when Lazarus had been offered a post at St. Julian's, a fine church in London where the Polite World went to worship, and there had been talk of him being in line to serve as a bishop in the future, Aunt Cordelia had not been appeased.

Even so, the relationship between Priscilla and her aunt had been cordial until Papa died, and Isaac became the earl. Aunt Cordelia had announced at the funeral that she doubted if Priscilla, who had, after all, married a clergyman, was the best person to guide the next earl in his duties.

Priscilla checked her appearance in the glass beside the bay window that overlooked one corner of the Muirs' garden. She looked fine . . . for someone who had not slept in almost three days.

A motion caught her eye, and she saw Irwin Muir digging in a corner of the garden. She watched, perplexed, for he seemed to be tossing dirt with rare gusto. Why was he digging such a deep hole in that one spot?

*To hide another body?*

Priscilla chided herself for the untoward thought. She could not allow Constable Forshaw's suspicions to taint her own thoughts. The Muir brothers were described—kindly—as eccentric. Those who were not in a generous mood used words like half-mad. She had learned to accept their odd ways, for they were pleasant to her family. Even when Isaac had kicked a ball into their prize peonies, they had not complained. Rather, they had spent hours showing her son how to kick the ball straighter, so it would not soar into their garden.

Priscilla reached the parlor only moments before Gilbert ushered Aunt Cordelia in. Cordelia Emberley Smith Gray Dexter was slender. Not a hint of gray lightened her ebony hair, and her face was almost unlined. That was, Priscilla believed, because her aunt gave others white hair and wrinkles. Cordelia clung to the highest standards of the Polite World, considering herself the equal of the *grand dames* at Almack's.

Her pink-sprigged gown gave no clue that she had been traveling for the past day from Emberson Park where she had returned after the death of her third husband two years ago. A stylish bonnet perched on her perfectly coiffed hair and a paisley shawl draped its fringe along her arms. Around her neck, hanging from a fine gold chain, her quizzing glass bounced with each step.

That feminine fragility was only an illusion. Priscilla had heard that her aunt once gave a scold to the Regent's brother, when his carriage cut off hers. Even though the Duke of Clarence, well known for having retained the salty turn of a phrase that he had acquired in the navy, had had no choice but to accept being dressed down by Aunt Cordelia.

Now, as Aunt Cordelia untied that pert bonnet and held it out to Gilbert, she said in her crisp voice, "You look appalling, Priscilla."

"Aunt Cordelia, what an unexpected surprise." Priscilla hoped her aunt did not hear her hypocrisy. Not to worry, she reminded herself, for Aunt Cordelia heard only what she wanted to hear and discounted everything else as folly.

Giving her aunt the required kiss on her heavily powdered cheek, Priscilla was glad that her children were nowhere in sight. She hoped they did not come to check on who had arrived in the grand carriage Aunt Cordelia preferred to use. She was unsure how much longer she could restrain Daphne from speaking up when Aunt Cordelia made another demure hit about Priscilla's unsuitability as the mother of an earl.

"I did mention in my last letter to you that I was paying you a call soon," Aunt Cordelia replied. "Didn't you receive it?"

"Yes, I did." She smiled, refraining from adding that she had read no further than the first page that had been a listing of suggestions on how Priscilla could improve her maternal skills. She wondered what had given her father's sister the idea that Priscilla did not revere the title her father had bequeathed to her son or that Aunt Cordelia, who was childless, knew more about raising a boisterous boy than Priscilla did.

"Then you should not be astonished to see me," her aunt replied.

"You know you are always welcome here, Aunt Cordelia." She motioned for her aunt to precede her to the gold settee and matching chairs in the parlor. "Gilbert, please inform Mrs. Dunham that my aunt has arrived."

He nodded. She thought he was about to say something, but he must have decided to remain silent, because he walked away.

"Would you like to sit?" Priscilla asked, turning back to her aunt.

"You are the one who looks as if the slightest breeze could topple you." Aunt Cordelia eyed her up and down. "Black is such a horrible color for you. I thought you would have dispensed with it by now."

"I am just out of first mourning. I have not had a chance to visit a *modiste* to have new clothes made."

"I'm glad to hear you are not about to wear your old gowns. But it is more than the color of your dress. Have the children been ill and keeping you from your rest?"

She shook her head. "Aunt Cordelia, I think this conversation would be handled better if we both were seated."

"What can be so horrid that you cannot speak of it standing?"

"Please sit down."

With a mumble that Priscilla did not attempt to decipher, her aunt sat. Aunt Cordelia glared, so Priscilla quickly perched on one of the chairs that faced the settee.

Before she could say a single word, the door opened again. She turned, ready to greet the children. Instead she gasped when Neville entered.

He glanced in her direction for only the length of time it took for her to draw in an uneven breath; then he walked to where Aunt Cordelia was watching with a frown. In his finely cut navy coat and tan breeches, he gave no sign of exhaustion. His smile was warm, but, if he thought he could bamboozle her aunt, he would learn how mistaken he was. Aunt Cordelia could see through any half-truths.

Priscilla came to her feet, then wished she had not. The lack of sleep made her lightheaded. "Aunt Cordelia, may I introduce Sir Neville Hathaway? Neville, this is my aunt Lady Cordelia Dexter."

"Sir Neville Hathaway?" Her aunt's voice sounded as if someone was strangling her.

"Have we met, my lady?" He bowed over her hand. "I cannot believe so, for I am certain I would have recalled it."

"No, we have not."

He did not act insulted by her frigid tone. "I am glad."

"Glad?" Aunt Cordelia asked sharply as Priscilla smothered a laugh.

"It would have been beastly of me to forget meeting you, my lady."

"You are as glib as *on dits* suggests."

"Guilty."

Priscilla flinched and hoped that no one had seen her motion. A futile hope, for Neville moved to assist her to sit with the same grace that he had shown while he bowed in his greeting to her aunt. When she thanked him, she was aware of Aunt Cordelia's glower focused on them.

Before Priscilla could speak her mind, telling her aunt that she was not in the mood to be chastised again, the door opened and a maid came in with a tray topped with the chocolate pot, small cakes, and a quartet of cups. She set the tray on a table next to Priscilla's chair.

"Thank you, June," Priscilla said.

The maid curtseyed and hurried from the room. No doubt, Gilbert had warned the household. Aunt Cordelia's last visit had ended with both Mrs. Dunham and Mrs. Moore threatening to leave, even without a recommendation. It had taken Priscilla a fortnight and an increase in wages to placate them.

"Chocolate?" Aunt Cordelia smiled as she took the cup Priscilla held out to her. "How kind of you, Priscilla, to recall that I am fond of it."

She silently thanked Mrs. Dunham who never forgot what any guest liked, even Aunt Cordelia. As Neville queried her aunt about her journey, Priscilla poured two more cups. She handed one to Neville. When he winked at her, she was not sure if she should ask him to leave or beg him to stay to help her deal with her cantankerous aunt.

"Priscilla," said her aunt, "I believe you were about to tell me why you are wearing such a haggard appearance."

It did not take Priscilla long to explain what had happened. She had thought Neville might interject a word or two, but he remained as silent as Aunt Cordelia.

Her aunt pursed her lips, revealing that her youthful appearance was aided with rice powder. "Really, Priscilla, have you considered how this looks?"

"It looks as if the duke is dead."

Aunt Cordelia put down her cup and scowled more fiercely. "Do not be flippant, young lady."

"Forgive me, Aunt Cordelia." She did not dare look in Neville's direction, for she was having a difficult time not smiling at being called "young lady" in that chastising tone. If he smiled, she was sure to dissolve into tired giggles. Sweet heavens, she was so exhausted that she was giddy.

Neville added, "My dear Lady Cordelia, you can be most assuredly reassured that Priscilla knows the gravity of this situation. However, she has gotten little or no sleep in the nights since the duke's body was discovered."

Raising her quizzing glass as if she were looking at him like a child peering through a magnifying glass at some insect, she asked, "Is that so? I do not find much comfort in hearing that you are privy to such information, Sir Neville."

"I am not the only one privy to it." He kept his smile in place as he marveled at how the old tough's mind seemed to slide into salacious thoughts far too often. "We spent much of the recent nights talking with the constable and Priscilla's neighbors on either side of Mermaid Cottage."

With a frown at Priscilla, she said, "I am sure that Sir Neville shall be willing to excuse us to speak privately."

Neville said, "Of course, if that is your wish, Pris."

Her aunt bristled at his familiar address.

"Will you be certain that Isaac has finished his work for Mr. Ackerley?" Priscilla asked before her aunt could explode with fury. "I trust you recall some of your basic Latin."

"I will endeavor to dredge my mind for what little Latin was forced upon it." Coming to his feet, he bowed his head. "Have a pleasant conversation, ladies."

Priscilla was as certain that this conversation would be anything but pleasant as she was that her life was in a wild spiral that was getting more complicated and vexing with each passing minute.

The door had barely closed behind Neville when Aunt Cordelia announced, "This is a disaster."

"Yes, the duke is—"

Aunt Cordelia waved her to silence. "Bother, Priscilla, will you look to the future rather than the past? The duke is dead. In *your* garden. That fact is sure to taint this family for years to come. You have your daughters to think of." She paused, then said in her most stentorian *Voice of Doom* tone, "And your son, the earl."

"I have thought of little else." Priscilla set her cup down. "That is why I have the ragged appearance of no sleep. I have been lying awake trying to determine how I might discover who killed the duke, so that I am no longer suspected of the crime."

*"You? You* are accused of committing this crime?"

"I am a suspect."

"How is that possible?" Aunt Cordelia stood and paced the room as if she wished to punish each inch of the carpet. "You are the daughter of an earl. You would not do such a thing." She threw her hands up in the air. "You are the wife—the widow of a clergyman. I shall go and speak with your constable as soon as I have recovered from my journey."

Priscilla came to her feet. "We must not interfere with the constable's investigation. There was a murderer in my garden, and I want to be certain sure that horrible fiend doesn't return to prey on my children."

"The children!"

"Aunt Cordelia, are you unwell?" Priscilla rushed to

her aunt's side as the older woman's cheeks became a sickly shade.

"Of course, I am unwell. The very thought of what has happened has made me sick. So sick that I can barely bring myself to speak of this."

Priscilla hastened to say, "You should take some time to recover from your trip as well as from the shock of discovering what has happened here."

"How could I rest at a time like this? This is the very worst thing that could have happened."

"Aunt Cordelia, we need to remain calm."

"Calm?" Her voice became a moan. "Once word of this reaches London—"

"A man is dead. We should be thinking of that rather than our family's reputation."

Aunt Cordelia scowled. "You must clear your name immediately, or I shall have Isaac removed from this house."

"Removed?" Priscilla had been foolish to say aloud that matters could not worsen. Now she was going to have to eat those malodorous words . . . again and again.

"It is not right for an earl to have his name sullied by such events."

"He would not be the first earl to be implicated in a scandal."

"Are you suggesting that your son is involved with this?"

"Of course not."

Aunt Cordelia crossed her arms over her chest. "You must put an end to this posthaste, Priscilla. Word of this tragedy is certain to reach many ears, and then you and your children will be ostracized." She gasped and pressed her hand to her full bosom. "And so shall I!"

"No one can consider that you had anything to do with this mess when you were not even here."

Waving her to silence, Aunt Cordelia sighed. "You never have understood the Polite World."

"I do believe I understand it quite well. Even if they prattle about this—"

"It will be far worse than prattle. You must put an end to this, or I shall have Isaac taken to Emberson Park where he can be properly overseen while he receives an education worthy of an earl." She wagged her finger at Priscilla. "Do not give me back-talk and tell me that you will halt me. I am not the only one who has expressed concerns about Isaac."

"Not the only one?"

"Your Aunt Wilma has said she believes you have more burdens than you can handle."

Priscilla smiled coolly. She had heard her other aunt say that—at Lazarus's funeral when Aunt Wilma had spoken of her sorrow about Priscilla having to raise three children on her own. Then her aunt had added if anyone could manage it, that person would be Priscilla.

"Aunt Cordelia, why don't you rest after your trip? We can talk more about this tonight."

"And we shall." She paused and added as a final threat, "Put an end to your name being associated with this by week's end, Priscilla, or I swear I shall take all the children out of this house."

"You cannot be serious."

"I am, and you need to be serious about clearing your name before more damage is done."

Priscilla sighed as her aunt left the threat in her wake. For once, she would be happy to comply with her aunt's commands. She just had to figure out how.

When the door opened—*again*—Priscilla was not surprised to see Neville. She would have accused him of listening at the hinges, but he needed only watch for her aunt to burst out. He left the door ajar, and she was amazed until she heard her aunt speaking in that same "heed me if you are wise" tone to her daughters.

Priscilla took a single step toward the door, then paused. Going out to oversee the situation would infuriate Aunt Cordelia more. Later, she would apologize to Daphne and Leah for not warning them their great-aunt was here.

"That termagant does not seem to have done you great damage." Neville smiled tightly.

"The damage inflicted by Aunt Cordelia is not obvious." She rubbed her forehead that had begun to ache when Gilbert announced who was calling. It had grown worse during the conversation with Aunt Cordelia.

"You could ask her to leave."

She laughed tersely. "You know that is impossible."

"Just say: Get the hel—" He paused and looked at the girls being interrogated in the foyer. "I mean . . . Get the perdition out of my house."

"My aunt doesn't heed even a not-so-subtle suggestion. Now that she is certain that I am unfit to raise the Earl of Emberson, she will beleaguer me like a hound after a fox."

"You? Unfit to raise Isaac?"

She raised her hands. "She holds on to her belief that I could have married more advantageously than Lazarus."

"You could have." He sighed. "And you could have been as miserable as I have heard that your aunt was in each of her *advantageous* marriages. You and Lazarus were meant for each other. I doubt if I ever have seen a husband and a wife who were more of a team." His lips straightened. "If I believed in such things, I swear Lazarus's spirit would be headed here to haunt your aunt."

"Thank you, Neville." She patted his arm. In the face of Aunt Cordelia's attempt to vex her, his confidence in her was special.

"I would be glad to tell the old serpent that she should spew her venom elsewhere."

"Thank you, but no."

"Or I can—"

"Neville, she is *my* problem."

"If there is anything I can do to help—"

"I will let you know." She went to the window that looked out over the sea. Staring out at the water turning a thick gray beneath lowering clouds, she said, "If you wish to take that button to Constable Forshaw, you should do so without me."

"He isn't in." He gave her a lopsided grin. "I went to check while you were enjoying your aunt."

Sitting on the windowseat, she said, "Leah has a lesson with Mr. Ackerley just before midday. After I take her there, we can pay a call on the constable to see if he has returned."

Neville walked over to where she sat. Putting his hand on the window frame, he said, "I thought we might want to call on the new Duke of Meresden first. If the button belonged to his father, he may recognize it. Then we can share that information with the constable as well."

"An excellent idea."

"I thought so."

She came to her feet. "Don't preen, Neville. It is a most unattractive trait."

"Among the many I possess."

When she laughed, his smile told her that he was trying to help her ease her unhappiness. "I will not argue with you about that. If you will excuse me . . ."

"Where are you bound?"

"I have to speak with Mrs. Dunham about tomorrow's meals."

"Mrs. Moore can do that for you."

She smiled. "It is my task. If you would like to help me, keep my aunt busy so she does not notice I am in the kitchen."

He grimaced. "That is quite a request."

"You did say you would be glad to do anything to help."

"Words I suspect I shall come to rue many times in the next few days."

"Few days? Aunt Cordelia never stays for less than a fortnight." Her brow furrowed as she frowned. "Or are you thinking of leaving?"

"Not until I know who killed the duke in your garden so that the finger of guilt would be pointed at someone in Mermaid Cottage."

That assurance made Priscilla feel better than she had since she had gone into the garden the evening of his arrival. It added a lightness to her steps as she made good her escape from her aunt and went into the kitchen where she had to think of nothing more important than what sauce should be served with tomorrow's leg of mutton.

"'Tain't right," Muriel said as the door closed behind Lady Priscilla.

"What 'tain't right?" asked June, who was fixing a tray to take up to Lady Cordelia. Everything must be perfect, for the last time the old earl's daughter visited, she had chastised June for a full hour about how a tray should be arranged.

"'Ow Lady Priscilla is bein' plagued by the constable and now by 'er own aunt."

"The constable thinks 'er ladyship is mixed up with the duke's death."

Muriel's nose wrinkled as she scrubbed a stubborn pot. "*I* was with 'er when she found the duke. She was as surprised as anyone."

Mrs. Dunham, the cook, came into the kitchen with dried carrots in her apron. "Enough of the chatterin'. Ye'll never 'elp Lady Priscilla by prattlin'."

"Do you think there is someone mad out there stalkin' good folks in the dark?" asked June, undaunted by the cook's scowl. It was less than what she would face when she could no longer delay taking this tray upstairs to Lady Cordelia.

"No."

"Why not?" Muriel put down the pot. "The duke is dead."

"But not in the dark," said Mrs. Dunham as she set the carrots on the table and motioned for Muriel to scrape and cut them when she finished the last pot.

"Who knows 'ow long he was lyin' there?" persisted June. "'E could've been there for a long time."

Mrs. Dunham's tone became more impatient. "I know! I was in the garden with Lady Priscilla to get the flowers for the table that afternoon. No one was there."

"Then the killer is bold." June shuddered. "We aren't safe in the daylight."

"Yer safe as long as ye stay in the kitchen and do yer chores."

A knock came on the back door. Firing another scowl at the girls when one of them shrieked, Mrs. Dunham opened it. One of the Muir brothers stood there. She was not sure which.

He tipped his cap. "We have finished replanting the flowers in Lady Priscilla's garden. Will you let her know?"

"Yes, Mr. Muir."

"Tell her that within a fortnight, no one will ever know that anything happened out of the ordinary in the garden."

"Yes, sir."

When he walked away, she closed the door. She turned and saw both of the maids regarding her with wide eyes.

"Wot are ye starin' at?" she asked, her voice sharp.

"Where be the other one?" June glanced at Muriel fearfully.

Muriel said, "The other was not in sight."

"Never seen one without the other," seconded June.

"Never. They always be together."

"Do you think 'e killed the other one?"

"And the duke?" Muriel shivered. "The gate was open to their garden. 'E could have snuck in here and whacked the duke on the 'ead."

June moaned. "Do you think 'e will 'urt us next?"

Mrs. Dunham took each girl by the arm. With a shake, she snapped, "Listen to ye! Ye sound just like those two 'alf-crazy brothers."

"They be all crazy!" Muriel gasped.

"I 'ave 'eard enough." The cook released them. "Get to yer chores. No more dawdlin'."

As Mrs. Dunham went to check the bread in the oven, Muriel lowered her voice to a whisper, "It be strange, June, that 'e was all alone."

"D'ye think I should speak of this to 'er ladyship?"

"If ye 'ave a chance." She paused, then added, "Or may'ap to Sir Neville."

"'Im? 'E could 'ave killed the duke. Ye saw wot 'e did to Gilbert! Pinned 'im to the wall with that sword."

Muriel shook her head. "'E was jestin'."

"May'ap so. May'ap not. I ain't speakin' to 'im

about this." Picking up the tray, June added, "May'ap 'er ladyship. That's all."

"Say somethin' to 'er! Don't want someone in this 'ouse to be the next one to 'ave a cudgel scuttle m'nob." She put her hand up to her head as if feeling for a lump.

"I will. I—"

A crash came from the other side of the kitchen, and the tray fell from June's quivering hands. Glass and china shattered on the stone floor. With a gasp, she put her hands over her face and began to weep.

Mrs. Dunham came across the room. More gently than she had before, she said, "June, get another tray. Muriel will 'elp me clean this up."

"Yes, Mrs. Dunham," she gulped through her tears.

As the cook bent to pick up the broken pieces of china, she knew *she* must speak with Lady Priscilla straightaway. The girls were too skittish. The footmen and Mrs. Moore were not much better. Even Gilbert's serenity was showing signs of disintegrating. If this continued, one of them was sure to hurt themselves in their attempts to flee what they believed hid in the shadows.

They were fools. They should listen when she said that whoever had killed the duke had not lurked in the darkness. If the murderer struck again, it could be at any time.

She moaned at her own thoughts. Mayhap it was for the best that the girls were not heeding her, for that would make them even more nervous.

If that was possible.

# Six

Priscilla was not deceived by the sight of her children clustered together reading in the parlor while Neville perused the paper on the windowseat. The domestic scene was as false as her own smile, because she could hear how Daphne's voice quavered as she read aloud to her sister and brother.

"Leah," Priscilla called, "'tis time for your French lesson with Mr. Ackerley."

Leah grimaced when her brother gave her a superior smile that suggested she had worn the same when he had gone for his lessons. "I don't understand why I need to learn French when we are at war with France."

Looking over the newspaper, Neville said, "So you will understand what is being said when Napoleon's troops pay a call on England."

"You think they will come here?" Isaac leaped about like a toad and waved an invisible sword. "If they try it, we will drive them back into the sea."

"But first you have to shout for them to surrender, and then you need to question them." Neville raised the paper up again. "For that, you will need French."

"That is true," Leah said in amazement. "Mama, how do you say surrender in French?"

Priscilla put her hand on Leah's shoulder and

steered her toward the door. "Why don't you ask Mr. Ackerley?"

A wind that was chilly enough for winter lashed through the trees and beneath Priscilla's black bonnet, threatening to pull it off, as they hurried to the small cottage next door. She was amazed to hear voices from the Muir garden, for she had not guessed they would be working there in this weather.

She was further astonished when the door to the Ackerley cottage was opened by Martha's brother, Thomas. A tall and lanky man with stooped shoulders, as if he carried all the volumes in his book-room upon them, he had dull, light brown hair. His cravat was askew, and ink stained the front of his plain waistcoat. With a pair of glasses perched on his nose, he reminded her of a thoughtful dog watching over its flock.

"Lady Priscilla!" He smiled, and his whole countenance altered. Stepping back so she and Leah could enter the narrow vestibule, he added, "You are always so punctual. You have no idea how pleasant a change that is from my other students."

Leah walked past him to his book-room two doors on the left. Pausing in the doorway, she looked back. "How much longer will you be talking, Mama? I want to start my lesson."

Mr. Ackerley could not hide his astonishment.

Priscilla said in a near whisper, "She has decided she needs to know enough French to make sure she can demand any invasion troops to surrender to her."

He chuckled. "'Tis as good a reason as any. If you could inspire young Isaac as thoroughly, he might turn his mind to his lessons more readily."

"I doubt if he will believe that Roman legions are returning to England."

When Mr. Ackerley laughed again, Martha peeked

out from the kitchen on the opposite side of the hall-way from his book-room. "What is so amusing? Oh, Lady Priscilla, is it time for Miss Leah's lesson already?" She came out of the kitchen, wiping her hands on her apron. Giving her brother a warm smile, she put her hand on his arm with obvious affection before he went to his book-room. "Thomas is very distressed."

"Distressed? He seemed in a rather jolly mood just now," Priscilla replied. She did not add that Martha seemed far more agitated than her brother.

"Thomas is very good at keeping his true feelings to himself. Since you found the duke in your flower bed, he has been talking of us leaving Stonehall-on-Sea."

"And going where?"

"I don't know." A hint of a smile eased her taut lips. "I often have thought how I would like to see London."

"London? You are thinking of moving there?"

"No, not really. It is too expensive, and Thomas's students are here." She smiled for the first time, and her voice lightened from its near hysteria. "Forgive me, Lady Priscilla. I am letting my own dismals carry me away. Thomas is right to be concerned, but this cottage and Stonehall-on-Sea will be our home until we can return home to New York."

"May I?" Priscilla motioned the small parlor.

"Of course." Martha flushed as she added, "May I bring you something to drink or eat?"

"No, no. I do not want to disturb your day."

Martha smiled, albeit weakly. "I am glad to have you linger. I wanted to ask you some questions, if I might."

"Of course," she replied as Martha had. If Martha posed some questions, then Priscilla could do the same thing back.

"Have you been having trouble sleeping?"

"Why do you ask?" Priscilla asked.

"I see the lights on in Mermaid Cottage all night long." Martha's smile disappeared. "I know your lamps are lit because I find it impossible to sleep as well."

"It has been very stressful."

"Do you have any idea who might have killed the duke?" Martha asked, sitting on a footstool near Priscilla's chair.

"None. Do you?"

"Me? Why would you ask such a thing?"

Putting her hand on the young woman's trembling arm, Priscilla said, "Your kitchen has a good view of my garden, which my dining room does not. I do not mean to interrogate you as the constable has, but I was wondering if you had remembered anything pertinent."

"I don't mind telling you, Lady Priscilla. You are not badgering me as Constable Forshaw did. I did notice that both gates were open in your garden. I thought that was strange, because they usually are kept closed so the village dogs and children don't run through down to the shore."

"When did you notice that the gates were open?"

She frowned in concentration. "I would say sometime in the latter part of that afternoon. Yes, it was when Mrs. Bigley brought her daughter for her Greek and mathematics lessons." Her forehead ruffled. "Now that I think of it, I believe I saw someone in the garden. I did not get a good look at him."

"Him?" She wanted to hug Martha. If her neighbor shared with Constable Forshaw that the duke had been attacked by a man, then Priscilla would no longer be a suspect. Then Aunt Cordelia would not be able to threaten to take Isaac away to be raised in the manner Aunt Cordelia deemed correct.

"Yes. A man I hadn't seen before. I thought you

might have a guest, but then I saw Sir Neville, and I realized he was not the same man."

Priscilla had not guessed how she had tensed until she released the breath she had been holding. Transferring the suspicion from her to Neville would not persuade Aunt Cordelia to set aside her threats, and Neville, as an outsider, might find it more difficult than she to find allies in the village.

"Will you describe him to me?"

"He was a tall man with light-colored hair."

"That would describe the Duke of Meresden himself," Priscilla said slowly, not adding that *tall with light-colored hair* also matched the late duke's heir, Lord Sherbourne. But was the new duke capable of patricide? Neville's description of the man had not been flattering, and he had said Lord Sherbourne was a coward. Would a coward slay his own father? She shivered. The duke had been struck from behind. A coward's way to commit murder.

"Blonde hair," Martha said quickly, "not white hair. I think he may have had a mustache, but I can't be certain. It might have been a trick of the light. He was quite muscular. Do you know anyone who matches that description in Stonehall-on-Sea?"

"I may." Priscilla clasped Martha's hand. "I just may."

The butler who had greeted Priscilla and Neville on their arrival at Meresden Court paused in front of an arch filled with ornate red velvet–brocade draperies. "If you will wait in here, my lady, Sir Neville," he intoned as if he wanted to let his voice echo everywhere in the house, "I will inform His Grace of your call."

"Thank you," Priscilla said as she sat on the closest chair. The white silk was slippery. She grasped the arms, not to keep from falling, but to calm her quivering hands. Neither she nor Neville had said more than a score of words on their way from Mermaid Cottage to this elegant house farther inland. Coming to Meresden Court to accuse the new duke of murdering his father made her uneasier than she had been while talking with her aunt. She had not thought that possible.

Now she was under the duke's roof and gazing at a grandeur that eclipsed anything she had seen in London. She and Lazarus had been invited into some of the finest homes of the *ton* as well as the hovels of those who lived in the slums of London. Many of the fancy houses had been splendid, but she had not visited any that had ceilings as sweeping or as covered with such exquisite paintings of what might be ancient gods or earthly revelers among the clouds. Gilt-accented columns stood guard, flanking the windows soaring toward the ceiling.

The furniture was as glorious. Mahogany and marble and white silk filled the room along with paintings of somber people and elevations of Meresden Court and a single painting of thick woods that might have been in Canada or the United States.

As Neville walked about the room, examining each piece of art and a stack of books set on a marble-topped lyre table with an odd intensity, Priscilla said, "Do sit. It would not do for our host to come in to see you prowling about like a fox appraising a henhouse."

He whistled lowly, and she shot him a frown. The *ton* in London might be accustomed to him acting like a ramshackle fellow, but Lord Sherbourne—the new Duke of Meresden—might not be as understanding when the house was in mourning.

"This is as grand as Carlton House," Neville said.

"I will have to take your word for it."

He gave her a cheerful grin. "You have never been to call on the Prince Regent?"

"I have been—if you recall, Neville—in mourning."

"Forgive me, Pris. I did not intend to remind you of that grief, even though I have not—for a single moment—forgotten it myself."

She patted his arm. "Do not be grim. Lazarus would not have approved."

"You are right."

Unable to let her thoughts stray from the reason for their call, Priscilla asked, "Do you know how to ask the duke about . . ."

"Querying a man about slaying his own father is not something that one learns in school."

"I had thought you might have gained that knowledge in one of your—um—experiences before you inherited your title."

He laughed. "You do not need to be delicate with me, Pris. I know what I was before the Polite World welcomed me into its bosom."

"Neville, would you please answer my question?"

Sitting beside her, he lowered his voice. "There is no good way, Pris, to ask a man if he is responsible for anyone's death. Asking him if he murdered his father to gain his title and wealth is even more difficult."

"I wish Constable Forshaw had come with us."

"He would have if he had been in his office when we stopped in on the way here."

"I hope nothing bad has happened to him."

Neville chuckled. "I suspect rather that he has taken my advice at last and sought his bed for a long nap."

"So we just wait for an opportunity to question the duke?"

"It is amazing what I have learned from simply waiting, as you say, for an opportunity. You—" He looked over his shoulder, and his smile hardened.

Priscilla came to her feet as Neville did. A man was entering the grand room. The newest Duke of Meresden was as imposing a figure as his father had been. Tall, his pale hair matching the portrait of his father's younger years, he gave the appearance of a man who would inspire others to great deeds. From what Neville had told her, that was an illusion.

He held a handkerchief to his nose as he put something beneath his coat. His snuff box, no doubt. With a body-shuddering sneeze, he dabbed at his nose again. Only then did he walk toward them with an air that suggested they should deem themselves grateful simply to wait for him.

"I understand you wish to see me." The duke's voice was a very pleasing tenor.

Much like his father's, Priscilla thought with a twinge of regret. She had had only a passing acquaintance with the duke through his good works for the village and the church, but whether he had been a good man or a bad, he had not deserved to die as he did.

"I am Lady Priscilla Flanders." She offered her hand, and he bowed over it perfunctorily. Withdrawing her fingers, she said, "This is my guest and friend, Sir Neville Hathaway."

"Hathaway?" The new duke scowled. "That name has a very familiar ring to it. Have we been introduced previously?"

"Once or twice. The most recent time was at one of Lady Arlington's soirees. I believe it was about a month ago." A smile slipped across Neville's lips. "At the card table, if you recall."

Meresden's shoulders stiffened, and he cleared his

throat. "Ah, yes, we were introduced by that obnoxious marquess."

"And then I introduced you to my companion that evening." He smiled broadly. "Lady Luck."

"Neville," Priscilla said under her breath. Annoying the duke would gain them nothing. As long as possible, they should keep this meeting cordial. She raised her voice and said, "I would like to offer my condolences, Your Grace."

"Thank you."

"Your father was well respected by my husband, the late Reverend Dr. Flanders."

At the mention of her husband's name, Meresden seemed to make the connection to her at last. "And may I say, my lady, I am sorry you have been the subject of so many evil rumors?"

"It is understandable. So many people are distressed." She glanced at Neville, then said, "Of course, *you* can understand why I would want to find the real murderer."

"Most certainly. You wish to clear your name."

"And find the person who killed your father."

"As I do." He motioned toward the settee where they had been sitting. "I have my doubts that well-meaning constable is capable of finding him."

Neville asked as the duke sat facing them, "Have you considered sending to Bow Street for help?"

"Bow Street?" The duke's nose wrinkled as if something disgusting had touched it. "I daresay they would not be much help in the country. Their work is best done in the city."

"They have been called for help in other cases in daisyville."

The duke waved aside the suggestion as absurd. "Their arrival would send the murderer into hiding so that he might never be caught. I would rather, at this time, continue to see what Constable Forshaw can discover."

Priscilla glanced at Neville who was smiling as if he agreed wholeheartedly with Meresden's decision. She was sure Neville was as aware as she at the contradictions in the duke's comments in this short conversation.

"Has anyone made a threat toward your late father?" she asked.

The duke's astonishment seemed genuine. "Why would anyone threaten him?"

"Is it possible that someone wished to repay your father for some slight or for being outsmarted in a business deal?"

"You have a baleful mind, Lady Priscilla, for a clergyman's widow."

"A clergyman's wife sees the sordid aspects of life far more often than you might guess."

Meresden looked at her steadily for the first time. When she met his gaze, he lowered his. "My father had retired from the Polite World, and anyone who had a quibble with him is probably of an age with him. I doubt if someone was going to send his second over to challenge my father to a duel."

"I was not speaking of a duel."

Meresden scowled. "Are you suggesting that my father was involved with someone who might have sent a despicable creature to prey on my father in your garden, Lady Priscilla? That farfetched tale might shift the constable's attention from any complicity you might have in this matter, but you will find that you cannot play the jack so easily with me."

"She has no intention of trying to fool you," Neville said quietly. "She and I simply wish to know—as I assume you do, Meresden—who might have wished your father harm."

"My father had no enemies. Certainly nobody in Stonehall-on-Sea."

Priscilla frowned at Neville. Her hope that she could depend on him to speak man-to-man with the duke was futile. Every word he spoke was aimed at infuriating the duke further.

Quietly she said, "I agree. My husband always had the highest praise for your late father."

"Thank you," the duke replied.

"That is why we are puzzled about who would have wished him harm." She put her hand over her heart. "I have been so worried for my family, you must understand. If this was some sort of random attack, it could mean my children are in grave danger."

Meresden shook his head. "It was not a random attack."

"How can you be so certain of that?" asked Neville in a tone that suggested he was curious for no reason other than what they had already discussed.

"I cannot be, but I believe this sense of intuition that I have about this crime against my family."

Neville laughed shortly. "I hope your intuition is serving you better today than it did at the card table."

"Neville!" chided Priscilla, much to the duke's delight, she noted as she looked back at Meresden. "Do you know any reason your father would have been in my garden?"

"None." He tapped his finger against his full, lower lip. "I know he has paid calls infrequently on the Muir brothers, but that does not explain why he would be in your garden."

Neville leaned forward. "Did you notice anything out of the ordinary about your father in the days before his death?"

"Out of the ordinary?" The duke laughed tightly. "My father chose to be eccentric, staying here on his dirty acres instead of enjoying London. At first, I thought it was because my mother did not like the Season. I was wrong, for when they . . . when they found it expedient to live separate lives, Mother was one of the first to return to Town the next Season."

"So he did not seem agitated or distressed?"

"Not that I took note of."

"Then, mayhap, he had no idea that he was in danger."

Priscilla opened her reticule and drew out the bright button. "I found this in my garden. Do you recognize this, Your Grace?"

A satisfied, but fleeting smile spread across Meresden's lips. No one could mistake how pleased this man was to have the family's prestigious title. He grew somber again as he took the button and examined it.

"This is from a military uniform," the duke said.

"That was our guess as well." She took it back, noting that he did not seem agitated when confronted with what might be a damning piece of evidence. "Could it be your father's?"

He shook his head. "Impossible."

"Your father never served the king?" Neville asked.

"Of course, he did his duty." Meresden squared his shoulders. "However, that could not be his, for his uniforms were destroyed, along with many other family heirlooms, when there was a fire in the house in London when I was not much more than a babe."

"All of his uniforms?"

He scowled. "That is what I just said, Hathaway."

Priscilla jabbed Neville with her elbow. Making Meresden hostile would gain them nothing. Pasting on her sweetest smile, the one she had practiced often when she was required to speak to someone she did not care for at the church, she said, "It was a question we had to ask, Your Grace. The button belongs to no-body in my house."

"It may have been left by the murderer." Meresden focused his scowl at Neville. "Did you give that any thought?"

"I trust my intuition, too. My intuition tells me that this button has something to do with why your father was in Lady Priscilla's garden and why he died."

Meresden stood. Even though he waved aside Neville's words as insignificant, Priscilla noted how his hands quivered. The man was more unsettled by their questions than he wished for them to guess.

"Bah!" he retorted. "Hathaway, you may be able to trust your feelings at the card table, but this is something else."

"At last, we agree." Getting up, Neville added, "And one other thing we agree about is that your father must have had a reason to be where he was. Someone may have lured him there."

"Lady Priscilla—"

She rose with dignity. "I assure you, Your Grace, that I had no idea that your father was there until I chanced upon him."

Meresden blanched. "My lady, I did not mean to suggest that *you* had lured my father there for any illicit reasons."

"I should hope not." She placed the button into her reticule. "Your Grace, I would like to ask you to gather any items your father might have used in the days before he died."

"How could I know what those things might be? I arrived only the day before he was slain."

Neville said in a casual tone, "There may be some clue amid his papers."

"Papers?" The duke reminded Priscilla of Isaac when her son was trying to avoid doing the assignments that Mr. Ackerley had given him. "You expect me to go through his papers? That could take weeks, months. Even years."

"But," she hurried to say, "if you learn anything to help, surely it will have been worth the time expended."

The duke stared at her for a long minute. She wondered if he was trying to devise an excuse—any excuse at all—to avoid this chore he did not want to undertake.

"Your Grace," she added when he did not answer, "your father's valet would be the best help to determine if something is out of the ordinary."

He smiled, glad to turn the task over to someone else. "Very well. As you insist there might be something of import in his private papers, I shall endeavor to ascertain that."

"And you will alert Constable Forshaw if something is found?"

"Of course." He smiled, once again the beneficent duke. "If it would please you, Lady Priscilla, I shall inform you as well."

"How kind of you! That would greatly please me." She held out her hand and smiled as he bowed over it while they bid each other a good day.

Priscilla sighed as Neville handed her into his carriage. She started to speak, but he hushed her as they drove along the long avenue to the gate of Meresden Court. Only when they were on the road leading toward Stonehall-on-Sea did he speak.

"He is hiding something," Neville said in a tight voice.

"I know."

"Do you have any idea what?"

She shook her head. "Not yet, but I think when we

hear what he decides to share with Constable Forshaw—"

"And with you."

"And with me." She slapped his arm. "Don't sound like a jealous lover, Neville." She smiled. "Or an anxious father."

"Don't believe his act of being a gentleman. He has long wanted this title."

"He will do everything he can to keep it, even if that means working with us and the constable to pinpoint the person who killed his father."

"Or he will do everything he can to hide that truth."

# Seven

Neville opened the door to Constable Forshaw's office. He smiled when he saw the constable with his head down on his desk. The rumble of snores filled the small room. Nobody could complain about how hard Forshaw was working. He frowned. The man was sleeping as if he had not had a chance to since he left his supper to come to Mermaid Cottage. If Forshaw had not been sleeping when they came looking for him on their way to confront Meresden, where had he been?

Closing the door, Neville set down the basket of food Priscilla had sent to the constable. He walked to the small stove where a cast-iron pot was not steaming. He took the constable's coat off a peg and used it to lift the pot off the stove. As he had guessed, the pot was empty. Forshaw must have arrived back here shortly after Neville and Priscilla had left for Meresden Court.

He grimaced. Meresden was being as slippery as a hooked fish. Neville doubted if the new duke had the courage to kill his father, so what was he hiding?

The constable was deeply asleep, so Neville decided this was the very best time to look around the office. A pile of papers was balanced on the second chair. Picking up the top one, he saw it was covered with the notes Forshaw had taken during a conversation with Vicar

Kenyon. Beneath it was one from when the constable spoke with the Muir brothers. That one was a jumble. No surprise, for Neville's conversations with the elderly twins had been baffling. He suspected that the brothers did not listen to anyone but each other. Beneath those pages were the notes made while speaking with the Ackerleys and Priscilla's servants. On the bottom were the statements he and Priscilla had given.

With a frown, he restacked the pages. Nothing from any conversations with Meresden. The only thing on the desk was Forshaw's head atop his arms. Surely the constable had questioned the new duke when Meresden had requested that there be no coroner's inquest.

"Sir Neville!" Forshaw lifted his head, then rubbed his eyes. "When did you come in? Why didn't you wake me?"

"You looked as if you were enjoying your nap, so I didn't want to disturb you." He set the basket on the desk. "Lady Priscilla hopes this will atone for calling you away from your dinner the other night."

"There was no need for her to apologize," the constable said even as he was drawing back the cloth covering it. He lifted out some of Mrs. Dunham's excellent chutney and thick slices of roast beef. As he was unwrapping some bread, he paused and frowned.

"Don't even say it," Neville warned. "You know that Lady Priscilla would never use kindness to persuade you of her innocence."

"Are you a mind-reader, Sir Neville?"

He laughed. "I am only assuming that you are thinking what I would if our places were reversed. I did see a man purported to be a mind-reader at a low theater in London. It was fascinating." He picked up the papers and placed them on the desk. "Mayhap we should send for him."

"Mayhap."

Forshaw's reluctant agreement startled Neville. During their last conversation, the constable had been so insistent that he could handle this investigation.

He made sure his voice remained dispassionate as he asked, "Are you hitting a dead end?"

"Yes."

Again Neville was amazed. Forshaw must be exhausted if he was being so blunt. "I may be of some help."

"Unlikely." He rocked a slice of roast beef. "I went to call on my predecessor, Constable Kensfield. He lives with his daughter near Romney Marsh. I thought he might have some ideas of how to handle apprehending the duke's murderer."

"And?"

Forshaw put the meat onto the table. "He was constable of Stonehall-on-Sea for forty years, and he never had a single crime worse than a want-witted highwayman preying on travelers on the shore road. That knight of the pad was caught within a fortnight and sent to his reward on the gallows." He sighed. "As for the duke's death, I have discovered nothing that I can share with you at this time."

"We may have discovered something that you should know."

"We?"

"Lady Priscilla and I."

He stood and clasped his hands behind his back. "With all due respect, Sir Neville, I must ask you *again* to refrain from becoming involved in this investigation."

"I am involved already. As Lady Priscilla's guest, and as her husband's friend, it behooves me to find out everything I can to prove that she had nothing to do with this crime."

Forshaw deflated like one of the giant balloons that carried people about the countryside on holiday. "Have you discovered something?"

Neville drew up a chair and sat next to the constable's immaculate desk. As Forshaw sank back to his own chair, Neville said, "We have spoken with the duke."

"The duke? He is dead."

"His son. The *new* duke."

The constable's mouth tightened, and Neville knew embarrassing the young man would gain him nothing. He had come to gain the constable's camaraderie.

"It is," Neville continued, "going to take us awhile to become accustomed to this unexpected passing of the title."

"If anyone should be adapted to it, I should be. I have thought of nothing, night and day, but this murder."

"And you are exhausted."

Forshaw picked up the slice of beef and smiled. "You are being pleasant, Sir Neville. That tells me that I shall not find a way to ask you to leave until you share with me what you and Lady Priscilla have discovered."

Neville tossed the button onto the desk.

Forshaw caught it before it stopped spinning. "This is a button off a military uniform."

"It is." His respect for the young constable increased. He had met Bow Street Runners who could not have identified it as quickly. "Lady Priscilla found it in her garden near where the duke was discovered. As well, Miss Ackerley reports seeing a man she did not know, a tall man with light-colored hair, in the garden earlier that day."

"Was he wearing a military uniform?"

Neville laughed. "That would have made the whole far too easy, wouldn't it?"

"I would gladly have it be easy . . . and done with."
That Neville had to agree with wholeheartedly.

Priscilla breathed a sigh of relief. She had taken the
children to call on friends, as an excuse for all of
them to leave Mermaid Cottage. They had been glad
to escape the dreary cloud of the duke's death and
Aunt Cordelia's attempts to correct them on everything they said and did.

How much easier it would be if her aunt was hateful and doing this out of spite! But Aunt Cordelia
cared about the children, the family, and the title.
Some of her comments were valuable while others
were nitpicking. Like her most recent complaint that
Priscilla should make sure that Isaac received more
regular haircuts. So Priscilla had found taking the
children to visit friends a good excuse to slip out.
Fresh air would strengthen her for the next discussion
with Aunt Cordelia.

Her name was called, and she turned to see Martha
Ackerley walking toward her.

Pausing in front of the gate to the Muirs' house,
Priscilla said, "I see you are about to do some errands."

"Yes." She looked down at her covered basket. "Did
you hear anything other than the same rumors in the
village?"

"Not really. Do you expect there will be new rumors?"

She started to answer, then looked at the Muirs'
house. "I do not want to linger here where those two
horrible men might be listening."

Priscilla nodded, although she was sure her astonishment was visible. She had known that Martha

disliked the Muir brothers, but she had not guessed the young woman's antipathy was so bitter.

"I'm walking toward the old orchard. Would you join me?" Priscilla asked. "I was hoping to find some early apple blossoms for the table."

"Yes." Such gratitude filled her voice that Priscilla was startled. "I am quite amazed, Lady Priscilla."

"At what?"

"At your buoyant tone. How can you sound as if nothing were out of the ordinary now?"

"I do not wish to upset my children more." *Or Aunt Cordelia.*

"The poor dears."

"How is your brother? You said he was deeply upset."

"He is." She drew the basket off her arm. "Let me leave this on the steps."

"If you need to take it inside, I will be glad to wait."

Martha smiled as they put Mermaid Cottage between them and the Muirs. "I was on my way into the village to deliver something." Her smile wavered. "For Thomas. He is so forgetful, and I am often taking books to his students to read for their next lesson."

"You are a good sister." Priscilla waited while Martha set the basket on the steps of the Ackerleys' cottage, then continued along the road away from the village. "I hope he realizes that."

"I suspect he might . . . if he gave it any thought. You know how men are when they are busy with something."

Priscilla laughed. "That is very true."

"Is it?" asked Neville, startling her again.

"Why are you skulking up on us?" she asked as she turned.

"I did not skulk. I was walking along the road and

saw two pretty ladies." He bowed toward Martha, who dimpled with delight.

"You have met Sir Neville Hathaway, I assume," Priscilla said.

"We have spoken, but we have not been introduced." She held out her hand as if they were standing in an elegant ballroom instead of the narrow, twisting path. "It is a pleasure, Sir Neville."

"Neville is sufficient." He bowed again, this time over her hand. "And the pleasure is mine, Miss Ackerley."

"Oh, you must call me Martha."

Priscilla bit her lower lip to keep it from tilting up in a smile. She had never seen Martha simper before.

"We were walking to the apple orchard," Priscilla said. "Would you like to come along?"

"Yes."

His answer was the greatest surprise of the day. Neville was not one to spend a day strolling about, so what reason did he have for accepting her invitation? She wanted to ask what he had discussed with the constable, but she could not when Martha was listening. Mayhap *that* was why Neville had agreed to this promenade.

Martha clearly had no doubts why Neville had accepted the invitation. She matched her steps to his and began to chatter as Priscilla had never heard her do before. When the path narrowed past the Ackerleys' cottage, Priscilla let the other two walk ahead of her. She pretended not to see Neville's glance back. If he did not know enough to be careful around an innocent young woman, he must learn.

"I trust," he said, "you are well in the wake of what has happened."

"Yes," Martha replied.

Neville looked back at Priscilla again. She shrugged.

Martha's terse answer revealed she was more distressed by what had happened than she had suggested before.

"Are you otherwise enjoying your stay in Stonehall-on-Sea and England, Martha?" he asked.

"For the most part." Running her fingers along the stones on the low wall, Martha said, "I do so wish to go back to New York, but I know how impossible that is."

"It would be very dangerous to try to cross the Atlantic now with the French trying to blockade England. Who knows what the silly Americans are up to or will do?" He halted, then said, "Forgive me, Martha. My comment was not meant to suggest that you are silly."

She laughed, her face brightening. "Of course you didn't. You are far too kind a gentleman to speak so of me."

Priscilla put her hand over her mouth to silence her laughter. *Kind* and *gentleman* were words seldom associated with Neville. When Neville looked at her, his face was screwed up in a frightful frown. He had started flirting with Martha, so *he* would have to extract himself from this. Just now, she was content to walk along this path and enjoy the sea air.

They reached the orchard too quickly for Priscilla. She would have gladly continued walking to Rye and beyond, but escaping her problems would not be that simple.

Drawing up her skirt, Priscilla climbed over the wooden stile on the wall separating the orchard from the path. She smiled, for the apple trees were snowy white with blossoms. She went to the closest tree, reached up for a branch, then paused as she realized Martha and Neville remained on the far side of the wall. She started to ask what was amiss, then saw Martha hold out her hand.

"Will you assist me, Neville?" the young woman cooed.

"Most certainly."

This time, Priscilla made no effort to hide either her smile or her laugh. She received another glower from Neville, but Martha was too enrapt to take notice of anyone but him.

As he assisted her over the stile so gracefully that Priscilla would have guessed they were dancing a quadrille, Martha's smile widened. The young woman waited at the bottom for him to join her. Then she put her hand on his arm, startling Priscilla as much as Neville. Martha had never been so brazen before.

"You are not like the men in Stonehall-on-Sea." Martha put her other hand over the one on his arm. "I appreciate how you do not treat me as if I am inferior to everyone else."

"I do not judge someone by their birth," Neville replied.

Priscilla laughed again as she broke off the small branches that were heavy with blossoms. Now Neville was being honest. He treated everyone he met with the same polite graciousness, unless it behooved him not to.

"Allow me," Neville said, stepping forward and holding out his arms to take the blossoms.

"You looked as if you could use an excuse to dodge some eager fingers," she whispered as Martha went to another tree and picked a blossom to weave through her hair.

"More than you could guess."

"You should know better than to trifle with an innocent lass." She put more blossoms in his arms.

"Innocent? She had a stranglehold on my arm."

"Your arm cannot be strangled, Neville."

He arched a dark brow. "That is what *you* think." He

raised his voice. "How much do you need? I shall not be able to see if you pile this much higher."

"I would be glad to help guide you," Martha said, rushing to him. "I have helped Thomas when he carries heavy loads from the barn."

"Barn?" asked Priscilla.

Martha glanced at her with a frown that suggested she had forgotten Priscilla was there. It was replaced by a tepid smile as she said, "At home in America."

"I believe I can manage," Neville said, striding toward the stile rapidly. "Blast!"

With a laugh, Priscilla took pity on him and, holding his arm, steered him over the stile before Martha could. That did not keep Martha from finding a place beside him on the path so she could babble all the way back to the trio of cottages.

"Would you like to come in?" Martha asked as they reached her house.

"I need to get these in water," Priscilla said. "Neville, if you would—"

"You cannot carry these yourself," he hastened to reply.

"Thank you for your company, Neville." Martha batted her golden lashes. "I do look forward to another promenade."

"As do I."

"Tomorrow afternoon?"

"Tomorrow afternoon?" he repeated.

Martha must not have heard his questioning tone, because she said, "After luncheon, call and we can take another walk."

"Tomorrow afternoon," he began.

"Wonderful!" Martha hurried through the gate and to the front door. Picking up her basket, she waved before going into the house.

Neville grumbled something as they continued on

to Mermaid Cottage. Priscilla chuckled as he stepped through the gate. She closed it behind them.

"You are enjoying this too much," he growled.

"It is about time you were caught in your own flirtatious trap."

"'Tis not a flirting trap she is eager to get me into, but the parson's mouse-trap."

"Marriage would be good for you, Neville."

He shuddered. "I thought you were my friend."

"I am."

"No friend of mine would suggest such a thing to me."

She laughed. "I suspect that you will remain wily enough to keep yourself free of such a trap."

"I always have been." He put the branches on a bench in the front garden. "Let me knock the dirt from my boots before I add to Mrs. Moore's distress by tracking it inside."

She picked up some branches. "I shall order tea, and you can tell me what you learned at the constable's office."

"It shall not take long to tell."

Priscilla's smile wavered. She had not guessed—until now—how much she had hoped Neville would bring the word that she was no longer a suspect in the duke's death.

Neville patted her arm. "Don't worry. I have a few more ideas to try before they send you off to the gallows."

"How comforting," she retorted, turning toward the front door.

As she reached the top step, her foot struck something. Something soft. Looking over the apple blossoms, she grimaced as she saw a dead bird. She backed away a step, then another. The blossoms fell from her hands, and she pressed her hand over her churning stomach. She usually was not queasy, but the bird brought forth memories of the duke lying in her back garden.

"What is it?" asked Neville from behind her.

Anger surged through her. If she had not chanced upon this poor, dead creature before the children arrived home, they would have been met by this appalling sight.

"It is a dead bird," she said. "I don't know why it would have crashed into the front door. I shall have one of the footmen remove it before—"

Neville's curse silenced her. He knelt and stared at the bird as he had at the duke. "It did not bash into your door. At least, not on its own." He stood and turned to her. "Someone smashed in its skull."

"Smashed its skull?"

"Just like the duke's was."

# Eight

Neville drew the parlor doors closed before seating Priscilla on the closest chair. Her face was too pale.

"It isn't like you, Pris, to be so melodramatic."

"It isn't like you, Neville, to dismiss my heartfelt words as feminine vapors."

That comment brought him up short. She was a woman who had an orderly mind that was a match for her late husband's. That was why Neville had found it easy to welcome her into the discourses he had with Lazarus. But had he found it so easy that he had forgotten she possessed feminine sensitivities?

He knew that he could not forget she was a woman. He had always enjoyed admiring her, even when she had been Lazarus's wife instead of his widow. Her deep blue eyes fascinated him. Lines crinkled around them and bespoke of how often her full lips tilted in a smile. From their first meeting, he had discovered that he should not dismiss her because the top of her head barely reached his chin. Those eyes could snap like a hot ember, and woe be to the person her gaze was aimed at.

She was a woman who could turn men's heads, and yet she seemed unaware of that. No, it was more that she did not consider it important. He doubted if she had learned that after marrying Lazarus. She had not been the usual wife for a vicar in many ways, so he could not imagine her putting aside earthly concerns. It could be as simple as she had the ability to see beyond an outer appearance, and she assumed others did as well.

He went to the sideboard and poured himself a generous serving of wine. He took a deep drink, refilled his glass, then filled another for her. Taking it to where she was sitting, he made no comment about how her fingers trembled.

She took a sip. "Someone must have put that poor dead creature there as a warning to me."

"A warning?" He shook his head. "I daresay it was more likely a prank perpetrated by one of young Isaac's friends."

"His friends are not involved in such horrible antics."

"You don't understand how young boys think when they get together. The more disgusting the possibilities, the better they like it. On this matter, I do have experience."

"I am not surprised." She took another sip and sighed. "I suppose we should leave it there until the constable can be contacted."

He sat facing her. "By Jove, Pris, you haven't heeded a single thing I have said. You cannot let a childish hoax unsettle you so."

"And you haven't heard a single word I said. I know my son, Neville, and he would not be party to such a prank."

A scream came from beyond the parlor door. Neville recognized Lady Cordelia's voice. Standing, he went to the door and opened it. He was not surprised to see Priscilla's aunt staring through the open front door.

"Remove this! Immediately!" she was calling to Priscilla's butler who was trying to edge past her to obey.

"No," Neville said. "Leave it be."

She glowered at him. "I cannot believe you would suggest we leave this carrion here."

Priscilla said from behind him, "Neville is expressing *my* wishes, Aunt Cordelia."

"*You* want a dead bird on the front steps?"

"Gilbert, send someone for the constable. Mrs. Moore, please have tea delivered to the parlor with an extra cup for Constable Forshaw."

Neville stepped hastily out of the way as Lady Cordelia followed Priscilla back into the parlor. Exchanging a glance with Gilbert, he suspected he would be wise to take his leave. He could not leave Priscilla to face her aunt—and the constable—alone. She needed an ally when she explained her silly theory about the bird. He did not want to consider that she might be right.

Lady Cordelia had launched into her scold before Neville walked into the room. Surprised that Priscilla said nothing, he waited until the older woman took a breath. Then he said, "Lady Cordelia, you cannot blame Priscilla for someone else's actions."

"Stay out of this, Neville," Priscilla said in a tone he heard so seldom. The last time, he recalled with a pinch of consternation, was when she had stood by her husband's grave on the day Lazarus was buried.

"Yes," Lady Cordelia seconded. "This is a family matter, and you are, most fortunately, not part of this family."

Priscilla's voice did not warm. "Aunt Cordelia, as I have mentioned to you many times since your arrival, Neville is my guest. Please remember that when you speak to him."

Her aunt bristled.

"And," Priscilla continued before Lady Cordelia could respond, "I will thank you to allow me to handle matters as I see fit in my own house. At the moment, I see fit to send for the constable, even though there may not be any relationship between that dead bird and the Duke of Meresden's death."

"Mama!" Isaac rushed into the parlor, followed at nearly the same pace by his sisters. Isaac did not slow, although his sisters did when they saw their great-aunt. Isaac threw his arms around Priscilla. "I thought you were dead!"

Priscilla knelt and put her hands on either side of his face. All fury vanished from her as she asked softly, "Whatever made you think that?"

Leah threw her arms around Priscilla, and Daphne, after a glance at her great-aunt, embraced both her sister and mother. Neville was not sure if it was Leah or Daphne who cried, "The constable is on his way here! We thought something horrible had happened."

"I want the constable to check something for me." She smiled as she touched each one on the cheek. "Do not fret."

"But, Mama—" Daphne began.

"Will you take your sister and brother to the kitchen?" Priscilla asked, standing. "Mrs. Dunham told me that she would be making special tarts today. Why don't you go and check if she has them baked?"

All three children hesitated, then nodded. Neville gave them a bolstering smile as they walked out of the parlor slowly. Isaac grinned when he ruffled the boy's hair. When he winked at the girls, they gave him a smile.

The door had just closed before it opened again. Gilbert bowed toward Priscilla and said, "Constable Forshaw, my lady."

"Are you going to continue with this foolishness?" demanded Lady Cordelia. "Priscilla, you are making yourself and this family the topic on every tongue in London."

"Aunt Cordelia," she replied with more restraint than Neville believed he could have mustered, "I need to speak with Constable Forshaw. You are welcome to stay or go, as you wish." Looking at the startled constable, she asked, "Will you join us, Constable Forshaw?"

Her aunt harrumphed, then strode to the door. She wagged a finger at Priscilla. "You shall rue this day when you spoke so discourteously to me. I see, without question, that you are not fit for the duties that have been thrust upon you."

Priscilla did not reply as her aunt stormed out, but Neville saw her shoulders flinch at her aunt's threat. He wanted to say something to give her solace. She gave him no chance as she began to tell the constable what they had found and both her and Neville's opinions.

Constable Forshaw took off his cap and wiped his nape. "I believe Sir Neville's assessment is correct, my lady."

A footman came into the room. He looked at the constable and gulped, but hurried to Lady Priscilla. "My lady, pardon me for intruding." He turned to Neville. "May I speak with you privately?"

Astonished at how the young man's voice quivered, Neville went with the footman into the dining room. "What is it?"

"I was not sure if I should have interrupted with the constable here and . . ." He gulped again and held out a piece of paper. "I thought you should see this."

A stained piece of paper, Neville noted, as he took it. Stained with blood, if he was not mistaken. "Where did you find this?"

"Beneath the bird."

He scanned it. "You were right to bring it to me." He crossed the hallway and into the parlor.

Priscilla looked toward him, anxiety dimming her eyes. "Is there something else amiss?"

"I think this may change your opinion, Forshaw, as it changed mine." He handed the page to the constable.

The constable read it and snarled an oath. A flush burst out of his collar to climb his cheeks.

"What does it say?" asked Priscilla.

The constable hesitated, then handed the paper to Neville. He tipped his cap to Priscilla. "I will want to see where you found the bird and the bird itself posthaste."

"Layden," Neville ordered to the footman, "show Constable Forshaw what he needs to see."

As they went out the door, Priscilla asked, almost as coldly as she had to her aunt, "Are you going to show that to everyone, save me?"

"Save you?" He laughed without humor. "Your question may be more appropriate than you have guessed."

Priscilla took the page. Her eyes widened, and his lips straightened, for he knew what she was reading. He doubted he could forget a single word.

*Stop asking questions or you may find one of your children lying here next time.*

# Nine

The funeral at St. Elizabeth's Church hardly befit a duke. That surprised Priscilla as she entered the church filled with most of the villagers. She would have guessed his son would want to have a huge ceremony, so that everyone—not just the villagers—was quite aware that he had inherited his father's title. She noticed a strange man and woman sitting next to the new duke in the front pew. He was a handsome, well-dressed man and the woman's clothes were apropos for London. They must be the new duke's friends, who had come to Stonehall-on-Sea to attend the funeral.

As every time she entered St. Elizabeth's Church, Priscilla had the odd feeling that she was coming home and yet was as much a stranger as that man and woman who were garnering curious glances. Vicar Kenyon had not made any changes to the stone building since he had assumed the pulpit from her late husband. That would be considered by Stonehall-on-Sea to be blasphemy, if not outright heresy. Music came from the pipe organ set in a loft at the back of the church. The first four rows of pews were stone, for they had been brought from the ruined monastery along with the altar that had been stripped of anything that hinted of popery. The other pews were carved from the same oak as the lacy work above the altar and the rafters that usually had a bird or two on them.

She shivered at that thought. Just as when the duke had died, no one had seen anyone put the bird on the front steps of Mermaid Cottage.

Pushing that memory aside, she walked along the center aisle. Stained glass was set into the leaded windows, save for the grandest window that was set in an arch over the altar, and the walls were decorated with paintings of the apostles in their martyrdom. In the farthest corner was a portrait that was said to be of St. Elizabeth. The herald of the king hung behind the pulpit.

Sitting in the third row where she had moved after Lazarus no longer served this parish, Priscilla was glad she did not have to hush her children. Even Isaac seemed to comprehend the need to curb his usual exuberance. He nestled close as he had not since he had deemed himself too old to be, in his words, "treated like a baby." He was more upset than she had guessed that something had happened to her. What if something *had* happened to her? She frowned. She could not leave her children in her aunt's care. Her aunt would think first of the family's reputation, not the children's happiness.

Putting her arm around her son's shoulders, Priscilla looked at the altar. There was no coffin set in front of it, because the duke had had his father interred in the fancy mausoleum at Meresden Court. This was a memorial service, which puzzled her even more, because it could have waited until the duke's friends and political associates came down from London.

Neville slid into the pew just as the choir sitting to the left of the altar began a dirge. He gave Isaac a bolstering smile, then leaned past him and murmured, "How appropriate this is at St. Elizabeth's."

She glanced at him, but did not speak.

"St. Elizabeth is the patron saint of falsely accused people, after all," Neville continued.

This time, she stared at him. How did he gather this seemingly obscure information? She would be wiser not to ask. What she did know was that she was glad he was sitting with them. By being here, he did not stop the glances—in fact he might have caused a few more—but she was glad to have him beside her when a threat had been aimed at her children. Now it was not just Aunt Cordelia who was trying to tear them apart, but whoever had left the dead bird on her step. If Neville was not here . . .

As the choir completed its song, Vicar Kenyon stepped to the pulpit. Priscilla lowered her eyes. In the past year, she had become accustomed to the loss of her husband. Everywhere, but here. His voice still seemed to echo against the ceiling, as full and rich as the pipe organ.

A hand patted hers. She looked at Neville, whose face was long with sorrow. Other than her children, no one shared her grief as much as Neville.

Giving him an unsteady smile, she listened to Vicar Kenyon who was extolling the duke's life. The eulogy with a few changes could have been spoken at the passing of anyone in Stonehall-on-Sea. That was as odd as every other part of this memorial service, because Vicar Kenyon usually was an inspired orator. She glanced at the duke. He was nodding, pleased with each word the clergyman spoke. Trying to force her shoulders to relax, she told herself that if the Duke of Meresden was satisfied, then the clergyman was doing as he should. She fought to concentrate on Vicar Kenyon's words, but her mind drifted in directions she did not want it to go.

After examining the bird yesterday, Constable Forshaw had requested that Priscilla give the slip of paper to him. She could not guess what he might need it for, because it was a common sort of paper and the block letters could have been written by anyone.

She had heard Mrs. Moore whispering with Mrs. Dunham that the bird may have been left by the duke's ghost which could not rest in peace as long as his murderer was uncaught. Priscilla's attempts to make the housekeeper and the cook see reason, for the note had wanted her to *stop* trying to find answers, had been for naught.

The only saving grace had been that Aunt Cordelia had avoided Priscilla the rest of the day. Priscilla guessed her aunt was busy with correspondence, for she had heard Gilbert explain to one of the footmen how letters would be delivered beyond Stonehall-on-Sea. She did not want to think to whom Aunt Cordelia had been writing and why.

"Pris?"

At Neville's whisper, Priscilla tore herself from her bleak thoughts to realize the surprisingly brief service was over. She let him bring her to her feet, then took Isaac's and Leah's hands. When Neville offered his arm to Daphne, her daughter's eyes grew wide and she smiled. Daphne enjoyed the rare opportunities when she was treated as an adult instead of a child.

The mourners milled on the green, nobody ready to go home and resume their customary day. Or, more likely, everyone was hoping to hear the latest gossip. When the man and woman Priscilla had not known came out of the church, a buzz of whispers rushed along the green.

"I guess no one expected to see the prime minister and his wife here," Neville said as he paused next to where Priscilla was standing in the shade of a great horse chestnut.

"That is the prime minister?" Daphne asked.

"Hush," Priscilla warned, but wondered why she had not recognized Spencer Perceval. She had seen him on several occasions when he called on Lazarus. She had not been surprised a prime minister would call on a vicar, for her husband had been respected in so many homes—both high and low—in London.

"Did you know," Daphne continued, "that he and his wife were wed in secret because her father refused to allow the match? It is said that she wore nothing fancier than her riding habit."

She realized that her daughter was talking to Martha who must have come out of the church while Priscilla was watching the prime minister and Mrs. Perceval.

Neville chuckled. "Much like your mother and father, Daphne."

"Grandfather did not deny them the chance to marry!" Daphne argued.

*"Finally* he agreed."

"Is that true, Mama?" asked Daphne, wide-eyed.

Priscilla gave Neville a vexed look, but it was useless, for he left her to deal with her curious children and Martha. She should have guessed that Neville would not have sympathy for her for very long. Like Lazarus, he expected her to stand on her own and deal with her problems. She had appreciated Lazarus's faith in her . . . and she did Neville's as well. *Although,* she had to own, *I would have appreciated his solace for at least a full day.*

"He is exaggerating a bit," Priscilla said when she saw her daughter waiting for an answer. "Your grandfather was surprised at my choice of a husband. Once he recovered from that astonishment, he was quite accepting of your father's and my plans to wed."

Daphne looked a bit deflated at the explanation, which was almost completely true.

Priscilla wanted to keep this tale from being interesting, because her aunt would be glad to go on for hours about how foolish the earl had been to grant his daughter's request to marry a mere clergyman. Changing the topic back to the prime minister and his wife, Priscilla walked with the children and Martha toward the road leading to their cottages.

"Lady Priscilla?"

She turned to see the duke waving to her. Telling the children to wait in front of the bakery, she hurried to the duke. She preferred, in the wake of the threatening note, not to leave her children alone, but she would be able to see them while she spoke with the Duke of Meresden.

"Thank you so much for attending this service," the duke said when she reached him.

Was that all he wanted to tell her? She glanced at where the children were talking to some friends. Martha must have continued on to her cottage.

"It was a lovely service," she said, not sure what else to say.

"My father was well known to all of you. He told me often that this village was his true home. I believe he deemed each and every one of you a part of his family."

"I believe that was true." She had to say something else. But what? "The eulogy was heartfelt."

"Thank you, Lady Priscilla. I wrote it."

That explained why the words were not up to the clergyman's usual standard. "Your father would have been pleased."

"I suppose he would have been, although I suspect he would just as well not had it read today."

She knew she was about to overstep the bounds of propriety. Glancing about, she saw her aunt in conversation with Mrs. Perceval. This morning, Priscilla had overhead Aunt Cordelia talking to Isaac about a boarding school that she believed would be "perfect for a young lord." Playing on his vanity at having such a respected title was sure to persuade Isaac to heed his great-aunt. If her aunt heard her now . . .

"Your Grace, have you had the opportunity to search your father's papers?" Priscilla asked.

He frowned. "I had thought to do that after the memorial ceremony."

"But every minute that passes allows his murderer to cover his trail."

"Or hers."

She raised her chin and gave him the look that quelled even Neville. "I am a suspect because your father died in my garden, but I can assure you that I had no knowledge of his death until I saw him lying prone in my flowers."

"Lady Priscilla, I did not mean to suggest that *you* slew my father. I am simply repeating what Constable Forshaw has said."

"And many others." She halted as the church bell began to ring.

The green became silent while everyone listened to the slow peal of the bell that had been given to St. Elizabeth's by the late Duke of Meresden. A stricken expression, the first she had seen, crossed the new duke's face, and she saw tears well up in his eyes. He was not so heartless, after all. When he walked away without saying anything else, Priscilla was not offended. She knew how consuming sorrow could be, blinding and deafening one to every other emotion.

"Poor man," said Constable Forshaw as he stepped out of the way of the prime minister's coach. "I think he is only now believing that his father is dead."

"I suspect you are right," she replied. "Constable

Forshaw, after your call yesterday, I realized that I should have drawn a likeness of that button I found. Then I can look at it enough times so I will recognize its like if I chance upon another."

"Impossible."

"If I could examine it—"

"You can't, Lady Priscilla."

"I know you have rules and regulations you must adhere to as the constable, but I did bring you the button, after all. And as you still consider me a suspect in this crime, the very least you can do is let me look at the button once more."

"You can't because I don't have it."

"What?"

His face turned red as he bowed his head sheepishly. "The button has vanished."

"Buttons don't just vanish."

"This one has."

Priscilla counted to ten in Latin, Greek, and German before speaking. Even that pause did not ease her fury as she said, "Constable Forshaw, please explain how this button disappeared."

"I would if I could. All I know is that it is no longer in the drawer of my desk where I put it for safekeeping."

"A locked drawer?"

His eyes widened. "I never thought to lock it."

Priscilla was torn between grasping him by the shoulders and shaking him or trying to knock some good sense into his head, but she did neither. Constable Forshaw was inexperienced and not prepared to deal with such a crime. Now their single clue to the duke's murderer had vanished.

An icy chill raced down her back. The only one who would have taken the button was the murderer, which meant that person had not left Stonehall-on-Sea.

\* \* \*

Priscilla had never been fond of needlework, but Isaac had snagged the knees of another set of breeches. She suspected he had been sliding down the ruined walls of the monastery on the shore, because sand still clung to the fabric even after the breeches had been laundered.

Each time footfalls passed the arbor where she sat in her side garden between her house and the low wall of the Muir brothers' garden, she looked up. Neville had been in a pelter about Constable Forshaw losing the button, and he had vowed to tear the constable's office apart to find it. Only then would he acquiesce that the button had been stolen from the office.

"Why would a murderer risk everything to get a *button?*" she had asked more than once last night.

"It is the only clue we have to the murderer's identity."

"A clue that has us stymied."

"The murderer may not know that."

Priscilla had not been able to argue with that. Now she was waiting to hear if, by some chance, the button had been found.

A knock was placed on one of the gazebo's uprights. Gilbert stood rod-straight in front of the gazebo. "Lady Priscilla, you have a caller. A Mr. Ledyard Pritchard."

Although she did not recognize the name, she instructed the butler to bring Mr. Pritchard to the garden and to have some refreshments prepared. She finished the last two stitches on the right knee of Isaac's breeches, then set them and her needle, thread and scissors on the bench. Brushing bits of thread off her dress, she went to greet her guest.

A tall white-haired man was standing in the middle of the path that led from the front door to this garden, tugging at his gloves. He was looking around nervously, and she wondered why he should be unsettled. He must have heard of the discovery of the duke in her back garden. She was tempted to tell him, from where he stood, that flower bed could not be seen.

"I am Lady Priscilla Flanders," she said, holding out her hand. "Welcome to Mermaid Cottage."

"Ledyard Pritchard, my lady." He bowed over her hand, then offered a calling card.

Taking it, she did not look at it. The card would have nothing more than his name, for he was not a tradesman. His diction was too perfect, and his clothes, despite the dust from his journey, too well made.

"Forgive me, Mr. Pritchard," she said. "I do not believe I was previously informed that you intended to call."

"Surely your aunt mentioned I would be visiting to discuss your son's future." His voice boomed more on each word.

Aunt Cordelia had not heeded a single word Priscilla had spoken in the past year about Isaac. It was a struggle, but she managed to ask in her customary tone, "What aspect of my son's future, Mr. Pritchard?"

"His education, of course. I am the headmaster of Elsworth Academy."

"Elsworth Academy?"

He struck a pose that would have better suited a statue in a London square as he intoned, "The finest school for young men in England. We are proud that our students have gone on to be leaders of this nation as well as great industrialists. We prepare our students for the finest universities. As you must know, all the earls in your family have studied there."

"Is that so?" She tried to remember if her father had ever spoken of this school. In his later years, her father had enjoyed reminiscing about his youth, but only the parts he wanted to recall. He never talked about aspects he found distasteful or troublesome. Not once had he said anything about Elsworth Academy. "I am not familiar with your academy, Mr. Pritchard."

"How can that be?" His voice became even louder.

Wanting to put her hands over her ears, she replied, "I do not believe my father mentioned it in my hearing."

"Odd."

Not half as odd as this tall man, she decided. "Mr. Pritchard, if my aunt suggested that I had decided upon a boarding school for my son, you have been brought here under a false impression."

"You will find the decision simple, for all you need to do is agree to send Lord Emberson to Elsworth Academy. Then you need have no other concerns about his education." He tugged at his gloves. "In light of what you have endured recently—"

"You can understand why I do not wish to make a hasty decision."

"Surely it is not a hasty decision. I have been in correspondence with Lady Cordelia for almost six months. It was my understanding that she wished for Lord Emberson to return with me to Elsworth Academy."

"I think there has been a mistake."

Mr. Pritchard looked down his nose. "Lady Cordelia did mention that you would not be receptive to the idea. She is very concerned about your son's future."

"As I am."

"Then you must see that the only choice is—"

"Lady Priscilla, how are you doing on this lovely day?" Irwin Muir walked into the garden with his brother following like a well-trained pup. What hair they had remaining was white, and their faces were lined with an identical pattern of wrinkles. She suspected it was because the two brothers never had spent a moment apart from the moment of their conception.

And she had never been happier to see her quirky neighbors.

"It is a lovely day." Walden would not be left out of any conversation.

"The finest one we have had this year," said his brother.

"No, last week, the air was fresher off the sea."

Irwin glowered. "But the sunshine was not as warm."

"Good day to you," Priscilla interrupted as Walden drew in a breath to retort. When the brothers looked at her, she motioned toward Mr. Pritchard who was wearing a scowl as fierce as Irwin's. "May I introduce you to Mr. Pritchard of the Elsworth Academy? Mr. Pritchard, my neighbors Mr. Irwin Muir and Mr. Walden Muir."

"Mr. Pritchard," Irwin said with a slight nod. Even though he must be approaching his seventieth year, he stood as straight as a soldier at attention.

"Mr. Pritchard," echoed Walden.

"Lady Priscilla," continued Irwin, "I know I promised you yesterday that I would show you the way we transplant roses."

Walden's smile returned. "Yes, we have a foolproof way."

"We shall have beautiful roses next summer."

"Red and white roses."

"In alternating vines that will be climbing this wall."

Irwin slapped the wall. "They will creep right up and over these stones."

"If you do not mind, Lady Priscilla."

Mr. Pritchard cleared his throat. "Lady Priscilla, if *you* do not mind—"

"She will not mind," Irwin said with a smile.

"You do like roses, don't you, Lady Priscilla?"asked Walden.

Again Mr. Pritchard tried to interrupt. "Lady Priscilla, this is of vital—"

The brothers paid him no mind, continuing to talk about roses. Mr. Pritchard muttered about continuing their conversation inside the house where they would not be interrupted. Before she could answer, he strode toward the front of the house.

Irwin and Walden paused in midword and grinned.

"He's gone," Irwin said needlessly.

"Not much of a conversationalist," Walden added.

Priscilla chuckled. "Thank you so much. I should not sound so relieved, but I am."

"He seemed officious." Irwin smiled, clearly seeing Mr. Pritchard's leave-taking as a retreat.

"And loud." Walden wrinkled his nose in disgust.

"I need to ask you something," Priscilla said before they could start into another cycle of conversation. "Miss Ackerley told me she saw a light-haired man in my garden several hours before I chanced upon the duke's body. Did you perchance see him, too?"

Irwin frowned in concentration. "A light-haired man."

"Tall," added his brother. "And he was in Lady Priscilla's garden during the afternoon before the duke was found."

"No," both of them said in unison.

"We did not see such a man," Irwin went on.

Walden scratched his nose. "We were in *our* garden all day that day."

"All day."

"First time we saw a tall light-haired man in your garden is that irritating man."

"Mr. Pritchard."

"Yes, his name is Mr. Pritchard."

Priscilla knew she was letting herself in for another storm of comments, but she had to ask, "You didn't see the duke either?"

"Not until we saw him facedown in your flowers," Irwin answered.

"He did not call on us."

"Hasn't in nearly two months."

Walden frowned. "He was due to visit."

"Yes, he was, but he did not visit that day."

"Then," Priscilla said to herself, for she was unsure if they would listen, "the duke must have entered my garden through the Ackerley's garden."

Irwin's lips turned down farther. "Why would the Duke of Meresden call there?"

"He wouldn't," Walden chimed in. "He never spoke to those Americans."

"Never."

"If he had come here of his own free will, he would have visited us."

"Very strange," Irwin said.

"Yes, very, very strange." Walden paused, then asked, "What else have you discovered about the duke's murder?"

She sighed. "Too little. I thought I might have found a clue, but it has disappeared."

"How?" asked Irwin.

"Did you lose it?" Walden's scowl became sharper. "The only clue you have discovered?"

"It was misplaced." She did not want to accuse Constable Forshaw, who was surely trying his best to deal with this horrible crime. "What I found was a button in the flower bed."

Irwin glanced at his brother, then said, "A button is a poor clue."

"It is all we have so far," she said before Walden could add his comment.

"Well, anything is better than nothing," Irwin replied.

"But this is nothing," Walden added.

"Less than nothing."

"Yes, for the button could have come from anyone at anytime."

Priscilla excused herself and left the brothers to their conversation on her garden path. She was unsure if they had heard her until she looked back to see them walking toward the gate to their garden, still talking in perfect rhythms.

"Mr. Pritchard has been settled into the green guest room," Mrs. Moore said as Priscilla entered.

Untying her bonnet, she replied, "I did not realize that he was staying here."

"Lady Cordelia invited him." The housekeeper reached for Priscilla's bonnet. "I wanted to let you know right away."

"Thank you." She took a deep breath.

"And Lady Cordelia requested that you come to the parlor as soon as you came inside."

"That is not unexpected." Drawing in another deep breath, she said, "Please have someone retrieve my sewing from the gazebo. I am afraid I forgot about it."

Mrs. Moore glanced over her shoulder and then held out Priscilla's bonnet. "If you wish to go back to your sewing, my lady, your aunt will not learn from me that you came in."

"You are tempting me to be wicked."

"I am tempting you to be sensible."

With a smile, Priscilla thanked her housekeeper before going to the parlor. She had a few things she needed to say to her aunt.

"Good afternoon, Aunt Cordelia," she said as she entered the parlor.

Aunt Cordelia scowled. "I had thought your manners were better than this."

"My manners are fine." She walked to the window to look out on the off-chance that Neville might be returning. She could use him standing beside her now that her aunt had brought in reinforcements in her battle to decide Isaac's future.

"Do sit, Priscilla. You are jumping about like an Indian monkey."

How was it that Aunt Cordelia could make her forget that she was a woman grown with children and compel her to act like a disobedient child? Asking that question aloud would lengthen the lecture that was about to begin.

"I know you are upset," Aunt Cordelia said, "but I expected better of you than how you have treated dear Mr. Pritchard."

"Dear?"

The wrong thing to say, for her aunt snapped, "He was horrified to be treated so by those two strange men. I have no idea how *they* were raised, but I know that *you* were instructed in proper manners."

"Mr. Pritchard was overmastered by the Muir brothers and their conversation that allows no one else to say much." She kept her chin high. "If he had remained and spoken with them instead of racing away as if a dog nipped his heels, he would have seen that they were speaking of nothing more troublesome than the transplanting of roses."

Aunt Cordelia gave an emoted shiver. "I have never

liked you living here, Priscilla, with those men next door. Now with your husband gone and those Americans on the other side of your cottage . . ." She picked up a fan from the table beside her, snapped it open, and waved it as if the very thought undid her.

Her pose of outrage was ruined when Mrs. Moore rushed in. "My lady, Vicar Kenyon requests to speak to you." She lowered her voice to a whisper. "Alone."

Priscilla tried to ignore the dismay in her stomach. "Please show him to my study. I will speak with him there."

"Priscilla," her aunt said as the housekeeper went out, "our conversation is of utmost importance. It cannot be delayed."

"It must. Vicar Kenyon would not request to speak to me alone unless it was about something very consequential."

"A clergyman is always in a tizzy. They are so full of tales of death and saving lost souls and—"

"May I remind you that my late husband was a clergyman, Aunt Cordelia?"

"And may I remind you that your son is an earl?"

"I never forget that." She sighed as she left the parlor. Why couldn't she despise her aunt for her meddling? Later, she would explain to her aunt that it was Isaac's mother's duty to plan for his future. Mayhap, this time, her aunt would listen.

# Ten

"And what do you enjoy most about London, Neville?"

Trying to keep his smile in place, Neville walked with Martha along a path beside the sea. Martha was not quiet and unassuming. By Jove, Priscilla was wrong about this young woman. Priscilla was seldom mistaken, but this time she had wildly missed the truth.

Or it could be simply that he wished he could have found a way to avoid this walk. In the wake of a futile search of the constable's office, he had wanted to have a chance to consider the reasons a murderer might steal the button. Assuming, he reminded himself, that the button had not been lost through the constable's bungling.

That would be the easiest answer, but Neville did not believe it. Forshaw still had much to learn, but he had kept the peace here since he assumed his position. Even in a quiet village like Stonehall-on-Sea, there were petty disturbances. The constable had handled those with skill, according to the people Neville had asked.

So that left only Neville's original assumption: Someone had stolen the button for a reason he had yet to comprehend.

"Neville?"

At Martha's persistent voice, he said, "I enjoy the company of my friends."

"I guess that you have many, many friends." Slipping her hand through his arm, she gave him a provocative smile.

"Not as many as you might think."

"Then those folks in London are fools." She fluttered her lashes. "I am glad that we are friends."

"Yes." He was feeling more and more empathy with a maiden being pursued by a rake. A most peculiar sensation and one that would bring peals of laughter from Priscilla. *She* would never be coy. She spoke her mind, and, although he had appreciated it from their first meeting, he never had yearned for her straightforward speech as much as he did now.

"And possibly more than friends?"

He disentangled his arm from hers. "I fear you are reading more into a walk than was intended."

"You are reading far less." She grabbed him by the lapels and kissed him soundly.

After his first moment of shock, Neville pushed her back. She grinned and took a step forward. He held up his hands to keep her away, but she grasped them.

"Martha—Miss Ackerley," he said as he drew his hands away, "you are not thinking clearly."

"Oh, but I am! I have never met a man like you."

"Nor I a woman like you."

He was surprised when she took his words as a compliment and clung to his arm as they continued back toward her cottage. He bid her a good afternoon and slipped through the gate to the sanctuary of Priscilla's front garden. Were all Americans as forthright as Martha Ackerley? She had fawned over him as if he were a conquering hero. And to kiss him like that . . .

He chuckled. English lasses could learn a bit from American ones and keep Englishmen a bit more on their guard. It would be an interesting change for the *ton.*

As he came into the house, Gilbert popped out of the dining room. The butler must have been waiting for him, proving again how proficient Priscilla's staff was.

"Sir Neville, you might want to join Lady Priscilla and the vicar in her study."

He handed his hat and gloves to the butler. "Vicar Kenyon is here? Why?"

"I am not certain, but it must be important because Lady Priscilla walked out on her aunt in the midst of an argument."

"Thank you, Gilbert." He strode along the hall.

When Priscilla saw Neville enter her study, she was grateful he had not spent more time with Martha. "Please join us." She looked at Vicar Kenyon's drawn face. The only color came from his eyes. Even his lips had the appearance of a death mask. "Do sit, Vicar Kenyon," she said, for she feared the clergyman would collapse any second.

"Thank you." He lowered himself to a chair before she reached another, warning how upset he was. He would never sit while a lady was standing unless something was terribly wrong.

Something *else* was terribly wrong.

She sat. Neville remained standing, but moved to lean one shoulder against a bookcase. Knowing him, she guessed he wanted to gauge every word spoken and every motion made. She must do the same, and then they could compare their reactions when this conversation was done.

"What is amiss, Vicar Kenyon?" she asked.

"I am not certain anything is," the vicar replied.

"I don't understand."

"At the duke's funeral, I overheard you talking to Constable Forshaw about a button." The tips of his ears reddened as he gave her a guilty glance. "I know eavesdropping is an intolerable habit, and I assure you, Lady Priscilla, it was only by chance."

"Do not fret. I know how easy it is to hear bits of conversations when one is in a crowd."

He gave her a relieved smile. "It was because I heard you speaking of the button that I thought you might help me unravel a puzzling matter."

"I will be glad to help if I can. What is the puzzle?"

"A message for my uncle was found at the vicarage."

She sat straighter and saw Neville frown. "A message?"

"A slip of paper. Whoever wrote it used a childish hand." He reached under his coat and pulled out a small piece of paper. "The words are few. It says: *It is time to even the scales of fortune.*"

"May I?"

When he handed her the page, she recognized the simple lettering that had been used in the message left with the dead bird. It must have been written by the same person. She handed it to Neville who glanced at it and gave it back to the clergyman. She sighed, for she had hoped Neville might be able to make something of the note.

Then she realized how foolish she was being. Even if Constable Forshaw ordered everyone in Stonehall-on-Sea to copy the letters, she doubted he would find a match. A cunning murderer would disguise his handwriting.

"And you said something about a button?" she asked.

"Yes. One was wrapped in this note."

She held out her hand. "May I see the button?"

His fingers shook as he lifted the button out of his pocket. As it glistened, her breath caught. He placed it in her hand and looked at her expectantly.

"It is the same button," she said with another shudder. "Or its twin."

"What does it signify?"

"I wish I knew."

"Have you ever served in the military?" Neville asked as he took the button.

"I did." Vicar Kenyon rolled his cap nervously. "I served in India. Then, I found my vocation and came home to attend the university. I was never an officer, so the buttons on my uniform were white. Never gold." He swallowed tightly. "It was found with the note. It must be significant."

Neville tossed it in the air.

Priscilla came to her feet and caught it before he could. Giving him a fearsome frown, she turned to the clergyman who was standing. "I would like to keep this if you do not object."

Vicar Kenyon hesitated. "I should take it to the constable."

"I will deliver it to him as soon as I have spoken with the duke. If he has found something among his father's papers, it might offer us a clue to why this button keeps appearing."

Neville put his hand on the clergyman's shoulder. "In the meantime, I suggest that you do not go out without someone with you."

"You think whoever killed the duke will try to kill me?"

Priscilla was sure she could hear the clergyman's knees knocking in fear. Or was it the thud of her heart at the thought that the kindly clergyman might be the murderer's next target?

She sank back into her chair as Neville walked the vicar to the door. When she heard Neville ask Layden to escort the clergyman to the rectory, she stood and went to the parlor. She picked up a bottle and returned to the study where Neville was waiting for her.

Opening the decanter, she poured a glass of brandy. She held it out. "You look as if you could use this."

"Thank you. You are right." He took a sip, then looked about. "Where are the children?"

"Gilbert told me they went for a ride in the pony cart with Aunt Cordelia after I left in the middle of our conversation." She sat.

"You do not appear pleased."

"She is sure to fill their heads with nonsense."

He knocked sand off his boots. "Another reason I am grateful to have avoided being raised to expect the duties of a title."

"And I have another guest."

"Who?"

"Ledyard Pritchard, headmaster of the Elsworth Academy."

Neville sat where Vicar Kenyon had. "More of your aunt's machinations, I collect."

"Yes." She smiled. "Aunt Cordelia already has learned of my displeasure."

"A mighty thing indeed."

Growing serious, she looked at the button. "This appears to be the same one I found in the garden." She pointed to a scratch. "That's where I cleaned dirt off it."

"I believe you are right." He tilted back his glass. "And, from the glint in your eyes, I believe you have an idea of what the next step should be. I hope it will be a cautious one."

She smiled at him. Even in the midst of this fearsome situation, he knew just the way to lighten her spirits. "As I told the vicar, I intend to send a message to the duke."

"And until you hear back from him?"

"I do suspect I shall be making Aunt Cordelia distressed with me about Isaac's future."

He laughed. "If you need any assistance in that quarter, you will ask me."

"I doubt that I shall need assistance, but I still may ask you to join in."


Priscilla was grateful the rest of the afternoon for that hour when, while she wrote a short note to the Duke of Meresden, she and Neville had laughed together about her troublesome aunt and his amorous Martha. She wondered what sort of woman appealed to Neville. One of these days, he must settle down and produce an heir. That talk would send him scurrying, she knew, for she had tried more than once to introduce him to a suitable miss. He always found some fault with the young woman, usually citing her lack of good sense and adding, "unlike you, Pris." She was not sure where Neville went while she finished mending Isaac's breeches, but she knew he would avoid the Ackerley house.

When Gilbert brought a footman dressed in the elegant blue and gold livery of Meresden Court to her study just before dinner was to be served, she was pleased at the duke's quick response.

"From His Grace, my lady." The footman did not look at her, but at some point over her head.

"Thank you, and thank His Grace for his swift response."

The footman did not move.

"That is all," she said, wondering how anyone could be surrounded by such rigid servants. Her household might not meet Aunt Cordelia's expectations, but it was comfortable.

"Yes, my lady." He bowed his head, as stiff as one of Isaac's toy soldiers, and left.

She opened the folded sheet to discover it held another inside. The letter from the duke was terse, saying only that he had found this odd note and thought she might be interested in seeing it.

"Was that Meresden's man?" asked Neville, poking his head into her study.

"How do you do that?"

"Do what?"

"Always appear when things start getting interesting again. How do you do that?"

He smiled as he lounged against the door. "Well-honed instincts . . . and a fortunate glance out of a window to see Meresden's colors on that footman. I thought you might have something you wanted to share."

*My fear for this family,* she almost said, but replied, "The late duke received a note with nearly identical words as the vicar's." She handed Neville the page that had been inside the folded sheet delivered by the footman.

He compared the two letters. "The only difference is one word. The handwriting looks the same."

"That is what I thought."

"So why aren't you smiling? You have pieced together more information than anyone else has."

"This isn't a contest, Neville."

"To the contrary, Pris, it is a contest of the finest sort. Whoever murdered the duke is enjoying watching us blunder about looking for answers. The murderer is keeping the truth close, and we can find the truth only if we dare to get close enough to him to put ourselves in great danger."

"You have a wicked mind to be able to think of that."

"And you wish me to believe that you did not?"

She sighed as she glanced at the letter that had been wrapped around the note. "I prefer not to linger long in the malevolent realms of my soul."

"If you wish to stop this madman, you must become very familiar with the diabolical aspects that you have hidden behind your civilized veneer." He gave her a villainous smile.

"I will do what I must to protect my children."

"As I will."

"I know," she answered, delighted at how much consolation his words offered.

He chuckled. "I have noticed, upon encountering Mr. Pritchard, how he resembles the description Martha gave you of the stranger in your garden."

"But Mr. Pritchard is just arrived in Stonehall-on-Sea."

"Are you so certain of that?"

Priscilla stared at him as if she had never seen him before. Neville had a civilized veneer, but it was very thin. She recalled the rumors she had heard of his disreputable life, and she wondered, as she had before, how much of the gossip was based on the truth.

"You keep staring at that other page," Neville said when she did not answer.

"It is from the Duke of Meresden. He is demanding that I explain what I have discovered—"

"Not much more than a button and two identical notes."

"And that I explain why his father was in my garden at the moment of his death."

"A fact we all would like to know."

"And what I believe the reason is his father was murdered."

Neville snorted. "Apparently he has no wish to think for himself. He will leave that to others."

"Or he wishes to distance himself from the investigation."

"Possible."

She was startled when he agreed. "If my father had been slain, I would want to be involved in the capture of his murderer."

"But you have no reason to hide information that could be damaging to you."

"Do you think the duke does?"

"Most definitely."

"But what?"

His smile became icy. *"That,* Pris, is what I intend to find out."

# Eleven

The bonfire celebration had been held in Stonehall-on-Sea for so long that no one recalled why it first had come into being. Priscilla had heard that it was both to commemorate the victory of the Normans during the Conquest and that it was to mourn the loss by the Anglo-Saxons. Other stories suggested the fête had been ancient even at that time. Few cared why the festival had been started. They enjoyed a respite from spring chores and a preview of Midsummer's Eve that was not many weeks away.

Daphne bounced from one foot to the other as the family gathered in the foyer. "Mama, may I leave now for the celebration?"

"You must stay with either me or your Aunt Cordelia," Priscilla replied without looking up from giving Isaac's hair a final combing. Not that it mattered. Within seconds of their arrival on the beach, Isaac would look like an unloved, unkempt urchin.

"I can go with Neville, can't I?"

Priscilla saw Neville waving from behind her daughter, and she fought not to grin. During the past two days, Daphne had been as persistent in trying to spend time with Neville as Martha. Priscilla was unsure if Daphne was trying to avoid her younger sister or, after seeing Martha, had developed a calf-love herself for Neville—of all people!

"Neville will be busy tonight with the men," she replied with a motherly pat on Daphne's shoulder. "Isaac, all done. Now step back and let me see you."

Priscilla wondered how her daughters could be so different. Daphne looked as neat as a fashionplate while Leah appeared as if she had been blown about by a gale. Motioning for Leah to turn around, Priscilla picked up the brush and persuaded Leah's contrary light brown hair to twist into a pair of braids.

As she walked with her younger children and Neville down the cliffs that glowed white in the moonlight and along the shore toward where the gathering was held, she swung Isaac's and Leah's hands in hers. Daphne had decided, just before they left, that she was too mature to be seen in her mother's company, so she was arriving later with Aunt Cordelia.

Already the bonfire had been lit, and the flames shot so high in the air, she could believe they would lick the clouds. Each time a breeze lilted off the sea, the flames took on a new tempo. Surrounding the bonfire, like acolytes before a great idol, the villagers laughed and sang along with the small band, which consisted of several men playing barely in-tune violins and a lad beating a washtub like a drum.

"No, Isaac," Priscilla said for what she guessed was the fifth time since they had left Mermaid Cottage, "you may not jump through the bonfire this year."

"But, Mama, I am almost ten years old, and all the boys jump through the fire when they are ten."

She paused and adjusted his coat. "When you are ten, we will discuss it."

He pouted and turned to Neville, who held up his hands in a helpless pose.

"You heard your mother," Neville said with a laugh. "The rule is that you have to be ten years old."

Isaac grumbled and followed his sister toward where fish were being cooked over a smaller fire.

"Now that is something I never thought I would live long enough to hear," Priscilla said, chuckling.

Hooking his arm through hers, Neville asked, "What is that? I have a suspicion your laughter is at my expense."

"Most undoubtedly." She laughed again. "I never thought I would hear you laud any set of rules. You prefer to break them."

"Ah, there is the key. I do not offer myself as a persona to be copied by any lad."

"That is an inequitable standard."

"One that has worked for me. Young Isaac will be able to choose which rules to follow and which to break when he has had as many varied experiences as I have."

With an exaggerated shiver, she replied, "No one has as many varied experiences as you, Neville."

"I believe I have been insulted."

"Only if you find the truth insulting." Priscilla looked along the beach to where the young men were gathering to test their courage by jumping through the fire. Some of the lads were not any taller than her son. Thank heavens, Neville had persuaded Isaac to heed her. She wanted to thank him, but he would be discomfited by her gratitude. "'Tis good I have an excuse to keep Isaac from participating. Aunt Cordelia would be certain that I was unacceptable to raise an earl."

"You shouldn't let her bother you."

"I know." She gave him a wry smile. "I had thought she might be talked into being sensible. Then Mr. Pritchard arrived talking about that dreary-sounding boarding school."

"I cannot imagine wasting one's childhood in such a grim place with such a grim headmaster."

"I am sure *you* can't."

He grinned. "Now I know I have been insulted. How will I prove my worthiness to you?"

"You could jump through the flames as the others are."

"I have no wish to singe my breeches as well as my dignity."

"Wise of you."

Priscilla was grateful to him again, this time for his teasing as they strolled to where the villagers were gathered to watch the men jump through the fire. She did take note, as she wandered through the crowd while Neville spoke with Vicar Kenyon, how many people glanced askance at her and how many conversations seemed to come to an abrupt end when she neared. Tempted to ask them if any new rumors had sprouted about her apparent complicity in the duke's death, she held her tongue. Instead she spoke of the new baby in one cottage and a litter of puppies in another.

Cheers rose when the men lined up to challenge the flames. She saw Neville standing beside Isaac, his hand on her son's shoulder.

"This is the most absurd exercise I have ever seen," grumbled someone behind her.

Priscilla was astonished to see Thomas Ackerley leaning on a huge boulder that had crashed down the cliff long before there was a village here. The man, whose brown hair drooped over his eyes, was dressed in the perfectly pressed clothes that he had worn every time she had seen him.

"It may seem absurd to you, Mr. Ackerley," she replied, "but, in Stonehall-on-Sea, it's a rite of passage for lads."

"Someone could be killed."

"No one has."

"Other than the duke."

"That has nothing to do with this!" she retorted.

"I realize that." He kicked his boot back against the stone. "This tradition is another example of how different the English and the Americans have become."

"It is amazing when barely two centuries have separated us."

"Two centuries and a horrible war that seems doomed to be repeated. To be honest, Lady Priscilla, I would like to separate myself from this country posthaste. I never wanted to come here, but Martha was insistent. She developed an interest in England, and this part of England in particular, about two years before we arrived here."

"And now you are marooned here."

"A most disagreeable state." He gasped, facing her. "Forgive me, Lady Priscilla. I did not mean to suggest an insult to you or this village. It simply . . ."

"It isn't home."

"Thank you for understanding. If we had obtained a house closer to one of the universities, I might be able to endure this far better."

"I mean no insult to *you* when I suggest that you should move closer to Cambridge." She smiled. "You and your sister are good neighbors. Yet it might be better for you to leave."

"For me, but Martha will not hear of it. She says she intends to stay in Stonehall-on-Sea until we go back to America."

"Why?"

He shrugged. "I have no idea. She doesn't say, just clamps her lips shut. It is not as if she has made friends here other than you, Lady Priscilla. Many of the villagers are suspicious of us."

"If I speak with Martha, she might be more understanding."

"You can try, but she is stubborn." A hint of a smile pulled at his thin lips. "In that, we are much alike."

Leah ran up and tugged on Priscilla's hand. "Mama, come quick! Mama! Now!"

"What is it?" she asked, grasping her daughter's arm to keep the girl from jumping and spraying them with sand.

"'Tis Isaac, Mama! He is in trouble."

Drat! She had warned him to stay away from that fire. Why hadn't Neville halted him? That thought vanished as fear surged up through her.

"Is he hurt? Is he burned?" she asked.

"Burned?" Leah's eyes grew round. "Mama, he is up there!"

Priscilla followed her daughter's pointing finger to see Isaac clinging to the cliff nearly eight feet above the shore. As Mr. Ackerley called for someone to help, she rushed toward the cliff. Its chalky sides could crumble easily. Every step crunched the scree beneath her feet, reminding her how very fragile the cliff was. She screamed when she saw Isaac lose his grip and fall.

More shouts exploded from every direction as she raced across the beach. She knelt by her son and checked to be certain that he had no broken bones. When she ran her hands along his sides to be sure that his ribs were intact, he wiggled and laughed.

She stood and picked Isaac up off the ground, setting him on his feet and dusting white chalk off his clothes. "If you are giggling, you must not be hurt."

"You were tickling me."

"But are you hurt?"

"No." He held up a ball. "And I got this from that crevice on the cliff."

"So I see."

"Can I go back to the game?"

She shook her head in disbelief. "If you aren't injured, then there's nothing to keep you from continuing. Just no more climbing the cliffs, except on the paths."

She watched him race back to where the other boys waited. There was a slight limp each time he stepped onto his left leg, but she would not humiliate him by suggesting he might want to rest it. He would have all day tomorrow to rest.

Neville hurried over to her. "Did I just see Isaac plummeting down the cliff?"

"Yes. He went after the ball that got caught, and he came down more quickly than he had intended. He is fine."

"And you?"

She patted his arm. "I am not one of those mothers who swoons at the thought of her child doing something risky."

"The lad takes after you in so many ways."

"Is he all right?" asked Mr. Ackerley, pressing his hand to his side as he gasped for breath.

She smiled at him as she had at Neville, appreciating their concern for her sometimes obstreperous son. "He is fine. Thank you for asking."

When Neville glanced at her, then began talking with Mr. Ackerley about a book that he had recently read, Priscilla took the hint to leave them to their conversation. She was not certain what Neville intended.

As she walked toward the fire that was brightening the twilight, she gasped when someone bumped into her. Rocked back on her feet, she snapped, "Watch where you are going! Someone could be hurt."

"I would say the same to you."

In astonishment, she stared at the Duke of Meresden. She had not expected he would be here to take part in this celebration. Not once, since he had left Meresden Court to attend school, had he come.

His frown eased as he said, "Lady Priscilla, excuse me. I did not realize it was you."

"Good evening, Your Grace."

When he smiled, looking as excited as Isaac had upon retrieving the ball from the cliff, she knew he was still thrilled each time he was addressed so. "I trust you are enjoying yourself on this lovely evening," he said, once again the magnanimous lord deigning to wander among his subjects.

"Very much so."

"May I speak with you?" He glanced about as if he suspected everyone was heeding each word he uttered. "In private?"

"If we walk away from the bonfire, I doubt anyone will overhear us."

He nodded and said nothing else until they had almost reached the spot where the path curved up to the road that led past Mermaid Cottage. Pausing, he grimaced as he wiped sand and pebbles off his boots. Without looking up, the duke asked, "What did you make of the note I found?"

"It is very similar to one that the vicar's uncle recently received."

"What?" He straightened, and she knew she had his full attention. "How is it similar?"

"The handwriting and only one word was different. Odd."

"Odd?"

"The note was delivered to Vicar Kenyon's house rather than to the Dog and Crown."

"Do you believe it was written by my father's murderer?"

"Mayhap. Did your father's military career take him to India?"

The duke's mouth twisted in distaste. "India? Why would he go there? He had enough connections in the government to prevent himself from having to suffer that steam bath."

"Then where did he serve?"

"Many places. He was in the Caribbean and in the American colonies and in Canada. I believe he liked Canada the most, for he said he would gladly have returned there if he had been able to set aside his duties here."

"May I ask you one more question?"

"If you must."

She smiled coolly. "Yes, I must."

"Very well then. Ask what you wish." The benevolent lord now had become too busy to speak with the peasants and clearly wished to be on his way.

"You were not at Meresden Court when Constable Forshaw sent a message there on the evening of your father's death. Where were you?"

Even in the growing darkness, she could see him flinch. "Are you accusing me of murdering my father in *your* garden, Lady Priscilla?"

"No, I am asking a question."

"That was a Thursday evening, and it is well known that I spend one evening each week at the Dog and Crown."

"The public house belonging to Vicar Kenyon's uncle?" She held her breath. Was *this* the connection between the duke and the pubkeeper? She must be careful not to assume too much, but it was the first link she had discovered, feeble as it might be.

"Of course! How many Dog and Crown public houses do you believe there to be?" He scowled. "I believe your aunt is correct when she says that you have let this crime unsettle both you and your mind, my lady."

"I would be less than human not to be unsettled by

a murder in my garden!" Bother Aunt Cordelia! Priscilla had not guessed that her busybody aunt had spoken to the duke about how Isaac was being raised.

"Quite true." He walked away and up the path.

She believed that now *she* had been insulted.


"She said what to Aunt Cordelia about Mr. Pritchard?" Daphne asked in what was supposed to be a whisper.

Or mayhap not. Priscilla did not care. Her aunt had gone too far this time, and Priscilla would not allow Aunt Cordelia to overstep herself again. She loved her aunt . . . or she assumed she did, for that was what nieces did, but Aunt Cordelia would not set the direction of Isaac's life. She might be the fifth earl's aunt, but Priscilla was his *mother.* It was time for Aunt Cordelia to accept that.

"Daphne, gossiping is not a pretty pastime for a young lady," she chided.

"I am sorry, Mama."

Leah yawned.

Putting her arm around her younger daughter's shoulders, Priscilla said, "It is time for us to return home."

"So soon?" Daphne asked.

"Yes. Your Aunt Cordelia left almost two hours ago."

"With Mr. Pritchard," Leah added. "I was glad when they left. Aunt Cordelia wanted me to stand and say nothing. Nothing!"

With a commiserating smile, Priscilla said, "It is time to go." She looked around at the people still lingering by the bonfire that was fading to embers. Most of the children had already been taken home to bed. "Isaac!"

He hobbled toward her. When she told him to come along, he did not protest.

"Aren't we going to wait for Neville?" he asked, trying to stifle a yawn, but failing.

"He and Mr. Ackerley were in an intense conversation when I last saw him."

"Mr. Ackerley?"

She smiled at her son's astonishment that Neville would want to spend time with the tutor. She put her arm around him to help him along the path. As they walked, she listened to her children's voices exclaiming about everyone they had seen and spoken to tonight. It would be only a couple of years more— sooner if Daphne had her way—until her older daughter was discussing the very same thing, but about the *ton*. That thought saddened her, for she was not ready for Daphne to be fired-off into her first Season. As she watched her younger children teasing each other and laughing, she joined in and soon even Daphne was part of the silliness.

The Ackerleys' cottage was dark, and only a few lamps were lit in Mermaid Cottage. Overhead, the quarter moon was not too bright to block out the stars scattered through the ebony sky.

"There is Orion!" Leah called.

"That one is easy." Isaac pointed to another constellation, and they began to try to outdo each other in finding the most obscure grouping of stars.

Opening the gate, Priscilla ushered them toward the door. She tried to halt herself, but she could not keep from looking at the topmost step before she went up. She thought of the bird with the crushed skull each time she came this way.

The door did not open as they reached it, and she knew that Gilbert and the footmen must still be at the bonfire. A single lamp burned in the foyer. As she turned to bid the children a good night, something seemed wrong. She was not certain what it was.

"Wait here," she ordered quietly.

"What is wrong, Mama?" Daphne asked.

"Wait here."

The children nodded, silent, and she guessed her uneasy tone had upset them.

Priscilla took furtive steps along the hallway. She was not sure what she expected to see. When she looked toward her study and saw everything was as it should be, she sighed. She was looking for trouble.

"All right," she said as she turned to see her children's pale faces. "Why don't you go upstairs?"

"Mama!" Daphne's voice had a strangled, choking sound.

Priscilla looked at where she pointed and gasped. Shards of what had been a figurine of a lad holding up a brightly colored bird were scattered in the parlor's doorway. Amid the pieces was a book with its pages ripped out.

"Wait here," she said as she had before.

"Why?" Isaac was bouncing on one leg to try to see past her.

"Daphne, hold onto your brother." Thank heavens, one of her children was calm.

Daphne put her arms around her brother and sister. Priscilla decided her daughter was more mature than she had guessed.

Taking a deep breath, she inched toward the parlor door. She put her hands over her mouth as she stared at the upset furniture and the draperies that hung like shredded butterfly wings. Who had taken advantage of the household staff going to the bonfire and come in to ruin her parlor?

The lamp that she had left burning had gone out. Even though she had told Mrs. Moore and Gilbert to give the household the evening off to attend the celebration, she could not imagine Mrs. Dunham leaving the kitchen. Why hadn't Mrs. Dunham heard this destruction and investigated?

She froze. Mayhap this room was not the only one damaged. If the person who had done this had been interrupted by Mrs. Dunham—

A form burst out of a dark corner. She was slammed against a wall. A picture wobbled and crashed to the floor beside her as someone ran out of the room.

"Run!" she cried to her children.

Through her throbbing head, she heard Daphne repeat the order. The children shouted as the front door crashed back against the wall. She lurched to the doorway. What was she thinking? Isaac would not be restrained from giving chase, and then *he* could be hurt.

"Stay in the dining room!" she shouted when she saw her son peek out.

Oh, how her head ached! It had hit the wall. Hard. As she stepped away from the door, her legs threatened to buckle. She grasped a chair and sagged to her knees on the floor.

"Mama!" The cry added to the pain along her skull.

That was Isaac. When she heard other voices, she looked up to see her daughters running into the parlor.

One voice was louder in her ears than any others— Aunt Cordelia's—as her aunt asked in a most disgusted tone, "What have you done *now*, Priscilla?"

# Twelve

"Here," said Neville, handing a cool, damp cloth to Priscilla. "It will help with the pain."

"Thank you." She wanted to tell him that her throbbing head was the least of her worries. Then, she realized he knew that. She turned toward where Aunt Cordelia was sitting and holding a bottle of *sal volatile*. Not for if Priscilla swooned, but if Aunt Cordelia did. Placing the cool cloth on her aunt's head, she ignored how Mr. Pritchard was scowling.

"Take your time," Constable Forshaw was saying as he sat on the settee and looked at her children. "Think about what you saw. Start by describing the person you saw run out of the house." He gave Priscilla a glance. "If they can identify the person who attacked you, Lady Priscilla, we have a better chance of catching him."

"Go ahead," she said, knowing he awaited her permission.

He opened his notebook and a bottle of ink. Dipping his pen, he said, "Tell me about the person you saw, my lord. Tell me if the person was tall or short, what color hair, anything that will help."

Isaac puffed out his narrow chest as he did whenever anyone addressed him by his title, but let his breath go when Priscilla gave him a stern look. "It was a man, and he was taller than Neville. His hair was about the color of mine."

Constable Forshaw wrote in his notebook.

"No," argued Leah. "It was a woman. She was shorter than Mama, and I would guess by the way her hair shone in the dim light that she had hair about the same shade as Daphne and Mama."

The constable scratched out what he had written and dipped his pen into the bottle again.

Even as the pen inched along the paper again, Daphne stated, "You both are wrong. I am not certain if it was a man or a woman, but the person must have been about Mama's height. He or she wore some pale fabric covering his—or her—hair. *That* was what reflected in the moonlight."

Dismay lengthened the constable's face as he looked to Priscilla to corroborate one of the descriptions.

Taking another cool cloth from Neville, Priscilla started to hand it to her aunt. He put his hand on her arm and shook his head. She started to frown, then winced as the motion added to the pain across her forehead. He sat her in the nearest chair. She whispered her thanks as she held the cloth to her head. Then she said, "To be honest, Constable Forshaw, I did not get a clear look at the intruder. It all happened very fast, and my thoughts were on keeping my children from harm."

"So we have no more information than we had before." The constable stoppered the ink.

"Whoever came in here," Neville said in that tone which warned he would not be argued with, "may be the same person who left the dead bird on the front steps."

"That is possible, but . . ."

"And these notes." Neville reached beneath his coat and drew out the other notes.

Constable Forshaw took them. "Why didn't you show these to me before?"

"I have not had the opportunity. I trust you recognize the handwriting as very similar to the note Lady Priscilla's footman found beneath the dead bird."

"Oh, my!" gasped Constable Forshaw. "But who wrote these notes?"

"I think the answer is obvious," Priscilla replied. "Whoever murdered the duke."

"But you are the primary suspect," he blurted, then colored from his cheeks to the tips of his ears.

Neville said, "I believe you need to reconsider more than one of your opinions about this investigation, Forshaw."

He stood. "I want to look at the front door again." He held up the slips of paper. "I assume that you have no cause for me not to have these *now.*"

"Of course not."

Constable Forshaw frowned as he left.

He could not have reached the front door before Aunt Cordelia came to her feet. Pointing her finger at Priscilla, she cried, "How could you put these dear children in danger?" She put her hand to her head and wobbled. When Neville moved to help her, she jerked her arm away. That sent her dropping back into the chair.

"Are you all right, Aunt Cordelia?" Priscilla asked as her children stared in horror.

She had her answer when her aunt said in the same taut voice, "Really, Priscilla, I swear that you do not think of their welfare one bit."

When Neville drew in a deep breath, Priscilla looked at him and said softly, "Do not intrude. She will accuse me of arranging for you to embarrass her in front of Mr. Pritchard." Raising her voice, she added in a tone so sweet that she nearly gagged,

"These dear children were the only thing on my mind, Aunt Cordelia. Of that one thing you can be certain, dear aunt. I would do nothing to bring my children into danger."

"That's right!" crowed Isaac, jumping to his feet.

Priscilla wanted to groan when her aunt's eyes narrowed as both Daphne and Leah moved to flank Priscilla. This defiance was going to outrage Aunt Cordelia and offer further fodder for her assumption that Priscilla was an incompetent mother.

"Children, you should heed your aunt," interjected Mr. Pritchard. "She has wisdom that you have not yet gained."

Although it turned her stomach to agree with the officious man, Priscilla added, "Mr. Pritchard is correct. Go and get ready for bed. I shall be up to see you before you go to sleep." She stood.

"I will see to them," Aunt Cordelia said, pushing herself to her feet with Mr. Pritchard's assistance.

Priscilla smiled and took her aunt's hand. "Thank you, Aunt Cordelia," she whispered.

"Someone needs to make sure these children are properly taken care of," her aunt replied but offered Priscilla a small smile. Aunt Cordelia must believe that there was something salvageable in Priscilla.

As her aunt herded the children out with Mr. Pritchard following in case she stumbled, Priscilla dropped to the settee. A goblet appeared before her eyes, and she reached up for it. The sip of wine seared the cobwebs out of her head.

Neville sat across from her. "She's a tough one."

With a wry laugh, she said, "There is a reason they call women like her old toughs."

"She is not going to let up until she gets what she wants."

"Then she is going to be bothering me for a long

time. She will not accept that I refuse to send Isaac to that stuffy school. If Mr. Pritchard is representative of the staff there, it must be beyond intolerable."

"Yes."

"I know she means well, but she doesn't know the children."

"You should have someone you trust to guide them . . . if necessary."

She heard sorrow in his voice and knew that he was still angry that Lazarus had been taken so quickly by smallpox. Neville had said at her husband's funeral that he could not understand how a man could have his children and wife vaccinated and then refuse to do so himself. Being furious would not change anything.

"You're right," she said, thinking of her uneasy thoughts at the duke's memorial service. She had to think of her children's futures. "Would you consider being that person?"

He laughed loudly. When she did not join in, he stared at her. "Are you serious?"

"Much more than you, it would seem. The children love you, and you love them. You have a good feel for what is good for them."

"Anything I did *not* do."

"If that is to be your guide, fine." She stood. "Think about it, Neville. I plan to live long enough to bounce my grandchildren on my knee, but I agree that I need to think about what would happen if I'm not there to do that. Recent events have warned me I should consider—"

"I'll think about it," he said rather gruffly, and she knew she had unsettled him. He crossed the room and picked up a china dog. "Where does this go?"

"On the mantel. Is it unbroken?"

"Just a chip out of one ear."

She smiled. "It was chipped before. Daphne and

Leah were having a battle with the pillows on the settee, and one of their weapons slipped out of their hands and smashed into that poor dog."

She began to gather up other items strewn across the floor. She set her husband's favorite book on the small desk in a corner of the parlor. He had not used the study because he wanted to be available to anyone who might need him, even after he was no longer the vicar at St. Elizabeth's. Reaching for the bookends that had fallen beneath a chair, she set them on the desk and put the book between them. There should be another book. Where had it gone? She knelt and searched in the shadows beneath the desk.

Neville walked across the room. "It's gone."

"What is gone?"

"The button that was delivered to Vicar Kenyon's house."

"That shouldn't be a surprise."

"It isn't."

"But the button is not the only thing missing," she said as he handed her to her feet.

"What else is gone?"

She pointed to the book between the bookends. "There should be another book, a record of the births and deaths in this parish. Lazarus kept it here for his own use."

"But isn't there a copy at the church?"

"Yes." She frowned. "Why would someone steal this copy when the one at St. Elizabeth's could be taken easily?"

"What if it isn't at St. Elizabeth's any longer?"

"I think we should check on that right away."

Neville pounded again on the vicarage door. He saw lamps being lit in the houses nearby, but he got no reply. When he and Priscilla had gone to St. Elizabeth's and found the church register was not there, they had rushed here, hoping Vicar Kenyon had brought the valuable book to his house.

Holding a lantern high, he called, "Vicar Kenyon! Are you within?"

"Mayhap he cannot answer the door," Priscilla said as she peered through the window.

He knew what she would see, for he had called several times at this simple house when Lazarus served as vicar for the parish. The sitting room was smaller than the parlor at Mermaid Cottage, and he had had to watch his head to avoid bumping into the rafters crisscrossing its ceiling.

"What do you see?" he asked.

"Nothing. The draperies are closed."

Neville appraised the oak door. "I have never broken down the door of a clergyman's house."

"Until now."

"Until now," he said with a taut smile.

"Before you do . . ." She reached past him and lifted the latch. When the door swung open, she said, "You will have to wait awhile longer before you break down a clergyman's door."

"Thank you for saving my shoulder and my pride."

She gave him a quick smile as he pushed the door open wider and went into the small foyer. When he looked to his left past the narrow staircase, he spoke a phrase that had probably never been heard in this house. Then, he repeated it and added another oath. Behind him, he heard Priscilla's sharp intake of breath.

He walked to the middle of the room as he surveyed the jumble that had been made of the clergyman's office. The desk had been upended, and the contents of every drawer cast around the room. Not a single book remained on the shelves. An upholstered chair had been slashed open; its cushion tossed into the ashes on the hearth.

"If someone was looking for a book, much of this damage is needless," he said as he bent to pick up the closest book. It was a treatise on St. Elizabeth. Setting it on the shelf, he sighed. "Someone must be very angry to do this."

"And to murder the duke."

He shook his head. "Some murder is done in a very calculating, cold-blooded manner. It is not an act of passion but one of dispassion."

"I would rather not hear such things just now."

"I thought you would want to hear the truth."

"I do . . . just not so much of it." She went to the stairs and called on the chance the vicar might be upstairs.

"If he was knocked about as you were, he might not be able to answer," Neville said.

When she whirled to face him, her dismay was mixed with rage. "He is a man of the cloth! He should be sacrosanct from such violence."

"Thomas à Becket wasn't when King Henry's men stabbed him in the cathedral."

"I did not need to be reminded of that now, Neville."

He put his arm around her and gave her a gentle squeeze. No matter how brave Priscilla was, she saw the world through the eyes of an earl's daughter. She had seen the worst side of the people in her husband's parishes while she had been a clergyman's wife, but she had been sheltered from the darkest voids in a madman's soul.

"Oh, dear God!" came the moan from behind them.

Priscilla rushed to where Vicar Kenyon was reeling toward them. She steered him to a chair that Neville hastily set upright.

"Help . . ." The clergyman gave a shudder that threatened to shatter him.

"Neville, is there any wine?"

Vicar Kenyon shook himself as if waking from a nightmare. "My uncle! In the back garden! I think he may be dead."

"Which way is the garden, Pris?"

Grabbing Neville's arm, she said, "This way."

He pushed past her when they reached the kitchen. Throwing open the door, he ran out. She caught the door as it struck the house and ricocheted back to her. She sent it flying again. She bumped into him in the darkness. Looking down, she discovered why he had stopped only a pair of steps from the back door.

Mr. Kenyon was stretched out in the middle of the kitchen garden, just as the duke had been in her flower bed. Blood stained the curve of his cheek against the ground. It was as if no time had passed since she had found the duke. Neville squatted next to Mr. Kenyon just as he had in her garden.

Swallowing past the clog in her throat, she whispered, "Is he dead?"

"No, he's alive. Barely."

"Go for the doctor and the constable. I will stay here with Vicar Kenyon and his uncle."

"I will send someone to help you."

"Hurry and get Mr. Semple before he has to decide whether to hold a coroner's inquest."

Neville put a hand on her shoulder and then ran back into the house.

Priscilla went into the kitchen, grabbed a rag, and then went to the well that was not far from the kitchen door. Dipping the rag in the bucket there, she dabbed at the blood on Mr. Kenyon's face. She was unsure where the wound was, and she did not want to cause him more damage.

He moaned but did not move. She bent to see if his eyes were open. They remained closed.

"Lady Priscilla?" called the vicar. He was carrying a lamp.

"Here." She took Vicar Kenyon's hand as he inched closer. "Mr. Kenyon is still alive."

"Thank God!" While he began to pray, she continued to wash away the blood.

The shout of her name resounded from within the house. Gilbert! Neville could not have chosen a better person to send.

"Sir Neville thought we might offer more help," Gilbert said as he came out into the garden.

She was about to ask who was with him, then saw Mr. Pritchard and Layden, her footman. Wishing she could send the headmaster away before he created a to-do with his questions, she motioned for them to come closer. She stepped aside as they, with Vicar Kenyon's help, lifted his uncle from the patch of onions. She held the lamp high so they could watch where they walked while they carried the senseless man into the house. When she saw that the settee had been righted, she whispered a silent thanks to Neville for his forethought.

Sending Vicar Kenyon to put on a pot of water for tea and another for the doctor's needs, Priscilla set Gilbert to overseeing the straightening of the room. Her butler and Layden began work. Mr. Pritchard hesitated but joined them when Priscilla frowned at him. If he was here, he was going to help.

No matter how many times she wrung out the cloth in the bucket Gilbert brought to her, the blood continued to pulse along the old man's face. It slipped into every wrinkle and crevice, outlining them in scarlet.

When the door opened, Priscilla motioned for Mr. Semple to hurry in. The doctor, who had helped when both Daphne and Leah had the measles, was not a good advertisement for his own services. His face was thin with skin pulled tightly across his sharp bones. Sticking out from funereal black sleeves, his long, bony fingers could have belonged to a skeleton. He carried a battered bag.

As the doctor bent over Mr. Kenyon, Priscilla stepped aside. She said nothing when she saw the fury on Constable Forshaw's face. Neville stood behind him as they waited for Mr. Semple to make his pronouncement on the old man's condition.

The doctor straightened. "He has suffered a serious blow to his head. To the side of his head not far above his ear. Whoever struck him must have been off to the side, or Mr. Kenyon was turning to face his attacker. Those are the only explanations I have for why it was a glancing blow. If it had been straight on, we would be having another funeral."

"Oh, dear me!" moaned Vicar Kenyon, pausing in his pacing. "Will he recover?"

"I cannot say. I have cleaned the wound and stitched it closed. If his brain does not swell, he may recover."

"What can we do to prevent that swelling?"

Mr. Semple closed his bag. "Praying might be a good idea, Vicar. Otherwise, there is nothing much anyone can do but wait and see." He crooked his finger to Priscilla. "My lady, if you please."

She followed him out into the hallway, wondering what he could not say in front of the others. When he reopened his bag and drew out a handful of packets, he pressed them into her hand.

"You are a sensible woman, my lady. You will see that Vicar Kenyon uses one of these, if necessary, I assume."

"These are for *Vicar* Kenyon?"

"As you have seen, he is distressed." The doctor tapped the packets. "This in some wine may help him sleep."

"I don't think he wishes to sleep. I think he wants to be awake so he can know when his uncle wakes."

"It may be days . . . if ever."

"I know that, and so does Vicar Kenyon."

The doctor frowned. "I am not as certain of that as you are. I have never seen him so agitated."

"His uncle was viciously attacked." She held out the packets. "Vicar Kenyon won't want these."

"He needs to rest tonight, so he does not suffer such a *crise de nerfs* that he is as prostrate as his uncle."

Realizing that arguing with Mr. Semple was only creating more strain, she acquiesced. She closed the door as the doctor took his leave after telling the clergyman to send for him if there was any change in his uncle's condition and that Mr. Semple would return after dawn.

Neville edged over to where she was tossing the packets onto a nearby table. "Do you wish me to ask the vicar about the church register?"

"While you do that, I will check among the books on the floor."

She started to turn away, but he asked, "How are you faring?"

"Not well."

"I understand."

"I am glad *you* do," she retorted tartly, "because I don't understand why the duke and Mr. Kenyon were attacked."

"They both are elderly and unlikely to be able to fight off a young man."

"But that does not explain why they were attacked." Her eyes grew round. "Or does it? Were they attacked *because* they are elderly? Is that the connection?"

Neville wished he had an answer to give her, but he did not. Not yet. There was some shared aspect. If he could find it, he could find the murderer. Then Priscilla and her children would be out of danger.

As she went to the desk, he walked to where Vicar Kenyon was sitting with his head in his hands. Neville put his hand on the clergyman's shoulder and asked, "Vicar Kenyon?"

"Yes?" He raised his head.

"Do you know where we could find the church register?"

"The church register?" Vicar Kenyon repeated dully.

"Where do you keep it?"

He pointed to the desk. "I keep it there when I do not need it at St. Elizabeth's.

Priscilla shook her head when Neville glanced at her. "It is not here," she said. "I have checked every drawer."

Neville clasped his hands behind his back as he stared out the window toward the church's steeple that was awash in moonlight. This puzzle was becoming more complex. There was some link between these events. Two attacks on two old men and two houses vandalized. In both cases, the events had taken place on property that belonged to a clergyman. Was that the connection? If so, that did not account for the duke's death. He was overlooking something.

"The church register is missing?" Vicar Kenyon came to his feet. "Who would want it? Other than a listing of births, marriages, and deaths in this parish, it contains little more than an annual update of what happened in Stonehall-on-Sea. When residents moved away and when they came back. That sort of thing. Why would anyone want it?"

"I suspect, Vicar Kenyon," Neville said with a sigh, "if we find the answer to that, we will find the person who murdered the duke and tried to do the same thing to your uncle."

# Thirteen

Priscilla broke the thread and tossed aside Isaac's breeches. Keeping her hands busy had failed to allow her to escape the spinning wheel of her thoughts. Endlessly, around and around, her mind spewed forth images of what she had witnessed tonight.

She went to the window that gave her a view past the stables and out to the inky sea. Leaning her cheek against the cool glass, she wished, as she had not in so long, that Lazarus was here. She could use his common sense and clear thinking and his gentle heart.

"Should I listen to my aunt?" she asked aloud. Running her fingers along a mullion, she sighed. "Aunt Cordelia believes I am endangering the children by staying here, but you would never leave the village prey to a madman."

She did not believe in ghosts, but she could almost sense Lazarus's presence nearby. And she could guess what he would tell her. Neville was her ally. He was more than an ally. He had been Lazarus's best friend, and, over the years, he had become hers. If she had not known that before, his actions in Stonehall-on-Sea had proved that. She could depend on him as she could no one else.

Pushing away from the glass, she blew out the lamp. The children would be awake early, and she must be up to answer all their questions. She did not want

Aunt Cordelia using this latest attack to gain control of her children.

She climbed the two steps to the large bed where she now slept alone. She drew back the covers and plumped up the pillows. Setting them against the carved headboard, she leaned back on them. She brushed down her white nightdress's lacy collar and stared up at the top of her bed. The wooden design was lost in the darkness beyond the open bed curtains. She never had wanted to lose herself in sleep as much as she did tonight.

It was impossible. Each time she closed her eyes, she saw the two old men lying on the ground, their heads bloody. She pulled a pillow over her head, but the images were within her mind. She tossed the pillow to the other side of the bed.

Something squeaked.

Slowly Priscilla sat as she heard the latch rattle. If the person who had ransacked the house had returned . . . She held her breath as the door creaked open more. The poker beside the hearth would be a good weapon, but it was too far away. She might not be seen if she was very still.

*As still as death,* her aggravatingly honest mind added.

A slender form peeked in, and she gasped, "Isaac!"

"You sound scared, Mama."

"*You* scared me by sneaking in like a thief."

"Can I get into bed with you?" He wrapped his arms around his thin chest. "'Tis chilly."

She patted the bed. When he climbed up the steps and bounced toward her, settling on her left side, she pulled the covers over his bare feet.

"Can't you sleep?" she asked.

"I can sleep." He put his head on her lap. "But I am scared to."

"Did you have a nightmare?"

He nodded.

Priscilla closed her eyes as she thought of the right thing to say. Her son had not suffered from nightmares in the past three months, but he had endured many after his father died. What had happened tonight must have resurrected those night terrors.

"Isaac, you know that nothing in a nightmare can hurt you, don't you?"

He nodded again.

"But?" she asked as she brushed his hair out of his eyes.

"It was horrible."

"Do you want to talk about it? Will that make it go away?"

Her question opened a floodgate as he explained, in such a convoluted manner that she could not follow the story in his dream, everything that had happened. She tried not to tense with anger when he spoke of being at Mr. Pritchard's boarding school. Bother! Aunt Cordelia had gone too far bringing that meddlesome headmaster here to upset Isaac. On the morrow, Aunt Cordelia must own to that.

The door to the hall swung open again, but this time Priscilla did not tense. She was not surprised when Leah peered in.

"Come in and close the door so you do not wake anyone else," Priscilla said.

As she slipped into the bedroom, Leah said, "I saw Isaac was not in his bed, and . . ."

"Come here." She motioned for Leah to sit on her right side. "He is right here. He has been telling me about his nightmare."

Leah scrambled up onto the bed, her nightgown ghostly in the dim light. "Did you have a nightmare, too, Isaac?"

Lifting his head, he nodded. "I wager mine was worse than yours."

"I doubt it. Mine had horrible creatures in it."

"Mine had Mr. Pritchard."

Leah shivered as she took one of the pillows and nestled next to Priscilla. "You win. No monster in my nightmare could be worse than him."

"Leah!" chided Priscilla, but laughed.

"Mama, you know you agree."

"I shall not own to that." She laughed again as the children giggled.

When the door opened a third time, Priscilla saw Daphne shoving her arm into her wrapper. Her daughter must have hurried from her room.

"I saw Leah sneaking along the hallway," Daphne said, "and I wanted to be certain she was all right."

Priscilla laughed. "Come and join us. You can sleep on the other side of Isaac. This bed is big enough to hold all of us tonight."

Daphne climbed over the end of the bed and up to the pillows. As she pulled the covers over her, Isaac grumbled.

"Hush," Priscilla said. "If you want to stay here tonight, you have to get along." She stroked Isaac's hair, then Leah's. "Do you think you can get to sleep now?"

Isaac mumbled something, and Leah was already asleep. With care, Priscilla shifted down under the covers as well. She smiled when her son turned to curl up against his older sister. Daphne's arm curved around him.

Priscilla gazed up at the wooden top of her bed. She needed to find a solution for the puzzle surrounding them, but not tonight. For tonight, she would be grateful that the wickedness that had come to Stonehall-on-Sea had spared her children. At dawn, she would try to unravel the cobweb of lies that had been spun about the village.

She closed her eyes and let her thoughts drift away. Even with Isaac kicking her and Leah jabbing her with an elbow and Daphne's soft snores, Priscilla slept better than she had in many nights.

# Fourteen

When Priscilla took her children for their regular lessons with Mr. Ackerley after breakfast, she was amazed Martha did not open the door. Mr. Ackerley seemed distracted as he ushered them into the cottage.

"Martha is not ill, is she?" Priscilla asked a second time.

He blinked, then smiled tightly. "Forgive me, Lady Priscilla. My thoughts are not here."

"Martha? Is she fine?"

"Yes, yes." His eyes focused on her for the first time. "She mentioned that she had to arrange for a delivery. I must have forgotten again to send a book home with a student." Without a pause, he asked, "How do *you* fare? I heard of the horrible events at the vicarage."

"I would prefer not to speak of it now." She glanced at the children.

"I understand. Later, then."

"That would be better." She did not add that she never wanted to speak of it again. But she must, for Constable Forshaw had asked if he might stop by this afternoon. She doubted she could add anything to what she had already told him—and what Neville and Vicar Kenyon had told him—but she shared his determination to find the murderer before someone else was hurt.

Bidding him a good morning and telling her children to heed Mr. Ackerley brought a sense of the commonplace to her. She appreciated it more when she reached Mermaid Cottage and was met by a request to join her aunt in the study.

"She has flown up to the boughs," Mrs. Moore said, clearly sorry to deliver the message. "I would be glad to send one of the girls in to tidy up now."

"I believe I can handle my aunt on my own."

"Of course, my lady," she replied, chagrined.

Priscilla had not intended to distress her housekeeper and said so before adding, "I appreciate your concerns, Mrs. Moore. Do tell Mrs. Dunham to listen for a bell from the study and to send a girl posthaste if she hears it."

The housekeeper's smile returned. "That I shall do right now, my lady."

Priscilla took a deep breath as she walked to her study, preparing herself for battle. She was not disappointed.

Even as she was giving her aunt a kiss on the cheek and sitting, Aunt Cordelia stated, "This has gone on long enough." Her aunt set herself on her feet. "How much longer are you going to imperil your children?"

"The children are safest with me, because I am aware of the threat to them." Priscilla remained sitting. She had to be grateful Aunt Cordelia was in a pelter when the children were not witnesses. Daphne had gone with Neville to take a basket of Mrs. Dunham's fresh bread and some roast meat to the vicarage.

"How can you say that?"

"Here, with me, there are many people to watch over the children. I have had plenty of time to consider this."

"Plenty of time? The latest attack was last night."

"Last *evening*. I had all night to consider this."

"Yes," mumbled Aunt Cordelia, unable to argue with that.

"Both men who have been attacked are elderly. Someone is trying to exterminate old men in this village."

Aunt Cordelia scowled. "You cannot be certain of that."

"No, but the late duke and Mr. Kenyon were born within weeks of each other. That much we have learned."

"We? Sir Neville, I suppose. Priscilla, I do not understand how you can let *that* man be near you and your children. He—"

Interrupting before Aunt Cordelia began to list all of Neville's shortcomings, she said, "I suspect the Muir brothers also were born about the same time. I intend to warn them to take care."

"How much longer are you going to pursue what is not your business?"

"Would you rather that I did nothing and let someone else be hurt?"

"I would rather," Aunt Cordelia said in an imperious voice, "you did not do everything you can in an effort to prove to everyone that, not only are you inadequate to raise an earl, but your daughters as well."

Priscilla stood. "I see no reason to continue this conversation. Good morning, Aunt Cordelia."

She made her exit before she added something she would regret. Her dignity was ruined when she walked straight into Mr. Pritchard.

"Lady Priscilla!" he gasped as if she had done something nobody else ever had.

Eyeing him up and down, she doubted if any other woman had ever come so close to this irritating man. "Ah, Mr. Pritchard," she said with a cool smile. "I had hoped I would have a chance to tell you farewell in person."

"Farewell?" His eyes widened.

"I do hope you will have a pleasant journey back to Elsworth Academy." She held out her hand.

As he bowed over it, correct as always, she knew he understood that she had given him his *congé*. One problem taken care of. Now if only her others would be solved so easily . . .

When Priscilla went to call on the Muir brothers, she was flabbergasted to see them sitting on the small terrace overlooking the sea. She could not recall the last time she had seen them *not* working in their garden.

"Lady Priscilla!" called Irwin, coming to his feet with a spryness that suggested he was several decades younger.

"This is a wondrous surprise," added Walden. He moved a bit more slowly, keeping a hand on his left hip.

"You have been so busy that we have seen little of you."

"Yes, little."

"Do sit, Lady Priscilla," urged Irwin.

"Yes, do."

Priscilla smiled and sat on a bench. Before the brothers could begin prattling again, she asked, "Have you heard about what happened last night?"

"Poor Kenyon," said Irwin, as always the first to speak.

"Good chap," echoed his brother.

"The vicar must be very upset." Irwin sat.

"Very upset." Walden followed his brother onto the other bench.

Priscilla nodded. "You are right, and so is Constable Forshaw."

Irwin glanced at his brother and shrugged. "We have no reason to be fearful. Unlike your house and Vicar Kenyon's house, there is nothing of value here for a thief."

"Our garden is valuable," Walden said, glaring at his brother.

"But," Priscilla argued, "the attack was not on me or Vicar Kenyon."

"So it appears."

Walden nodded. "There are too many questions that need answers."

"The constable should find the murderer and hang him!"

"From the tree in the center of the green."

Priscilla interjected, "Constable Forshaw and I do not believe that robbery was the reason for the attacks. I am beginning to believe—and Sir Neville concurs—that the murderer may well be preying on old men in Stonehall-on-Sea."

"That is absurd," Irwin replied.

"'Tis nonsense." Walden folded his arms. "I told that to Mr. Dunham when I saw him in the village this morning."

She nodded, not surprised that tales of her conversations with Constable Forshaw and Neville had already spread through the village. "You are calm in the light of these rumors."

"We were not born here as Kenyon and the duke were," Irwin said.

"Born closer to London."

Priscilla halted Irwin from adding more by saying, "I thought you had spent your whole lives in this village."

Irwin shook his head. "We came here after we returned to England from the American colonies."

"Glad to be done with the war," his brother grumbled.

"We wanted to find a peaceful place to live."

"A house with a nice garden. Better to grow things than kill things."

Priscilla looked from one to the other. "I didn't know you had fought in the colonies, too."

Irwin turned to his brother. "She is speaking of the duke."

"The Duke of Meresden was a hero in the American war," Walden said.

"A great hero."

"But," she said, "if you were there and he was there, it is possible—"

"Impossible," Irwin replied.

"Impossible." Walden nodded in agreement.

"We did not wear those fancy buttons. We were not officers."

"Only officers wore those buttons," Walden said with an air of finality.

"If you are looking for some common thread, Lady Priscilla," Irwin said with a frown, "it is not that, for the vicar never served in the New World. All of his service was in India, if I recall correctly."

Walden nodded again. "That is correct."

"If you are looking for a connection," continued Irwin, "you may wish to consider that Kenyon's public house is on land leased from Meresden Court."

"This house, like yours, is not."

"You should consider that the new duke might have other uses for the property than the low rent Kenyon pays for use of the land. If—"

Knowing that she was being rude to interrupt, but needing to halt them, she asked, "Are you suggesting that Mr. Kenyon's tenancy might be the cause of the attack on him?"

"It is possible," Irwin answered.

"Lord Sherbourne," began Walden.

*"His Grace,"* corrected his brother with a scowl.

"I prefer to address him as Lord Sherbourne. I don't believe he is worthy of the title his father held."

"But he now holds the title."

"And his father must be spinning in his grave." Walden glanced at Priscilla for confirmation.

His brother replied, "Which would not matter to his son, who has been long eager to obtain both the title and the income from the duke's holdings."

Priscilla wanted to put her hands up to her head as the conversation bounced back and forth between the two brothers like a tennis ball between skilled players. They were not telling her anything that others had not already suggested, although not so bluntly.

"Pris?" came a call from the front gate. "Are you still here?"

She never had been so grateful to hear Neville's voice. Excusing herself, she left the brothers to their conversation. They did not even pause to bid her good day.

Neville was waiting with what for him was rare patience as she hurried out. He smiled. *"You* look well rested, Pris."

"I had a good night's sleep."

"The sleep of the innocent."

"That," she retorted, "is not amusing."

He held up his hands. "Don't snarl at me, Pris. I am on your side."

She sighed, not wanting to quarrel when she wanted to tell him how seeing him here offered her comfort. If he had not been here, she would still have struggled to clear her name, but it would have been so much harder. His teasing, even when it was vexing, was a balm to her ravaged nerves. "I realize that."

"And I believe I have convinced the good constable of your innocence as well. Almost."

"At least he has doubts."

When he offered his arm as they went back toward Mermaid Cottage, she put her hand on it. She explained what the Muir brothers had told her about Mr. Kenyon's public house.

"I can find out which properties in the village belong to the duke," Neville said, "while you deal with your aunt."

"Thank you, although I would gladly switch our tasks."

He chuckled. "I am no beef-head. I want to avoid the inimitable Lady Cordelia and her sycophantic schoolmaster."

"Mr. Pritchard is taking his leave today."

"Really?"

She nodded. "I told him farewell before I called on the Muirs."

"Can you persuade him to stay?"

"Stay? Why?"

His face became grim. "Because Pritchard's arrival coincides too closely to the duke's death."

"It was several days later that Mr. Pritchard came to Mermaid Cottage."

"But the description Martha Ackerley gave you fits him. He may have been nearby and waited a few days to give his arrival countenance."

"I can ask Mr. Pritchard to stay." She sighed.

He patted her hand. "I'm sorry, Pris, to ask this. I know you must have been very pleased at having the man gone."

"Aunt Cordelia is going to believe she has won." She faced him. "Tell me one thing, Neville. What possible reason could Mr. Pritchard have for murdering the duke and attacking Mr. Kenyon?"

"None that I know of, but I intend to find out if there is any connection."

"Do it quickly, please."

He laughed. "As quickly as possible."


Priscilla swung the empty basket as she strode along the road. Beside her, Juster lagged behind each time she did not glance to determine if the footman was still with her. This afternoon was supposed to be his half-day, but Gilbert had allowed him to trade with Layden. Now, the young footman regretted his request.

Suddenly he grinned and squared his shoulders, throwing out his chest.

She looked along the road and saw Martha Ackerley. Like Priscilla, she had a basket over her arm, but it was filled with flowers.

Martha waved and hurried toward them. "Good afternoon!"

"I didn't expect to see you out this way." She glanced at Juster who was regarding Martha with the symptoms—sweat on his brow and a silly grin—of a serious case of calf-love. Martha Ackerley was pretty and of an age to appeal to Juster. Taking pity on the poor lad, she said, "What lovely flowers! Where did you pick them? I could send Juster."

Martha glanced at the footman and away so quickly he deflated. She did not seem to notice as she said, "Thomas prefers quiet in the afternoon when he is doing his own studies." She laughed, but with little amusement. "Even when I tiptoe about, I disturb him."

"You are always welcome to call at Mermaid Cottage."

She shook her head. "Do not take this the wrong way, but your aunt makes me uncomfortable."

*You aren't the only one,* Priscilla thought.

"I do not think," Martha continued, "Lady Cordelia is fond of Americans."

"The whispers of war have unsettled many people." Her lips tightened. "I wish we could go home."

"You want to go home?" Priscilla asked, firing a frown at Juster who had gasped when Martha spoke of leaving Stonehall-on-Sea. She would have Gilbert speak to the footman about his behavior.

The footman lowered his eyes, and Priscilla was sorry for glaring at him. Who was she to fault someone for falling in love, whether wisely or unwisely? She had followed her heart and married Lazarus.

"I thought Mr. Ackerley said you wanted to come here," Priscilla added.

"I did," Martha replied, "but not as much as he did."

Had she misunderstood Mr. Ackerley? She drew the conversation out of her memory. No, Mr. Ackerley had been definite that *Martha* was the one who had yearned to come to England.

"I see," Priscilla said, although she did not.

"Now I want to go home."

"I understand."

"You do, don't you?" Martha's smile became warmer. "You have such a kind heart. Just like my grandmother." Tears filled her eyes. "I do so miss my grandmother, and I hate being so far from her."

"She is in America?"

"Yes, and with war threatening, she is sure to suffer."

Priscilla put her hand on Martha's arm, not surprised to find it trembling. "Mayhap the war will not come. The British government and the American one may find a compromise."

"Oh, I do so hope you are correct." She looked at her flowers. "I should put these in water, so I can begin Thomas's supper. He gets cranky when it is served late."

Priscilla bid Martha a good afternoon, then told Juster to follow as they continued toward the Dog and Crown public house. She saw the footman glancing at Martha, but she said nothing. 'Twas good that Neville was going with Constable Forshaw to Meresden Court to obtain information on the duke's holdings around the village. Martha would have broken young Juster's heart when she bantered like a hoyden with Neville.

The public house appeared deserted in the early afternoon sunshine, but Priscilla was not fooled. She had heard how the men spent hour after hour within its walls, enjoying a few pints and exaggerating their prowess and woes.

"Please go in," she said to Juster as they paused by the low stone wall that enclosed the public house.

His eyes lit up with anticipation. "Yes, my lady."

"Find the person who is in charge in Mr. Kenyon's absence and send whoever it is out to speak with me." She pressed a coin into Juster's hand. "Sample some of Mr. Kenyon's ale until I send for you to return with me to Mermaid Cottage."

"Yes, my lady." He nearly ran into the public house.

Priscilla looked back toward the village. The church's spire was visible above the thatched roofs. It looked so serene that anyone passing by would have no idea of the tragedy stalking Stonehall-on-Sea.

"Lady Priscilla?"

She turned to see Lenore Gillen behind her. Smiling, she wondered if her luck had taken a turn for the better. The Gillens were honest, hardworking folks; and dark-haired Lenore had often come to play with Daphne when both were young.

"I didn't know you were working for Mr. Kenyon, Lenore," she said.

"For 'bout two months now." She raised her apron and dried her face that bore the stains of tears. "Mr. Kenyon's a fine man, my lady. 'E shouldn't 'ave been treated so bad. 'Ow is 'e? Do ye know?"

"He is unconscious, but Mr. Semple says he is doing as well as can be expected."

"Will 'e live?"

Priscilla squeezed the young woman's hand gently. "We can only pray and wait." She paused. "Will you answer a few questions for me?"

"If I can."

"You have been here for two months."

"Yes."

"Have you seen the Duke of Meresden—the new duke—come here often?"

"Yes. 'E's 'ere pretty regular."

"Was he here the night I found his father's body in my garden?"

"The new duke? 'Ere the night 'is father's lights were put out?" Lenore shook her head. "'E weren't 'ere that night. The new duke, 'e only comes in on Sunday evenings, my lady, and that weren't a Sunday."

"I see." Priscilla frowned. The duke had assured her that he had been at Mr. Kenyon's public house. He had lied about that. What else was he lying about?

"See wot?"

"That not everything is as I had hoped it would be."

# Fifteen

Rain splattered on the window. Priscilla heard her children laughing upstairs. From the dining room came the voices of Mrs. Moore and Gilbert as they coordinated the work for the staff. Her aunt and Mr. Pritchard were taking tea in the parlor and reminiscing about Elsworth Academy and its companion school for girls. The mention of the Elsworth Lyceum was further proof to Priscilla why she should not send Isaac there. Her father would have enrolled her in the Elsworth Lyceum if he had enjoyed his experiences at the boy's school.

Neville appeared in the study's doorway, swinging his soaked head to dislodge water in a wide arc around him.

"Neville!" she cried when drops struck her. "You are not a dog. Please do not shake like one."

"I thought you would be anxious to learn what I discovered, so I did not get out of these wet clothes first." He drew off his coat and draped it over a chair.

"You are soaked to the skin," she said when his shirtsleeves and his waistcoat clung to him. "Let me ring for something warm for you to drink."

He caught her hand as she was reaching for the bell. "Pris, you need to hear what Forshaw and I found out at Meresden Court. *You* need to hear it.

Not your household staff or your aunt or your children."

His grim tone struck her like a blow. Nodding, she sat again. He started to do the same, then paused.

She pointed to a wooden chair. "Bring that over and sit on it. The cushion can be dried out afterward."

"Thanks." He almost collapsed into the chair. Rubbing his eyes, he murmured, "I shall be cursed before I spend another dreary day going through those endless pages."

"You could ask Aunt Cordelia to borrow her quizzing glass."

His lips twitched. "I might do that. Now, do you wish to learn what I found out?"

"Yes, then I shall tell you what I discovered."

"You?"

"Go ahead and tell me what you learned first."

"We found out from property maps at Meresden Court that half of the buildings in Stonehall-on-Sea are constructed on land leased from the duke."

"Half?"

"I had hoped it would be fewer properties. However . . ."

"Am I to ask 'However what?' Neville?"

"If you wish to know what else I have discovered."

"You can be the most tiresome man."

"I know." He gave her the smile he had used to charm Martha.

She was astonished that she was no more immune to it than Martha was. In her head, Aunt Cordelia's voice rumbled with that long list of Neville's transgressions. It was muted when she heard the echo of her late husband's admonition not to let anyone else make judgments for her.

"So," she said, trying to ignore her amazement that,

after so many years, she was beguiled by Neville's easy grin, "it seems that you will not tell me until I say what you wish to hear. So I shall."

"Is that so?"

"Yes. However what?"

He chuckled. "You know how to dash a man's hopes, don't you?"

"Will you keep your mind on the subject of the duke's holdings?"

"Very well." He leaned forward, holding her gaze with his intense eyes. "There is but one house owned by a man who is a contemporary of the late duke and Rudolph Kenyon."

"Mr. Robertson!"

His smile vanished. "Blast it, Pris. I was hoping to dazzle you with this information."

"I have been living in Stonehall-on-Sea for many years. I know everyone in the village."

"True, but how did you guess it was him? There are plenty of old chaps around."

"The year before Isaac was born, the duke had a party to celebrate his sixtieth birthday. He invited the Muirs, Mr. Kenyon, and Mr. Robertson to share the celebration because they would be turning sixty within three months of each other."

"You remember that?" He gave her a suspicious frown. "Or did you check that while I was out? Was that what you wanted to tell me?"

"No." She watched his eyes narrow. "However, you should know that a clergyman's wife must be able to remember such apparently insignificant details, because someone is sure to ask about them in the future."

"Elderly men with birthdays within a few months of each other." He tapped his chin. "By Jove, Pris! That is why someone grabbed the parish records! Not everyone else would remember the details you do."

She nodded, realizing how much sense that made. "The current duke would recall that. Mayhap he wished no one else to."

"Meresden? What have you learned, Pris?"

He came to his feet as she explained what Lenore had told her at the Dog and Crown. Leaving wet footprints in his wake, he paced from one side of the room to the other.

"Why would Meresden lie about something we could check so easily?" he asked.

"Mayhap he thought, now that he is a duke, no one would question his word!"

Neville snorted. "I assume that you have not met many dukes, Pris. You wouldn't be so naïve otherwise."

"I will remind you that I am the one who went to confirm his story."

Dropping back into the chair, he said, "Forgive me. You are right."

She stood and picked up a handbell. She rang it. "There is nothing to forgive, Neville. We are both nearing our wits' end with this." Pulling out a piece of paper, she wrote a quick note.

When the door opened to reveal Gilbert, Priscilla asked him to have the message delivered to Mr. Robertson's house to either the old man or his daughter. She also requested a tea tray to be brought.

"And something for Sir Neville to dry off with?" the butler asked.

"Thank you," Neville said. "I have been dripping on Lady Priscilla's floor long enough." As soon as the door closed, he added, "I assume that message was a warning to Robertson."

"Yes, as well as word that we would call on the morrow."

"I hope he survives the night."

She shivered. "I believe I shall have a message delivered to Constable Forshaw. The constable may wish to pay the Robertsons a look-in also."

"An excellent idea."

"I hope it is enough."


"It is about time," Aunt Cordelia announced with satisfaction as she looked up from the page she held and around the dining room table. Her smile broadened as it slipped past Mr. Pritchard, widened even more for her grandnieces and Isaac, then vanished as her eyes met Neville's. She did not look, Priscilla noted, at her.

"Time for what?" Priscilla asked, knowing that her aunt would be cross if she did not. Tonight, with her head pounding, she had no interest in enduring another of Aunt Cordelia's scolds.

"An invitation to attend a garden *soirée* at Lord Wallingford's estate."

"That is near Brighton, is it not?" piped up Mr. Pritchard.

"Yes." Aunt Cordelia gave him an even warmer smile, and Priscilla wondered what the two were plotting now. Aunt Cordelia's expression revealed she had already spoken with the headmaster about the gathering.

"I do hope you have a pleasant time," Priscilla said.

"Me?" Aunt Cordelia lowered her quizzing glass. "Why, my dear child, we all are invited."

Ignoring the giggles that came from Leah and Isaac each time Aunt Cordelia addressed her as *my dear child,* Priscilla replied, "That is so generous of Lord Wallingford, but leaving Stonehall-on-Sea may not be possible."

"If you are worried about that impertinent Constable Forshaw insisting that you remain here because he thinks that you could be involved in that disgusting murder, you may rest assured that he will change his mind."

Neville put down his wine. "You may find the good constable will be less likely than usual to have his mind changed for him."

"Nonsense!" Aunt Cordelia's wave wafted away his words as if they were tiresome insects. "Anyone with a bit of sense knows Priscilla had nothing to do with the unfortunate incidents here."

"For once, we agree." He ignored how Aunt Cordelia bristled as he turned to Priscilla. "It might not be a bad idea to give the children a change of scenery."

"That is true," Priscilla replied. "I think they will enjoy going to such a gathering." *And it will get them away from Stonehall-on-Sea.* In spite of her words to her aunt, she never could forget how close the threat was to her children. Should she send them away with her aunt? If she did, she feared she would never get the children back from Aunt Cordelia. While they were in Brighton, Constable Forshaw might unmask the murderer.

She was rewarded with delighted squeals from her daughters that she hushed, reminding them that they were at the table.

Daphne said more quietly, "Mama, you are out of first mourning, so you should not remain in black." Her face fell as she added, "I mean no disrespect to Papa."

Priscilla stroked her daughter's cheek. "I realize that, Daphne. However, you are correct. I believe I shall send for Mrs. Bird to make dresses appropriate for the occasion."

"Mrs. Bird?" Aunt Cordelia wrinkled her nose in aristocratic distaste. "You must allow me to send to London for Madame Glasson. *She* will make you a stylish gown, instead of whatever frumpish thing a seamstress here might design."

Not wanting to argue, Priscilla joined her daughters' conversation as they began to chatter about what color they would wear and how they would arrange their hair. She glanced toward the windows when a flash of lightning brightened the dark sky. Thunder thudded in its wake. She hoped the storm would prevent the murderer from making a call on Mr. Robertson.

Her attention came back to the conversation when Mr. Pritchard bragged, "Lord Wallingford also attended Elsworth Academy."

"How fortunate for him," Priscilla said. The headmaster had become even more intolerable since she had asked him to stay at Mermaid Cottage.

Neville added under his breath, but loud enough so she could hear him, "Yes, how fortunate that he escaped relatively unscathed."

Priscilla put her hand over her mouth to keep her laugh from reaching her aunt's ears. Neville had a true skill for putting Mr. Pritchard's blustering into perspective.

"How long will we be there, Mama?" Daphne asked.

"The invitation is for a fortnight." Aunt Cordelia smiled as if all of this were her doing.

"Then we should say farewell to the Ackerleys before we leave."

"Farewell?" Priscilla asked. "Why?"

"When I went to bring Leah home from her French lesson, Martha told me that she and her brother are planning to leave Stonehall-on-Sea."

"She said nothing when I saw her on the way to . . ." Priscilla knew better than to speak in her aunt's hearing of her visit to the public house. "Did she say where they were going?"

"I do not recall."

Neville intruded to say, "Wallingford is a good host. I believe we shall have a pleasant time at his estate."

"You?" Aunt Cordelia bristled. "I do not recall saying anything about you being invited, Sir Neville."

He reached beneath his coat. "No need, for I have my own invitation. I have already sent word to the viscount to expect me and my guests for the gathering."

"Guests?"

"I thought the Ackerleys would be pulled out of their dismals by attending."

"You asked those . . . those . . . those . . ."

With a smile, he asked, "Is *neighbor* the word you are seeking?"

"No! Americans! Their presence will taint the party."

Neville put the folded page back beneath his coat. "Quite to the contrary." He looked across the table at Daphne and Leah. "I thought your daughters, Pris, would like to have a familiar face with them."

Daphne glanced at her aunt and then gave Neville a scintillating smile. "How thoughtful of you, Uncle Neville."

Moments ago, Priscilla would have been shocked that her daughter was pleased to have Martha at the party when Daphne had considered her a rival for Neville's attention. But if the Ackerleys were leaving Stonehall-on-Sea, Daphne could afford to be generous.

"You are very welcome," he replied with a warm smile.

Priscilla wanted to jab him with her elbow. She did not need him flirting with Daphne. Her daughter could devise enough thoughts that troubled her mother without his help. Then, she realized, he must have a reason for what he was doing. He always did, and he would do nothing to hurt Daphne or any member of this family.

"The Ackerleys have never had an opportunity to attend such an assembly," Daphne continued. "May I have another slice of bread, Mama?"

Neville watched Priscilla hand her daughter the bread plate. She glanced at him, and he saw her disquiet. Like her, he wondered why Martha had said nothing to Priscilla about the Ackerleys' intention to leave. He continued to talk with Isaac about the horses Wallingford was renowned for, but his gaze shifted to meet hers again. She was conversing with her excited daughters about new gowns. Only in her eyes was he able to see that she was thinking of anything other than how many ruffles would be appropriate for Daphne's dress.

He smiled when Priscilla suggested that they enjoy their dessert in the parlor. As her children were herded in that direction by her aunt, with Mr. Pritchard trailing close behind, he handed Priscilla to her feet.

"May I see your invitation?" she asked, holding out her hand.

"Don't you trust me, Pris?"

"Of course not. I know you too well to trust you."

He chuckled as he drew the folded sheet from beneath his coat.

"This isn't an invitation," she said, opening it. "It is blank."

"Yes, it is."

"How did you know my aunt had received an invitation?"

"I have my allies."

"In *this* house?"

He laughed again. "As much as Gilbert was furious for my prank upon my arrival, he prefers me over your aunt. Wallingford is an old friend, so he will not be distressed to see me."

"I believe it would be proper at this point to inform my aunt of your falsehoods."

"But?"

"I am glad you will be going along." She paused as one of the footmen brought the tray of tarts into the dining room. After telling him to take it to the parlor, she went on, "So may I assume that you have not asked the Ackerleys?"

"Not yet."

She glanced past him, and he knew she was watching for the footman to return, not wanting anyone to overhear. "What compelled you to offer the Ackerleys an invitation?"

"When Daphne mentioned they were leaving Stonehall-on-Sea."

"She may have misunderstood, because Martha surely would have said something when we met near the Dog and Crown."

"If she had known." He went to the window that offered a view of the Ackerleys' cottage. "Her brother may have made the decision. She seems agreeable to anything he suggests."

"She does dote on him."

"Enough to lie?" He heard Priscilla's gasp. "Enough to lie about what she saw the day of the duke's death?"

"Do you believe she lied about seeing a light-haired man in the garden?"

"A light-haired *stranger*. What if the man was no stranger to her?"

He saw understanding in her eyes, then horror as she realized that much of what they had believed was true might not be.

"You are right. Martha would do anything for her brother." She dampened her lips. "Even lie."

* * *

Neville gave the constable a nod as he handed Priscilla out of her carriage. Although Constable Forshaw had been grateful for Neville's suggestion of visiting Meresden Court to check the property maps, she knew the constable would be glad to see Neville take his leave of the village.

Dark circles hung beneath the constable's eyes. She wanted to tell him to get some sleep, but he would not be able to rest well until they put an end to the fear creeping through Stonehall-on-Sea.

"Thank you for your note," the constable said. "Miss Robertson is waiting to speak with you. Will this take long?"

"Why?"

"I promised Vicar Kenyon that I would sit with his uncle while the vicar went to call on some parishioners."

"Go ahead in, Pris," Neville added. "I have a few questions for the constable before I join you."

Wondering what he was planning now, Priscilla nodded. She left the two men by the carriage as she went through the wooden gate and into the Robertsons' unkempt garden. The house was in as poor condition as the garden, and she vowed to speak to Vicar Kenyon about seeing what help the parish might offer.

The door opened before she reached it. A chubby woman, who appeared to be in her third decade, pushed straight brown hair back toward her chignon. Her gown was simple, but as neat and clean as the foyer that could be seen behind her.

"My lady, do come in." Miss Robertson smiled, her face brightening. "I am so pleased that you have called. We have so few visitors."

"Do only you and your grandfather live here?" Priscilla went into the narrow hallway. Even though the walls were bare and the windows had no curtains, the few pieces of furniture glowed with tender care.

"Since my grandmother died several years ago."

"May I speak with Mr. Robertson?"

The young woman hesitated, then said, "Of course, my lady. Come this way."

Priscilla followed Miss Robertson up steep stairs and into the single room at the top. Like the room below, it was sparsely decorated. A narrow bed left only enough room for a washstand and chair.

An elderly man, his white hair as meager in number as the pieces of furniture, sat hunched in the chair. His clothes were so wrinkled that he could have slept in them. He did not move as they walked in.

"Grandfather?" asked Miss Robertson.

He did not reply . . . or even react.

Miss Robertson knelt beside him. "Grandfather, Lady Priscilla is here and would like to speak with you."

If he answered, Priscilla did not hear it.

Miss Robertson must have, because she motioned for Priscilla to come closer.

Priscilla said, "Mr. Robertson, thank you for . . ."

The old man raised his eyes, but they were as empty of thought as a newborn.

She looked at Miss Robertson, now aware of the burden this young woman was handling alone. No wonder the garden had been ignored. Miss Robertson must spend all her time taking care of her grandfather.

"Go ahead," Miss Robertson said. "Sometimes, when you talk to him, he seems to wake up."

"All right." Leaning toward the old man, she said, "I am Priscilla Flanders, Mr. Robertson. Do you remember my husband, the Vicar Dr. Flanders?"

Something flickered in the old man's eyes, and he said in a voice like a rusty hinge, "At St. Elizabeth's Church."

"Yes, that's right." She told herself not to become too excited.

"Good man."

"Yes, he was. Have you seen the Duke of Meresden lately?"

"He is dead."

"Mr. Robertson, did you ever serve the king in the army?"

"Good King George." He smiled.

"Yes. That's right. Did you serve in his army?"

He began to sing a song that Priscilla did not recognize until she heard the words *Yankee Doodle*.

"Mr. Robertson, does that mean you were in America?"

"How is the new duke?" he asked. "Is he doing well?"

"I believe he is."

"A good man."

Priscilla fought not to disagree. She looked back as Neville entered the room. The constable remained in the doorway.

"The duke is highly unsettled," she said, "by his father's sudden death."

"These things happen." The old man scratched his ribs, then his bewhiskered chin. "The duke knew he should not try to take that fence, but he never listened to anyone."

"Fence?" she asked, then stopped herself as the old man continued to talk. He was not speaking of the Duke of Meresden who had been found dead in her garden, but of that duke's father. This old man must be lost in time.

Mr. Robertson looked at his granddaughter. "Why

are you loitering here? Get our guests something to slake their thirst, Carol."

Miss Robertson appeared stricken as she murmured, "Carol was my mother's name, my lady."

"I understand." She turned to the door, then looked back. "Thank you for talking with us, Mr. Robertson."

"Lady Priscilla?" he asked, his eyes clearing.

"Yes?"

She tried not to let her hope return, but she did until he added, "Do send Dr. Flanders to call. I have not spoken with him in a long time."

In spite of herself, Priscilla choked out, "Yes, of course."

This old man lived in a world where Lazarus was still alive. Right after her husband's death, she had wished she could find a similar place. Then, with the help of her children, she had chosen to let the past go. She had decided to look to the present and the future and be happy as Lazarus would have wished. Mr. Robertson had made another choice.

Neville walked down the stairs behind her, silent. While she thanked Miss Robertson and they went through the neglected garden, neither he nor Constable Forshaw spoke.

"Thank you, Constable," she said, her voice cracking on the words. "Are you going directly to Vicar Kenyon's house?"

"Yes."

"Will you ask Vicar Kenyon to give Miss Robertson a look-in at his earliest convenience?"

He nodded. "I will mention Miss Robertson and her grandfather at the bakery shop. Mrs. Crockett will let everyone know that Miss Robertson needs help here."

"Thank you." She smiled as Neville assisted her into the open carriage. "Thank you very much."

Neville turned the carriage back toward Mermaid Cottage and said, "That was a dead end."

"Could you use another phrase?"

"Getting superstitious on me, Pris?"

"Not really. I feel so sorry for what that girl has to tend to every day for as long as her grandfather lives."

"Do not take this the wrong way, but I hope his death does not come soon and at the hands of the one who murdered the duke."

She nodded. "I agree. And I hope, as well, that he is the only one left in danger."

"If our assumptions that this has something to do with the holdings of the present duke are correct . . ."

"I wish I could be sure of that."

"So do I."

# Sixteen

"I would be glad to place the order alone," Mrs. Dunham said, pausing in front of the butcher shop. "I know you have many things to do before Lord Wallingford's gathering."

Priscilla was about to thank her cook and remind Mrs. Dunham, who was trying to protect her, that she would not let rumors dictate her life. She halted when she saw an elegant carriage in front of the church on the far side of the green.

"Thank you, Mrs. Dunham. That will be just perfect," she said and walked to the church.

The Duke of Meresden stepped out of his carriage and adjusted his perfectly tied cravat. Something glinted on his left hand. A pair of thick gold rings, she realized as she came closer. She wondered if they had belonged to his father or if he had obtained them since his father's death.

"Good morning, Your Grace," she called when he started toward the church.

He whirled, fear on his face. That terror vanished as his features hardened. "Lady Priscilla, it is not a good morning. I tire of you and your friend Hathaway trying to find ways to make me the scapegoat in my father's death."

"All we wish is to know the truth."

"The truth is that I did not kill my father."

"Nor did I."

He opened his mouth, then closed it. Staring at her, he drew out a small box. He took out a pinch of snuff. She waited, saying nothing, as he sniffed it, then sneezed.

As he put the box back under his coat, he asked, "Are you suggesting that we work together to find his murderer?"

"Are you suggesting that we do *not?*"

A reluctant smile stole across his expressive mouth. "By all that's blue, you have more wit than I would have expected in a clergyman's wife. And you speak your mind more."

"True."

"I suspect that habit was troublesome for your husband."

"Dr. Flanders preferred that everyone speak the truth. Will you?"

"Of course."

She met his eyes evenly. "Where were you when word was sent to Meresden Court about your father's death? You were not at the Dog and Crown, as you told me."

"Did I tell you that?"

"Yes."

"I was in error."

"Yes, you were." She was not going to let him squirm away from being truthful.

"I believe I was calling on a friend."

"Am I to believe that as well?"

His smile grew cold. "You may believe what you wish, Lady Priscilla, but that is the truth. I will say no more on that, because it is, if you will excuse my plain speech, none of your damnable business."

"Really, Your Grace! Do you forget that you are in the churchyard?"

When he glanced up as if he half-expected a lightning bolt to strike him, he replied sheepishly, "Forgive me for speaking so, Lady Priscilla. I forgot myself."

"I know you are distressed. We all are." Although she wanted to press further, she said, "Thank you for being honest with me."

"I collect that what you really wish to hear from me right now is what I am doing in the village and where I am bound."

Priscilla fought to keep her smile from betraying her delight in the course this awkward conversation was taking. "If you do not mind."

"No, for you are sure to see where I am bound." He adjusted his coat, although it was not wrinkled. "I thought to call on Vicar Kenyon to see if there has been any improvement in his uncle's condition."

"May I join you?"

"Were you bound in that direction?"

Unable to lie when she had just insisted on honesty, she said, "Eventually."

The duke smiled, then chuckled. "I am now forewarned, Lady Priscilla, to guard my words closely in your company." Offering his arm, he asked, "Shall we?"

Priscilla let him draw her hand within his arm. The muscles along it were hard, so he had the strength to wield a cudgel against a man's head. She wondered if Mr. Pritchard did. The very idea of touching the headmaster of the Elsworth Academy twisted her stomach.

A path made up of stones irregularly spaced through the grass led around the back of the church. When Daphne had been very young, she had tried to jump from one to the next. Each one she had conquered had been a victory to be celebrated.

"I understand you will be attending Wallingford's assembly, too," the duke said, startling her out of pleasant memories where she would have enjoyed lingering longer.

"Yes." Priscilla again kept her face from displaying her reaction. At the party, she might have a chance to pin the duke down further about where he had been the night of his father's death. She was tempted to ask him now to name the friend he had called upon, but she did not want to ruin his unanticipated camaraderie. So far, other than the lie about his whereabouts, he had cooperated, albeit with some resistance, in the search for his father's murderer.

"Will you save me a dance, Lady Priscilla, now that you are out of mourning?"

"I am honored," she replied as they reached the vicarage door.

As soon as it opened and the vicar peered out, she knew there had been no change. Vicar Kenyon's face was drawn, and he resembled the constable who was not sleeping either. She went in to offer some comfort, although she had very little.


The Ackerley house seemed deserted in the afternoon sunshine. Priscilla wondered why Martha had been delayed for her appointment with Mrs. Bird, who was going to remake one of Priscilla's gowns for Martha to wear to Lord Wallingford's gathering. Martha was so excited about attending.

Mr. Ackerley came to the door. As always, his thoughts seemed to be far away. Uneasiness teased her. Neville had warned that Martha might be lying about the murder to protect her brother. She did not like the idea of being alone in this house with a possible murderer. Then, she smiled. Mayhap Mr. Ackerley felt the same. After all, *she* had been accused of the crime by Constable Forshaw.

"Is something bothering you, Lady Priscilla?" he asked.

"Nothing new." She gave him a weak smile as she entered.

He pointed to the material draped over her arm. "What is that?"

"A gown that will be altered for Martha."

"You may wait for her in the parlor if you wish."

"I doubt," Priscilla said, "that she will want a fitting in the parlor when you have students coming and going."

"Fitting?" He frowned. "Oh, yes, the party. You can go up to her room if you wish. It is the second door on the right at the top of the stairs."

"Thank you." She hurried up the stairs, noting how he strode back to his office as if he could not wait to get there and shut out the world beyond his books.

Reaching the second door, she knocked on the door's frame, just in case Mr. Ackerley had failed to notice his sister returning. There was no answer. She looked into the room.

Not a hint of dust was on the worn chest of drawers. A double window was set into the sloping roof, casting light across the narrow bed topped with a quilt. Every shelf against the wall backing up to the hall was filled with books. She doubted they were Martha's, and she wondered how many Mr. Ackerley had brought from America. There were enough here to sink a ship. And he had more in his study.

Setting the white dress that would be the perfect foil for Martha's tawny hair over the wooden foot-board, Priscilla clasped her hands. Being in Martha's private room when the young woman was not made her uncomfortable.

She frowned when she saw another dress draped across a table by the window. Had Daphne sent over another dress while searching through Priscilla's gowns for ones for herself and her sister to have altered to wear at the viscount's house? As she lifted it up off the table, Priscilla realized its style had not been worn for over forty years. It was tattered and lovingly patched. This had not come from her dressing room.

She started to place it back on the table, then faltered as something glistened in the sunlight. Not something, but a gun. She placed the dress beside the one she had brought and picked up the pistol. Even though it was battered and showed its age, the barrel shone from as much attention as the furniture. If she was not mistaken, it must be almost as old as the dress. Were they family heirlooms?

Priscilla set the pistol on the table and put the gown over the table again. She frowned when she saw two items on the floor. Picking up a piece of paper that had fallen out of a small wooden box, she set them on the dress.

The paper was covered with writing that had been squeezed onto the page. A letter! She should not read it, for it was private correspondence. As she was about to turn away, her eyes were caught by the name on the upper corner. It was addressed to George Washington—General George Washington. In spite of her conscience warning that she was overstepping the bounds of friendship, she picked it up and began to read.

*Dear General Washington,*

*I am writing to you in the unflagging hope that you can see your way to help. After all we have suffered at the hands of the English, it behooves you and the new government to offer us assistance. I . . .*

"Lady Priscilla, are you here?" called Martha from downstairs.

"Up here." She slipped the page back under the dress and walked out of the room as Martha came up the stairs. "I hope you do not mind that I waited up here. Your brother suggested that I should."

"I owe you so much that you are welcome to run tame through my house whenever you wish."

Although Priscilla was surprised when Martha used that cant of the *ton,* she said only, "I wanted to call before Mrs. Bird arrived, so I could find out if you liked this gown."

Martha's eyes grew big as Priscilla picked up the dress from the footboard. "Oh, that is so beautiful! I don't know how to thank you."

"Thank me if Mrs. Bird can remake it into something stylish. This dress is more than three years old, for it was not new when I went into mourning."

"Oh, do say that you are going to wear something other than black silk, Lady Priscilla!"

"She is adding a white bodice and ruffles to one of my darker gowns, so I will not be wearing black."

Martha held the dress against herself. "You should wear pale pinks and blues. Those colors would be best for you." Raising her head, she added with a sly grin, "And Sir Neville would like to see you in such colors."

"He does not worry about the latest fashion."

"But he looks so fashionable."

She smiled. "I should have said he does not worry about the latest fashion for the ladies. Are you interested in fashion, Martha?"

"Oh, yes!"

"Did you do the repairs on this dress?" She pointed to the table.

Martha dropped the dress Priscilla had brought and rushed to the table, gathering up the old dress. Hugging it as if it were her child, she stared at Priscilla with accusing eyes. "Did you touch this?"

"I did look at it."

"You shouldn't have touched it! It . . . it . . ." She shivered.

"Martha?" she asked, perplexed.

Looking down at the dress she clutched, Martha's face crumbled into grief. She sat on the bed. As the dress fell over her knees, she bent forward and sobbed.

Priscilla knelt beside her. Putting a hand on Martha's quivering shoulders, she said, "Forgive me. I should not have touched this dress that is so precious to you."

"You didn't know, Lady Priscilla."

"May I ask a question?"

Martha nodded, her head still down.

"Did that dress belong to the woman who wrote the letter to General Washington?"

"You shouldn't have been looking at my things."

"The letter fell to the floor, and his name caught my eye. He is highly respected here in England, even though he was a traitor to the king."

"No, he wasn't! He was a great patriot and saved America from domination by the horrible, hateful British. I . . . Lady Priscilla, I should not have said that."

Priscilla grasped Martha's hand as she whispered, "You are always welcome to speak your mind in my company. After all, the only difference between a patriot and a traitor is which side you favor." Rising, she went to the chest of drawers and opened the top one. As she had hoped, a pair of handkerchiefs were inside. She took out one and handed it to Martha. "I am so sorry. If you do not wish to speak of this, we shall not."

"No, you are asking out of friendship." Martha raised her head and swept away her tears with the back of her hand. "I want to tell you about the dress.

Thomas will not speak of this, and I cannot bear the grief on my own any longer."

Priscilla wished she had never brought up this subject. She did not want to be burdened with trouble from forty years ago. There was enough trouble in Stonehall-on-Sea *now*. Certain she would regret her offer, she said, "Tell me if you wish, Martha."

"The dress belonged to my grandmother. She wore it to my grandfather's funeral."

"Oh, I am so very sorry."

"I know you are. You aren't like those horrible British soldiers who killed him."

"During the American War of Independence?"

Martha nodded and stroked the gown. "He was killed. And my grandmother, whose name is the same as mine, was left a cripple. Those soldiers did not care. They laughed."

"I understand that men do things in war that they would never do otherwise."

"Those beasts laughed!" she cried as if she had not heard Priscilla's attempt to calm her. "Then they left my grandmother to die. She didn't, although she found herself confined to a chair." Her voice grew soft and sad. "Now we are here, and she is alone. She nearly starved during the war when she had nobody to till the fields."

"So that is why she wrote to General Washington for assistance?"

Martha nodded again. "I fear what may be happening to her now when we are on the other side of the sea."

"And the pistol?"

"It was my grandfather's. His name was Thomas like my brother's." She blinked. "It is the only thing I have of my grandfather."

"So why did you want to come to England if you hate the British so?"

Martha stood and sighed. "Hate is something that must be healed. As a vicar's wife, you must know that."

"I do." Coming to her feet, she took the handkerchief and dabbed it at Martha's cheeks. "You are a very brave woman, Martha Ackerley."

"I have to be."

"Because you are marooned here." Priscilla gave her a sad smile. "I hope you have seen that all English are not like the men who killed your grandfather."

Martha threw her arms around Priscilla. "You are a dear friend, Lady Priscilla." Stepping back, she dashed away the tears dripping along her cheeks.

The sound of a door opening downstairs and Mrs. Bird's reedy voice trilling up the stairs brought back Martha's smile. She folded her grandmother's dress and placed it in a drawer with the pistol and the letter before she hurried down the stairs to invite the seamstress up for her fitting.

Priscilla sighed as she looked at the chest of drawers. Poor Martha! No wonder Martha had been so delighted to be invited to Lord Wallingford's estate. The young woman had suffered so much sorrow. This gathering might bring her a bit of joy. It would not make up for what had happened. Priscilla doubted if anything could, but she was going to try to make Martha's time there a memory she could enjoy when the dismals threatened to claim her again.

Doing that would give Priscilla a chance to think about something other than the tragedies in Stonehall-on-Sea. In helping Martha forget her sorrow, Priscilla might gain some perspective on the crimes. Then, she would be able to see past the madness and discover why the duke and Mr. Kenyon had been attacked.

It was an unlikely and possibly futile hope . . . but it was the only one she had.

Neville stood up as the door to the bedchamber in the vicarage opened. He kneaded his lower back. This chair by the vicar's uncle's bed had to be the most blasted hard one in the shire.

The vicar looked hopefully at him. "What is it, Sir Neville?"

"I did not want to interrupt you, Vicar—"

"It was no trouble. I was speaking with a young couple about the baptism of their baby, and they were willing to excuse me for a few minutes. You sent the constable for me?"

"There has been a change in your uncle's condition."

Vicar Kenyon clenched his hand in front of his heart. "For the better or the worse?"

"I am not sure. He has been moving and mumbling." He stepped aside so the vicar could go to his uncle.

"Uncle Rudolph!" called the vicar as he sat on the hard chair by the bed. He spoke his uncle's name twice more, then sighed. "He does not seem to hear me."

"Or he cannot yet reply."

The vicar nodded and folded his hands on his knees. Not in prayer, but in anger. "No matter how many different ways I try to look at this, I cannot determine why my uncle would be attacked."

"Is there any chance your uncle was dealing with owls?"

"Every tavernkeeper along the coast of England deals with the smugglers."

"Bad dealings, I should have said."

The vicar shook his head. "Uncle Rudolph is well known for paying his debts on time and keeping his mouth closed when the authorities come around. Even if he had been attacked by owls, that does not explain why the duke was murdered."

"We have been assuming the two crimes are related."

"You don't think they are?"

Neville's smile was brittle. "I am quite sure they are, but I want to consider any alternatives."

"The duke . . ." the vicar glanced toward the door—for the constable, it was clear—when he continued, "the duke has supported the efforts of the smugglers for many years."

"In exchange for a share of their profits?"

"That is the way of the world, Sir Neville." He turned back to his uncle. "I may be a man of the church, but a good clergyman always keeps his eye on the secular world."

Neville nodded, respecting the vicar's common sense. "I need to speak to some folks. Mrs. Crockett is coming over from her shop to sit with your uncle in a short time. Do you think the parents waiting to baptize their baby would excuse you a while longer?"

"Go." The vicar's lips slowly tilted in a smile, as if it required Herculean strength to lift each corner. "Let me know if you discover anything that will help stop the madman from hurting someone else."

His uncle shifted on the bed. Incoherent mumbles fell out of his mouth like drool along a baby's chin.

"Uncle Rudolph, can you hear me?" Vicar Kenyon leaned forward and seized his uncle's hand.

Neville slipped out of the room to leave the vicar with his hopes for his uncle's recovery. Fury gripped him, but he silenced it with the practice of many years of dealing with those who had little respect for others' lives.

The sun was falling toward the horizon, but there

was at least another hour of light remaining. He needed to use that time wisely.

The voices in the public house were low and furtive as if everyone within feared that the next assault would be aimed at them. When Neville closed the door, every eye—drunk or sober—appraised him. He must have passed some judgment because the patrons went back to their conversations and ale.

Going to where the screen was raised and a dark-haired lass was filling pewter mugs with golden ale, he leaned on the bar. She glanced at him and frowned. Not the best beginning to what was certain to be a difficult conversation.

He motioned for a mug and then asked, "Are you Lenore?"

"I am." She eyed him again, then smiled. "Ye be the gentleman wot's staying with Lady Priscilla."

"Yes. I am Sir Neville Hathaway." When she set a mug in front of him, he asked, "Can you talk for a few minutes?"

"Yes."

"About Mr. Kenyon."

"Figured that was wot ye wanted to talk 'bout." She used a rag to clean the counter as she glanced around the room. Lowering her voice, she asked, "What d'ye want to know?"

"How was he the night he was attacked at the vicarage?"

"'Ow? Wot d'ye mean?"

"Was he agitated? Was he watching for someone?"

She looked at him directly. "Sir Neville, 'e was as uneasy as a smuggler with the navy on 'is tail. Usually 'e sits and chats with the boys. That night, 'e paced from one side of the tavern to the other."

"Did he say anything to give you an insight into what was bothering him?"

"Insight? Wot's that?"

He hid his smile behind a swig of the ale. Putting the mug down, he asked, "Did he tell you why he was so upset?"

"Said somethin' 'bout lettin' sleepin' dogs lie."

This was not helping. "Did anyone unusual come into the Dog and Crown that evening?"

"The duke was 'ere. Early. 'Fore the celebration down on the shore. 'E don't usually come in any night but Sunday, but 'e must've been travelin' 'bout. 'E was all dusty."

"As if he had ridden a goodly distance?"

"Yes."

"What did he want?"

"Some ale to wet his throat. 'E flirted with Gracie who was workin' that night, askin' 'er if she be comin' to the bonfire."

Meresden had a reputation for being interested in every woman who crossed his path, be she quality or not. Nothing out of the ordinary here.

"Anyone else?" he asked.

"Irwin and Walden Muir." She wrinkled her nose and laughed. "Those two are as batty as my old granny."

"They don't come here often?"

She shrugged. "Often enough. I try to avoid them."

"Any strangers?"

"One." She raised one finger, and water dripped from the rag. She hurried to wipe it away. "There was a chap in 'ere. Didn't know 'im."

"Can you describe him? I may have seen him around Stonehall-on-Sea."

"Seen 'im?" She laughed. "Most likely, for 'e's stayin' with Lady Priscilla, too."

"Pritchard?"

"Aye, that was 'is name. Miserly chap. Didn't leave even a 'a'penny for me and Gracie, even though 'e was oglin' 'er all evenin'. Tried to get 'er to go off some place nice and private." Her lips twisted. "Gracie isn't a 'arlot, but 'e acted as if she should be pleased with 'is attentions. When she turned him down, 'e got vexed."

"Do you remember when he was here that evening?"

"Just before sunset, I believe, because some of the lads got right put out that he 'eld the door open and the sun 'it them in the eyes."

Tossing a coin on the bar, he said, "Thank you, Lenore."

"But this is a guinea."

"Consider it a gift from me *and* Pritchard."

She chuckled. "Thank *ye*, Sir Neville."

"Pritchard is going to pay his share of this." With a wink, he went out of the public house. He looked forward to asking Pritchard a few questions and getting some honest answers.

# Seventeen

"Excellent. It fits perfectly, and you look lovely."
Priscilla blinked back tears as she admired her older
daughter in front of the glass in her bedchamber.

Daphne was dressed in a translucent pink gown.
Her eyes glistened with excitement as she twirled
about, allowing the silk to flow around her ankles.
Mrs. Bird had worked magic in just days, for the gown
looked as stylish as one in London. At the same time,
the seamstress had kept it appropriately demure for a
young lady who had not yet been fired-off.

Throwing her arms around Priscilla, Daphne cried,
"Mama, I love this gown."

"It is perfect for you." She bit her lower lip to keep
herself from giving in to tears. Her daughter was becoming a young woman, a beauty who would capture
many men's attentions. As the granddaughter and sister of an earl, Daphne would be considered a good
match, so her suitors would be numerous. But
Priscilla wanted for her daughter what she had found
for herself: a true love that had nothing to do with
title or with wealth.

Going to her dressing table, Priscilla opened it and
withdrew a small brocade case. She held it out to her
daughter.

Daphne's fingers quivered as she opened the box.

A single pearl was set on a gold band between two sapphires.

"It was your grandmother's," Priscilla said. "She told me that I should give it to my firstborn daughter when she was old enough."

"It's beautiful!" She hugged Priscilla again. "Thank you, Mama."

"Take good care of it, so you may give it to your eldest daughter when it is her turn to attend her first *soirée.*"

From the doorway came, "This will be pretty with your gown as well."

Priscilla watched as Aunt Cordelia came in and handed Daphne another box, this one covered with navy blue velvet. Her aunt smiled as Daphne opened the box and squealed with delight as she held up a gold chain that held another pearl. This one was enclosed in thin gold wires.

As Daphne hooked the pendant around her neck, Priscilla squeezed her aunt's hand. Aunt Cordelia put her arm around Priscilla's shoulders and smiled.

"She is no longer a little girl," Aunt Cordelia said with a sigh.

"No, she is not." Priscilla reached out to straighten the chain.

As Daphne looked at her great-aunt, she hesitated. She glanced at Priscilla. When Priscilla nodded, Daphne gave Aunt Cordelia a big hug and a kiss on the cheek.

Aunt Cordelia chuckled. "My, my!"

"Daphne," said Priscilla when Aunt Cordelia repeated the word over and over, "change and come downstairs for a late tea. Your brother and sister are certain to be starved and threatening to chew on each other if we wait much longer."

Aunt Cordelia talked with giddy excitement while

they walked down the stairs. Priscilla smiled, glad to have her aunt speaking of something other than the children's future. Her aunt could be the most charming woman in the Polite World, as was proven by persuading three men to marry her. Priscilla hoped this kindly mood would continue.

Her hopes dimmed when they went into the parlor. Mr. Pritchard came to his feet, and Priscilla had the suspicion that Aunt Cordelia's visit to her room had another motive than just giving her daughter the beautiful necklace. She hoped she was wrong, but the headmaster's smile did not make her optimistic.

"Where are Leah and Isaac?" Priscilla asked.

"Having tea in the nursery." Aunt Cordelia sat in the middle of the settee and now wore her benevolent despot expression—a smile and steely eyes. "I thought it would be more pleasant for us to have tea without them today. They are quite boisterous children at times."

Priscilla chose a chair as far from Mr. Pritchard's as she could. "More pleasant or more propitious?"

"Why, both, Priscilla." Bestowing a smile on Mr. Pritchard, she added, "Our conversations about Elsworth Academy have been interrupted far too often. It is time to make arrangements for Isaac to attend the school as all previous earls have."

"I doubt if *all* previous earls have." Priscilla looked steadily at Mr. Pritchard. "I believe you said your academy was established in 1730."

"Yes, my lady," he replied reluctantly.

"Then my point is made," Priscilla replied. "The title is older than that."

"Do not quibble over such details," Aunt Cordelia chided. "We are speaking of your son's education. I would think you would want a voice in it."

"I do." She picked up the teapot that was decorated

with bright red roses. "I know Aunt Cordelia likes her tea sweet. And you, Mr. Pritchard?"

"Very sweet, my lady."

Priscilla gave him the smile she had borrowed from her aunt and said, "Of course." She added extra sugar to his cup before adding the steaming tea.

"So then you are in agreement that Isaac should attend Elsworth Academy," Aunt Cordelia said, taking her cup.

Offering another to Mr. Pritchard, Priscilla began to fix her own tea. "To the contrary, Aunt Cordelia. I am not at all in agreement with such a course of action."

"But it is a tradition!"

"Some traditions should not be observed simply because they are traditions." She held her cup without shaking and tried to keep her voice as steady. "Times change, and we need to reevaluate what we have taken for granted."

"My thoughts exactly," said Neville as he stood in the doorway, his shoulder against the frame. Past him, she could see her children gathered and grinning. He must have invited them to return to the parlor for tea. No entrance had, in Priscilla's opinion, ever been more timely.

"Sir Neville, this is a *private* conversation." Aunt Cordelia gave him a frightful glower.

Priscilla wondered what Neville was up to when he smiled as he turned to the headmaster. She stiffened. She appreciated his assistance, but he might make matters worse if he jumped to her defense too fervently.

The children came in at a decorous pace, she was happy to note. Their great-aunt's scowl would be warning enough to be on their very best behavior. As they sat, she passed them a plate that held small sandwiches. She motioned for them to take one and hand the plate to the next person.

At the same time, Neville walked over to the tea tray, picked up a small cake, and sat on the arm of Priscilla's chair as he took a bite. Only then did he ask off-handly, "Is this *private* conversation like the *private* one you had with Gracie at the Dog and Crown, Pritchard?"

Mr. Pritchard's face became gray, then a red as bright as the teapot as he choked out, "How do you know about that? I mean . . . You must be mistaken, Sir Neville."

"I don't believe so. Pris, will you pour me a cup of that tea? It smells delicious."

She smiled, glad that he was on *her* side. "No milk and no sugar, but lemon, right?"

"You are an excellent hostess to remember that when I have not called in almost a year." Without a pause, he said, "Pritchard, a word of advice, if I may. Being clutch-fisted will make you memorable to every tavern lass, even if she puts your clumsy attempts to seduce her out of her head."

Priscilla took a deep breath, preparing for what she knew was about to happen next. She did not have to wait long.

Aunt Cordelia put her cup on the table with a clatter that endangered the china. Pointing at Mr. Pritchard, a sure sign that she was so upset that she had misplaced her perfect manners, she tried to speak. All that came out was a sound that reminded Priscilla of water draining from a cracked bucket.

"My lady," Mr. Pritchard said, "I know this is distressing for you."

"Distressing?" Aunt Cordelia almost rose off the settee as her fury burst out. "Sir Neville is accusing you of flirting in a public house. Mr. Pritchard, is this true?"

"My lady," he said in a soothing tone, "the Dog and Crown is owned by the vicar's uncle. It is not a school of Venus."

"Mr. Pritchard! Do you forget that young ears are present?"

Priscilla put her finger to her lips as Isaac laughed. Then she poured some tea and handed it to him. Having to keep both his sandwich and the teacup balanced should keep him so occupied that he would not pay attention to the conversation.

The headmaster colored. "Forgive me, my lady."

Aunt Cordelia, Priscilla could have told Mr. Pritchard, was not about to accept an apology without making him suffer the edge of her tongue. Sitting ramrod straight, her aunt demanded, "Do you wish me to believe that you set an example—*this* example—for the youngsters at Elsworth Academy?"

"No . . . I mean . . . yes"—he gulped—"I would never do anything to bring dishonor to Elsworth Academy."

Neville started to speak, but Priscilla said, "I do recall, Aunt Cordelia, my father speaking of how he had to unlearn some of the rakish lessons he learned as a youth."

Aunt Cordelia set herself on her feet. "Mr. Pritchard, I will speak to you privately." She flushed. "Alone!"

Hearing Neville's hushed laugh, Priscilla took a sip of tea and gave her children a warning glance. Speaking might reaim her aunt's fury on them. Right now, Aunt Cordelia had her nose completely out of joint, and she would vent her spleen in whichever direction she could.

Mr. Pritchard followed her from the parlor. He wore such a pitiful expression that Priscilla found herself having sympathy for the poor man. She had suffered many a dressing-down from Aunt Cordelia, and she knew what a fearsome thrashing it could be.

Her aunt's raised voice reached back into the parlor, and the children exchanged amused smiles. Priscilla held up the teapot and refilled Neville's cup when he nodded.

He sipped and complimented Daphne on her ring and then teased Leah and Isaac. Anyone watching would guess he was ignoring the heated words from the hall. Yet, as soon as Aunt Cordelia stormed up the stairs, he stood and set his cup on the table. He walked out without a word.

"Excuse me, children," Priscilla said, coming to her feet.

"Where are you going?" Isaac asked.

She handed him another sandwich. "I will be back momentarily."

Priscilla stepped out into the hallway to see Neville steering Mr. Pritchard into her study. She followed the headmaster who looked as dazed as if he had run into a wall.

Slipping into the room before Neville could close the door, she remained by the door as Neville went to where Mr. Pritchard had dropped into a chair. Neville opened a bottle, and she realized he had been carrying a bottle of brandy with him. She rang for Gilbert to bring glasses. The room was silent until the butler returned. As Neville poured, Priscilla shut the door and waited.

Neville offered a glass to Mr. Pritchard, who took it and swallowed the contents in a single gulp. As Neville refilled the glass, he said, "Pritchard, you obviously had hoped that no one would learn you had left the bonfire celebration to go to the Dog and Crown."

His shoulders slumped. "I did not want Lady Cordelia to know." He flung out his hands but managed not to spill any brandy. "You have no idea how it has been with her insisting that I am at her elbow every hour of the day. She wishes to speak of nothing but ways to persuade you, Lady Priscilla, to send young Lord Emberson to my school."

Priscilla had never expected to have empathy for

this man she had dismissed as a toady. "I do have an idea of how Aunt Cordelia is."

"Yes, you do. Sir Neville, you must understand as well that a man needs to think of things other than his work."

"I do. And you should have known that, in Stone-hall-on-Sea, where everyone knows everyone else, you would stand out like a rose in a turnip patch, Pritchard."

"I should have known." He looked into his glass. "I had thought one small visit to the public house would go unnoticed."

"So you slipped away from the bonfire?"

He nodded.

"At the very hour the owner of that public house was ambushed in the vicarage garden." Neville rocked his glass. "There are some who would be suspicious that you were determined to keep Kenyon from revealing where you had been."

Mr. Pritchard gasped, "Are you accusing me of the crime?"

"Not necessarily, but did anyone see where you went after you left the Dog and Crown?"

The man's face became deathly pale. "No, the village was empty. You know that."

"Almost empty," Priscilla said quietly. "Someone was skulking through it on the way to attack Mr. Kenyon."

"I didn't see anyone!" the headmaster cried. "You have to believe me, my lady. I didn't try to kill Kenyon. I never even saw him at the public house."

"He was not there when you were?" asked Neville.

Mr. Pritchard shook his head. "I heard someone ask one of the lasses where he was, and she told him Kenyon was out."

"Where?"

"She didn't say." His cheeks flushed. "Or I did not hear her say. You have to believe me."

"Quite to the contrary, Pritchard. I don't have to believe a single word you speak." Neville arched a sardonic brow, and Priscilla fought not to smile. He was enjoying his role as chief high inquisitor.

"I didn't try to kill the man!" He brightened as he added, "I wasn't even here when the Duke of Meresden was murdered."

"You were not calling at Mermaid Cottage, no. So we have no idea where you might have been."

"I was visiting Lord Murray at his country seat." He took a deep drink. "If you wish me to obtain confirmation of that, I will."

Neville set his glass on Priscilla's desk. "I do not wish it, but Constable Forshaw may."

"*He* thinks I am involved in this?" His hand shook as he reached for the brandy. When Neville filled his glass yet again, Mr. Pritchard nodded his thanks. "I appreciate you telling me that."

Priscilla said, "You might wish to pay the constable's office a visit before you leave Stonehall-on-Sea, Mr. Pritchard."

"I shall . . . I shall the first thing on the morrow." He stood and wobbled. Finishing his brandy, he set his glass next to Neville's. "Thank you for your hospitality, my lady."

"Have a pleasant journey back to Elsworth Academy."

"It is a very lovely trip. When you bring—"

Irritated that he would try, even now, to persuade her to send Isaac to his school, she opened the door. "I shall have to take your word for it."

"Yes . . . yes. Quite." He made his escape.

Priscilla sighed as she closed the door. When Neville reached past her and set it partly ajar, she gave him a puzzled look.

"I prefer to hear who is trying to hear me," he said.

She smiled. "You allowed Aunt Cordelia to beat him down like Mrs. Dunham hammering on a piece of beef. Then, when his defenses were fragile, you asked him questions to get the truth."

He bowed. "Thank you, Pris. I do have a few useful tricks that I have picked up over the years."

"Did you really think *he* was the murderer?"

"No, but I had to be certain. Even a rat will turn to fight when cornered." He chuckled. "Fortunately, Pritchard is merely a mouse."

"He has been crossed off our list of possible suspects." She went to the window that gave her a view of her back garden in the moonlight. "It is easy to find the ones who are not suspects. The much harder task is to locate the murderer."

"We must be watchful, and the murderer may make a mistake."

"So you don't think this is over? If you believe Mr. Robertson is the next target—"

"I don't believe he is."

"Then who?"

He sighed. "That is another question I cannot answer."

As she opened her parasol and walked toward the closed carriage in front of Mermaid Cottage, Priscilla adjusted her best bonnet that was *not* lined with black silk. Last night, before retiring, she had looked for a hatbox in the back corner of her dressing room. Inside was the hat that Lazarus had given her for a gift to celebrate their sixteenth wedding anniversary. It had been the last anniversary they had before his death. The bonnet with pink roses sewn along the brim and ribbons of the same color might be a bit outmoded, but she did not care. It was a delight to wear this bonnet again. So often during this year of mourning, she had thought of donning it, but she knew that such an action could provoke a scandal, even though she *was* wearing it in memory of her late husband. He had enjoyed seeing her wear the roses that were the exact shade of her cheeks when he teased her.

Neville took the small case she was carrying and handed it to a footman. Smiling, he tapped the brim of her bonnet. "This is a pleasant change."

"I thought so." She straightened her bonnet as Isaac bounced around the back of the carriage and threw his arms around her. That made her bonnet slide toward her right ear again. "Up into the carriage with you, Isaac."

"Are we leaving now?"

"Shortly."

He made a face. "Then I would rather wait."

"Your aunt is sitting inside," Neville said in a stage whisper.

Priscilla nodded. Her aunt had been in a ferocious temper since Mr. Pritchard had taken his leave yesterday morning. Not wanting to inflict that bad mood on her son, she said, "Then help Juster make sure all the bags are secure in the boot."

He bounced away.

Not looking at Neville, she added, "I must do something before we leave. Keep everyone busy so they do not notice my absence. I will be only a short time."

"The vicar sent word at dawn that his uncle is still senseless."

She nodded, glad that Neville thought she was going to call on the vicar. "I shall be back as quickly as I can."

"Do you want an escort? It would be my pleasure to have you on my arm and garner the envy of any other man who walked by."

"Thank you, but no." She took a single step, then paused, "And, Neville, save your nothing-sayings for someone else. I thought we were friends who would always be honest with each other."

"I *was* being honest."

She dampened a pulse of pleasure that wanted to course through her like a springtide. This was not the time for teasing, although, when she saw the warmth in his eyes, she was unsure if he was jesting or not. It mattered little. She did not have time for this, whether she wished to continue flirting or not. When she walked away, he did not argue, and she was grateful yet again that Neville had called when he had. Others might not exhibit such a lack of curiosity this morning.

Or . . . She looked back to be certain that he was not sneaking after her. When she saw him picking up Isaac so her son could hand another box up to Layden on the top of the carriage, she forced her shoulders to relax.

The village was quiet in the midmorning sunshine. She was not lulled into thinking that she was crossing the green unobserved. Every window most likely had a set of eyes gazing out at her as she walked into the constable's office.

Constable Forshaw jumped to his feet. Straightening his unbuttoned waistcoat, he reached for his coat. "My lady, I did not expect you."

"I would think not." She leaned the tip of her parasol on the floor and pretended that she had not noticed he was in his stockinged-feet. The big toe on his left foot was poking through. "You are more likely to believe that I will do all I can to avoid you since you have accused me of something you should know, as well as I do, that I am incapable of."

The constable's face became the shade Mr. Pritchard's had in her parlor.

She held up her hand when he started to stutter an answer. "I am here to let you know that I am leaving Stonehall-on-Sea. Because I did not wish for you to believe I was fleeing justice, I thought you should know that my family and I will be joining Sir Neville and the Ackerleys at Lord Wallingford's estate near Brighton."

"It is good of you to keep me informed of your whereabouts, my lady." He finally met her eyes. "I trust you are planning to return here."

"I assume so." She had to ask. "Constable Forshaw, why do you still consider me a suspect? I was at the celebration on the beach when Mr. Kenyon was attacked."

"His attacker tried to be swift, which is why he survived. As you could have slipped away for a few minutes, I must keep you on my list of suspects."

"Who else is on that list?"

He stared at her in disbelief. "You cannot believe that I would discuss my investigation, can you, Lady Priscilla?" Shuffling the papers on his desk, he said, "Until Mr. Kenyon regains his senses and can identify his attacker, I must keep every possible option open."

"Which includes me as a suspect."

"Yes."

She nodded and opened the door and her parasol. "I, with the greatest sincerity, wish you good luck with your investigation, Constable."

She shut the door behind her and released the breath burning in her chest. Acting as if these accusations did not unsettle her was becoming more and more arduous. She was not foolish enough to believe that she would have a reprieve at Lord Wallingford's gathering.

Taking a deep breath, she walked back across the green and toward her cottage and the carriage waiting there. And Neville. She needed his lighthearted teasing today more than ever.

# Eighteen

Wallingford Manor was set on a hill with a view of Brighton and the sea. As Priscilla sat with Isaac's head on her lap and Daphne leaning on her shoulder and her arm around Leah to keep her daughter from bumping into the carriage wall, she could see the buildings of Brighton spread out from the pebbled shore. The stables set behind the Prince Regent's Marine Pavilion dominated the town.

As if he could read her thoughts, Neville said, "There are rumors the Prince Regent has plans to make the Pavilion as grand as the stables."

"They look big enough to provide stabling for a battalion."

"Not that many horses, but it is huge." He started to stretch and paused when Aunt Cordelia mumbled something in her sleep. He stuck his head out the window, then drew it back in. "The Ackerleys are still right behind us in the pony cart."

She frowned at her aunt who was oblivious in her sleep. Aunt Cordelia had been emphatic that she would not arrive at Lord Wallingford's estate in a carriage with *Americans*. Rather than embarrass the Ackerleys', Priscilla had had the pony cart brought so that Mr. Ackerley could drive himself and Martha here. They had not seemed to take offense. Mr. Ackerley had been concerned only with the books he was bringing to read during their sojourn at Wallingford Manor. Martha had been smiling so broadly that Priscilla half-expected the young woman could float to Brighton on her dreams of what she would experience here.

Her aunt roused from sleep and made enough noise adjusting her bonnet and shawl to wake the children. From that moment, Priscilla was peppered with questions. Many she could not answer. Others she was given no chance to answer as another one was fired at her.

She herded the children out of the carriage and into the house that she doubted had ever been a real manor. It appeared to be less than a century old with its even columns standing at attention along the front. Inside, her eyes were drawn to an elegant staircase of a pure black marble. No one entering this house could doubt the wealth that Lord Wallingford possessed. He would inherit even more when he became the Marquess of Tumbridge.

With quick efficiency, they were herded up the stairs and to rooms on an upper floor. She was happy to see there were two bedchambers, one decorated in a cool blue and the other in an elegant gold to match the antechamber, in the suite. She would use one bedchamber, the girls could share the other, and Isaac would sleep on the chaise longue.

Priscilla had barely taken off her bonnet when the door opened. Martha rushed in and twirled about.

"Isn't this wonderful?" Martha cried. "Do you think we shall meet Lord Wallingford and his family soon?"

"Lord Wallingford will greet us at the gathering this evening," Priscilla said, handing her bonnet to a maid. "I do not believe the marquess is in residence."

"Oh." Her disappointment stole her smile.

When Daphne walked over and put her arm around Martha, Priscilla was astonished. She had seen them talking together when they had paused on the way here to have an al fresco meal, but this friendship was something new.

She understood when her older daughter said, "Don't be disappointed, Martha. Who knows who will be at the gathering? That anticipation is part of the fun." Daphne frowned. "At least, you shall get to wear your hair the way you wish tonight."

Not wanting to get caught up in a discussion of how Daphne must act while still in the schoolroom, Priscilla said, "The evening will be worth waiting for, I can assure you."

The door opened again without the courtesy of a knock. When Aunt Cordelia walked in with another woman of her age, Martha and Daphne went into the girls' room with Leah and Isaac on their heels.

*Cowards*, Priscilla wanted to call after them.

The gray-haired woman with Aunt Cordelia was as tall as Priscilla's aunt was short. With a long neck and fingers, and a figure as thin as a vine, she resembled a bird. Yet her smile was warm when Aunt Cordelia introduced her as Lady Milingston.

"I have long wished to meet you," Lady Milingston said as she took Priscilla's hand. "When I heard you had arrived, I insisted that Cordelia introduce us straightaway. Your aunt has told me so many fine things about you."

"She has?" Priscilla clamped her mouth shut when Aunt Cordelia gave her a frown that suggested her aunt's next comment would not be laudatory.

"And," continued Lady Milingston as if she had not noticed either Priscilla's surprise or Aunt Cordelia's scowl, "I had the honor of meeting your husband on two occasions. He presided at my son's wedding and at my own husband's funeral. Dr. Flanders was a very fine man."

"Thank you. He was."

As she motioned for the other women to sit, Priscilla went and closed the bedroom door to shut out the children's voices.

Immediately Daphne reopened it. "Mama, Martha has never seen a country house, so I thought I would give her a tour."

Priscilla did not roll her eyes as she wanted to. "You may walk around the public areas, but remember this is not Emberson Park. Do not intrude where you do not belong."

Her daughter was not so reluctant to roll her eyes and did so. "I know that, Mama."

As the two young women left, Priscilla hushed her younger children as she gathered up the clothes Daphne had scattered across the bed. She should be glad that Daphne and Martha had finally found some common ground, but something about their sudden friendship bothered her. She was not sure what. She would have to talk with her daughter and find out what had brought about this abrupt change of heart.

Priscilla faltered, her hand on the doorway, when she realized her aunt and Lady Milingston were taking advantage of her absence to gossip . . . about her. She flinched when she heard Lady Milingston say, "Cordelia, she is out of mourning. Of course, she should be considering another marriage. She possesses that house in Stonehall-on-Sea and the house on Bedford Square in London that her husband bequeathed to her, along with her share of the earl's fortune."

"I know that. I also know that she is as innocent as a babe in the woods when it comes to men and their eagerness to get their hands on her fortune."

"You should introduce her to that viscount . . . What's his name? The one whose wife died within days of Dr. Flanders."

"I must arrange for her to marry before she is lured by Sir Neville Hathaway's ploys!" bemoaned Aunt Cordelia.

"Sir Neville? Oh, my! She is considering *him?*"

"He has been at Mermaid Cottage for days and days. He is determined to prove she had nothing to do with these attacks—which, of course, she didn't. I believe he is attempting to gain her gratitude, so that she will accept his proposal."

Priscilla almost laughed aloud. Neville marrying was an amusing idea, but Neville marrying *her* was ludicrous. Her smile faded. It *was* ludicrous, wasn't it? She recalled the look he had given her by the carriage in Stonehall-on-Sea. Even though she had tried to dismiss it as teasing, she had not been able to then or now. He never had explained why he had called at Mermaid Cottage. Could Aunt Cordelia be right?

Again she was tempted to chuckle. With any other man, her aunt's instincts might be on target, but not with Neville. He was not about to settle down with any one woman, and any woman who believed that he was considering giving up his free ways for her would soon learn she had been a fool.

She shut the bedchamber door a little harder than necessary. Both women immediately began to discuss who would be attending the gathering this evening.

"Oh, Priscilla!" Her aunt smiled and patted the cushion next to her. "Do come and join us so we may chat."

She wanted to ask if that topic would be something other than her possibilities of snaring another husband, but that would embarrass both her aunt and Lady Milingston. After all, their gossip was no different from what she had overheard in Stonehall-on-Sea. She had ignored that, and she must ignore this. As she sat next to her aunt, she heard Lady Milingston speak a familiar name.

"The Duke of Meresden is supposed to be here," Aunt Cordelia said. "He told Priscilla that himself."

"When he is in mourning?"

"That family has always followed its own ways."

"Why should he come here when he can entertain *her* at Meresden Court now?" Lady Milingston asked.

"Her?" Priscilla recognized the emphasis put on the single word. Her aunt's friend considered what she was about to share the most delicious gossip.

"Nancy Boch," said Lady Milingston with a laugh. "Surely you have heard his father would not allow him to bring her to Meresden Court. The late duke believed, quite rightly, that she, as the daughter of a shopkeeper, was not the proper woman for the next duchess."

"Is that so?" Priscilla noted how Aunt Cordelia was looking everywhere but at her.

"Yes." Lady Milingston was delighted to have someone to share this gossip with. "The current duke has had to sneak about to see his Nancy. I have heard that he calls every Thursday evening when his father thought he was in London."

"Thursday?" Priscilla leaned back against her chair. If the duke had been calling on his beloved the day his father died, he would not have wanted to own to that. Any misstep could bring the wrath of the Polite World down upon him, and, even though the *ton* admired a rake, not even a duke was completely excluded from the canons of Society.

Aunt Cordelia frowned. "Unsubstantiated rumors should not be repeated."

"I never said they were unsubstantiated," Lady Milingston returned. "It is something everyone knows."

"Not everyone, and gossip is often less than true."

"Cordelia, just because you had not heard the rumor before does not make it untrue."

Priscilla listened to the two women making guesses as to whether the duke would bring Miss Boch this evening. She had never guessed that *this* was what the duke had been trying to keep hidden. Instead of protecting himself from a charge of murder, the duke might have been protecting his beloved from the hateful gossips. Although she found it difficult to view him as a chivalrous hero, she could not discount the facts. The duke had an excellent alibi for that day.

And Constable Forshaw would have one less person to consider as the murderer. She needed to discover the truth of who had killed the duke before she was his *only* suspect.

Priscilla had no chance to share the news about the duke's mistress with Neville that afternoon. After Lady Milingston took her leave, she was kept busy supervising the children as she tried to get them to take some rest. She doubted if any of them got even a minute's sleep. Then, with Aunt Cordelia supervising *her,* she made certain they were properly dressed for the evening. She confiscated some rice powder from Daphne. A guilty face on one of the maids warned that Daphne had found an ally in Wallingford Manor.

Giving Isaac a piece of peppermint, for he was sure that he would fade away from starvation before the supper was served, even though he had eaten a huge tea, Priscilla adjusted Leah's hairbow. Daphne's hair was partially pinned up with fresh flowers. Sweeping her hair back from her face, but letting it fall over her shoulders was a compromise that she had accepted when Priscilla reminded her that, until she began her first Season, she should not wear her hair up.

Leaving the children to talk to their great-aunt or, more likely, getting a lecture from Aunt Cordelia,

Priscilla went to dress herself. Her gown was a deep blue appropriate for second mourning, but, for the first time since Lazarus's death, she wore the pearls that her father had given her at the beginning of her first Season.

A light breeze barely stirred the leaves as Priscilla led her children out into the garden where the *soirée* was being held. A trio of violins along with a cello and a harp created music that was as gentle as that breeze. A rumble of voices grew louder as she guided the children down the steps into the garden where the roses were waiting to bloom. They would have to wait for sunshine, because now the stars claimed the sky.

Brightly colored paper lanterns bounced on the trees. One near the house had a charred hole from where the breeze had gotten the paper too close to the candle inside it. The guests wore more subdued colors, but the sounds of silk and sharply pressed linen matched the motions of anyone who walked near Priscilla.

"There are Martha and Uncle Neville," Leah said, tugging on Priscilla's hand.

"Doesn't he look handsome?" Daphne asked.

Priscilla wanted to agree, for Neville wore his spotless black coat and white breeches with a rare verve, but rather she said, "Daphne, such comments should not be spoken at a volume that allows others to listen."

She was not sure if her daughter heard her as Daphne went to admire Martha's gown. Leah and Isaac followed, earning them a frown from their older sister, so they went to where lemonade was set out for the younger guests.

When Priscilla greeted Martha, the young woman grinned broadly.

"Thomas has chosen to remain indoors with his books," Martha said in answer to Priscilla's question about her brother. "I could not bear to remain inside a moment longer." She started to add more, then turned as Daphne pointed to a fountain.

Martha's reticule flew out at her motion, striking Priscilla's left wrist.

With a gasp of pain, Priscilla asked, "What do you have in there? A brick?"

"Oh, Lady Priscilla, I am so sorry. I put one of Thomas's books in there, and, in my hurry, I forgot to remove it." Tears glistened in her eyes. "I am so sorry. I would never want to hurt you."

"It was an accident." She put her hand on Martha's arm. "But you may want to take the book inside before it strikes someone else."

"I shall." Motioning for Daphne to follow, she walked toward the house.

Neville offered his arm to Priscilla. As he led her away from the children and her aunt, who was hovering over them, he said, "Thank heavens, Daphne has diverted Martha."

"Is something wrong?"

"Apparently, nothing is wrong with *me*." He chuckled. "She has offered me more gushing compliments than a tailor trying to sell another coat."

"Did you consider that her words may have been just as sincere as a greedy tailor's?"

"I have, after witnessing Martha's heartfelt apology to you, for she had a different tone when she spoke to you." Shaking his head, he said, "Mayhap I am not as well versed in the arts of flirtation as I had prided myself on being."

Priscilla laughed. "After all the tales I have heard about you, I cannot believe that you are unable to defend yourself against the attentions of one young lady."

"I am afraid my prowess in that quarter may be no more than a rumor."

Wincing as she moved her aching wrist, she said, "I have heard an interesting rumor, Neville." She shared what Lady Milingston had said about the duke attending this gathering with his beloved.

"By Jove, it would have been much far more interesting if Meresden still had no excuse for his absence."

"Neville!"

"Why are you so upset? If Meresden had no excuse, that might have kept some of the suspicion from you."

"I know. I have been considering how the number of suspects is dwindling."

He paused as the musicians struck a trio of notes that were loud enough to get everyone's attention. As the other guests formed up for a quadrille, a man walked toward them.

The man was even taller than Neville but had hair as red as the vicar. His clothing was elegant, and he wore even more rings than the new duke. When he smiled as he approached, she suspected this was their host. He wore a strained smile, and his eyes were not gleaming with the pleasure of hosting what had all the makings of being a very successful assembly.

"Wallingford," Neville said, confirming her guess.

"Hathaway!" He pumped Neville's hand. "Just the man I need to see."

"Need to see? For what?"

Lord Wallingford glanced at Priscilla and again tried to smile as he said, "We can discuss that later when we play that round of cards that you have avoided playing. I wondered if you had become so pudding-hearted that you would not show your face here. Where have you been dawdling?"

Priscilla drew in her breath sharply. If Neville had been bound here to gamble more of his fortune, why hadn't he been honest with her?

"I had some business to take care of in London," Neville replied, "before calling upon a friend."

She understood why he had been so elusive. Neville's business could mean anything from purchasing something as grand as a ship to stretching the very edges of the law. Lazarus had told her shortly after her first meeting with Neville that there were some matters Neville would not discuss, and she would be wise not to press. Had Lazarus known the truth amid the gossip? If so, he had never told her. Neville would, if he believed she must know. He would not allow his life to imperil her or the children. *That* was all she truly needed to know.

"Tell me," said their host. "What convinced you to join our gathering tonight? Was it this lovely creature you are keeping here to yourself?"

"You are quite right. Have you met Lady Priscilla Flanders?"

Lord Wallingford's smile faltered. "Lady Priscilla? But I thought—"

"It is a pleasure, Lord Wallingford," she said, extending her hand.

He bowed over her hand and excused himself, nonplused.

"You have an odd effect on gentleman, Pris," Neville murmured in Lord Wallingford's wake.

"It is clear the *on dits* of my guilt has preceded me here."

"You need to put it out of your mind tonight."

"Do I?"

He held up his hands. "Do not fire those daggers in your eyes at me. My suggestion was for your benefit."

"I know." She cradled her aching wrist. "I should gather the children and—"

"You will not convince Daphne to leave so soon."

He smiled and held out his hand. "Will you stand up with me?"

"Neville, do not be silly. I cannot dance. I need to watch over the children."

"Leah and Isaac are sitting with Lady Milingston while she feeds them cake. Daphne is chatting with Martha just beyond them. All of them are being overseen by your aunt."

"That is true, but I should not dance."

"Because you are just out of mourning? Do you think Lazarus would mind if you enjoyed a quadrille?"

She smiled even though she would have wagered that she could not. "Lazarus would not be distressed, for he knew how much I love to dance, but Aunt Cordelia might suffer apoplexy right here."

"All the more reason for you to dance with me. I believe she needs to be shaken up a bit." His lips tilted, and she wondered why she had never noticed before now how one side of his smile was higher than the other.

"Neville—"

"I realized this evening that you and I have never danced. I think that is something we should rectify posthaste."

"You are diabolical in your logic, you know."

He gave her that beguiling smile again. "I thought you would never notice, Pris."

Going with him out to where the others were gathering for the dance that had not yet started, she wished she could think of a way to tell him how indebted she was to him for bringing her smile back again and again. She saw the startled glances of the other dancers, but she turned and faced Neville. She was going to enjoy this dance and his company.

That plan failed the first time he took her left hand and started to twirl her through the pattern of the dance. When she winced, he grasped her right hand. He drew her away from the others and probed her left wrist with care.

"I don't think anything has been broken," he said with an honest concern she saw so seldom. "But it might be a good idea to have Wallingford send for the closest doctor."

"It should be fine."

"Pris, let Wallingford send for a doctor for you. Please."

Her gaze was caught by his. There was an odd intensity in his eyes, and it created an even more peculiar sensation within her, a sensation she had not planned to feel again after Lazarus died. It was a thrill that was as strong as when she had been a young woman who was welcoming the attentions of a handsome clergyman, and it was something she had never expected to experience in Neville's company. He was her dearest friend, not a man eager to court her . . .

She lowered her eyes quickly. Mayhap his concern was only for a friend, but, as she raised her eyes again, they were held by his once more. She waited for him to laugh at her for believing that he had any intent other than teasing her. He said nothing as he gently cupped her hand.

"It is not bad," she murmured.

"Pris, let a doctor check it." A gentleness she had never heard came into his voice. "Please . . . for me."

"Very well," she said, unsure if she could disagree now. "Send for a doctor."

When he turned and looked for their host, releasing her from this strange mesmerism, Lord Wallingford trotted over at once. Priscilla almost forgot the pain in her wrist as she realized the viscount had been watching them, eager to talk to Neville.

Before their host could say a single word, Neville

asked to have a doctor brought to tend to her wrist.
The viscount sent a footman running to fulfill that
order.

"While we wait," Lord Wallingford said, shifting
from one foot to other like a naughty child, "I must
speak with you, Hathaway."

"About?"

"Do you have any connections still with Bow Street?
I fear my life is in great danger."

# Nineteen

Priscilla sat in Lord Wallingford's comfortable book-room. The dark wood walls were lightened by a pair of lamps and the bindings of dozens of books. She said nothing as the viscount poured three glasses of wine and handed one to her and another to Neville. Although Lord Wallingford sat, Neville remained on his feet. That warned her he was preparing himself for anything.

"Why do you think your life is in danger?" Neville asked.

"I found an odd note in here this evening."

Priscilla set her glass on the table beside her chair, afraid her trembling fingers would spill it. "Was it a threat to even the scales of fortune? Was it wrapped around a button from a military uniform?"

"Yes." Lord Wallingford's forehead threaded with bafflement. "How did you know?"

"You are not the first to have such a note and a button delivered." She glanced at Neville, but his face was blank. "The first was delivered to the son of late Duke of Meresden."

"Who was murdered."

She nodded. "And the other was received by Vicar Kenyon in Stonehall-on-Sea. His uncle was viciously attacked and left for dead."

"Did he survive?" The viscount's voice grew higher on each word until he sounded Isaac's age.

Neville answered, "When we left Stonehall-on-Sea this morning, Mr. Kenyon remained senseless, and the doctor was unsure if he ever will wake."

"Oh, dear." Downing his wine in one gulp, he gripped the glass so fiercely, she feared it would shatter in his hand.

"Yes, it is very troubling," she said.

"Troubling?" he snapped, apparently fortified with the wine. "Lady Priscilla, you have a gift for understatement. One man is dead, and another could be, and you call it troubling."

"I am not trying to minimize the situation, Lord Wallingford. I am hoping to find some connection between you and the duke and Mr. Kenyon."

"Connection?" His eyes grew wide, and he jumped to his feet. "*You* are accused of Meresden's murder!"

Neville put his hand on the viscount's shoulder. "Calm yourself, Wallingford. Lady Priscilla had no hand in either incident. You can trust me on that."

The viscount nodded, terror draining out of his eyes. "I trust *you*, Hathaway."

"Then believe me when I tell you that Lady Priscilla is being accused of another's crimes."

Lord Wallingford nodded again but did not reply.

Priscilla said, "I believe you are too young to have this threat aimed at you, Lord Wallingford."

"A relief."

"For you, but not your father or grandfather."

His mouth straightened. "My father is dead for ten years now, Lady Priscilla."

"And your grandfather?"

"The marquess is well and on his way to join us this evening."

She came to her feet and grasped his arm, knowing

he must be starting to question again if she was sane or out of her mind. "Did the marquess ever serve in the military?"

"Yes, I believe he did."

"Where?"

Lord Wallingford shrugged. "I cannot say with certainty. He seldom talks of his experiences during those years."

"The years during the war with the American colonies?"

Again he shrugged. "Again, I cannot say for sure."

"Does he know either the late duke or Mr. Kenyon?"

"I assume he has met the duke either here in the country or in Town. As for Mr. Kenyon, I don't know. These are questions you need to ask my grandfather."

Neville put his glass next to Priscilla's. "Do you know which road he will take to get here?"

"Yes, he always travels the same way."

"It would be prudent for us to meet him."

Shouts came from outside the book-room. As Lord Wallingford rushed to find out what was amiss, he leaped back when it opened almost in his face. Two men struggled in the hallway.

One bellowed, "You cannot see his lordship until I have had you announced!"

"There is no time for formalities now!"

Priscilla recognized the second voice. "Constable Forshaw!"

Lord Wallingford ordered, "Masters, let the man go."

His butler obeyed, glowering at the constable.

Straightening his dusty coat, Constable Forshaw said, "I must speak with you right away, Lady Priscilla." He looked past her, his face grim. "Sir Neville, you need to hear this as well. Will you come with me and Lady Priscilla?"

"If you are planning to arrest her," Neville began with a scowl.

"I no longer have any reason to consider Lady Priscilla a suspect. May we speak privately?"

Neville motioned for him to enter. "Wallingford should hear this as well. What have you discovered?"

The constable closed the door, ignoring the angry butler. "Mr. Kenyon has regained his senses. He is coherent—"

"Thank heavens," Priscilla whispered.

"He gave me a poor description of his attacker," the constable continued, "but it was enough to prove that Lady Priscilla is not culpable. Mr. Kenyon identified his attacker as a woman dressed in white or something pale."

Priscilla looked down at her gown that, save for the lacy bodice, was dark blue. "But I have not worn anything but dark colors since Lazarus died."

"*That* is why you are no longer a suspect, my lady."

Lord Wallingford wore a sheepish expression. "Forgive me for doubting your innocence in this matter."

She did not have a chance to reply, because Neville tapped the constable on the shoulder and asked, "But the attacker is a woman?"

"So Mr. Kenyon said."

"That would make sense." Neville put his hand up to the side of his head. "Both men were struck about here. A short woman could not have reached much higher."

"Or a short man wearing a disguise," Priscilla added.

"Blast it, Pris! Don't complicate things."

"Complicating them isn't my goal. Figuring out who the murderer may be is."

The constable cleared his throat. "My lady, the question I must ask you next is not easy."

"I know what you intend to ask. The person who did these terrible things had access to my garden, but the murderer cannot be either of my daughters, for they were at the table when the duke was killed. As well, they have been wearing first mourning for my late husband, and I have not had new clothes, other than what they are wearing tonight, made for them. They have outgrown the clothes they wore a year ago." She counted on her fingers. "There are the two girls in the kitchen, but Mrs. Dunham allows no one out of the kitchen while a meal is being served."

"And they are wearing the dark colors of second mourning," added Neville. "Mrs. Moore is too tall."

"Yes, and the tweener and Mrs. Dunham as well."

"So who else has access to your garden?"

"Martha Ackerley!" she whispered in horror.

He shook his head. "That mouse? Other than the times when she flirted with me, she is under her brother's thumb."

"Even a mouse will turn when cornered."

"That is a rat, Pris. Mice scurry away. Remember how we discussed this about Pritchard?"

She grimaced at him. "You know what I mean."

"I do, but what reason would Martha have to take a cudgel to the heads of two old men? She is not happy in England, so being sent to the gallows and ending up beneath English soil will not bring her what she wants."

"I have no answer for that, but I believe we should find out if Martha does."

"What will you do? Walk up to her and accuse her of murder and attempted murder?"

Constable Forshaw nodded. "That is exactly what I intend to do."

As he turned to leave, Priscilla gasped, "Neville, Martha is with Daphne! They have been together all day." She gulped. "Martha could have left the note and button here when she and Daphne were exploring the house this afternoon. If she panics—"

"We'll be careful," Neville said.

"We?" retorted Constable Forshaw.

"How many murderers have you nabbed?"

"None, but—"

"Then I am unquestionably more experienced than you." Neville seized the constable's sleeve. "Let's stop her before she has another chance to hurt someone." He glanced at Priscilla, who could not hide her fear for her daughter. "Pris, stay here."

"I shall not! Daphne—"

He took her hand and said, "All right. Let's go."

An hour later, Neville was ready to spout every curse he knew. A search of Wallingford Manor and the grounds had turned up no sign of either Martha or Daphne. Lady Cordelia, who was lying on a chaise longue in her room with burned feathers ready if she swooned again, had told him that the last time she had seen the two girls, they were walking toward the house.

It did not take long to go from Lady Cordelia's suite to the rooms the Ackerleys had been given, but Neville begrudged every moment it took. He strode in without knocking and grasped the startled Thomas Ackerley by the lapels and jerked him from his chair. "Where is your sister?"

"Sir Neville . . ." The rest was garbled.

"You are choking him, Neville!" cried Priscilla. "Let him have air to speak."

Shoving the man away, Neville scowled at Priscilla. He did not need her aristocratic sensibilities getting in the way. He wanted to order her out of the room, but that would be just a waste of time.

And they might be running out of that fast.

Ackerley stared at him, then looked at Priscilla and

the constable, astonished. He flinched when Wallingford hurried into the room.

"What is wrong?" Ackerley asked.

Neville fired back a question of his own. "Where is
your sister?"

"At the party, I assume."

"She has vanished."

Ackerley's face became as gray as Kenyon's had
when they found him in the vicar's garden. "Vanished? Oh, dear God!" He groped for his chair and
dropped into it. "I didn't think she would do it."

"Do what?"

"Go back to Stonehall-on-Sea." He looked up, frightened. "She was complaining that she had forgotten her
best dress and said she must go back and get it."

"Best dress?" asked Priscilla. "But she was wearing it
tonight."

"I don't know what she meant." Ackerley hesitated,
then said, "Martha gets ideas sometimes. Nothing can
dislodge them. She may act odd for a while, but then
she is herself again."

"Odd?" Neville asked, glancing at Priscilla.

"She gets upset over things that happened long ago."

Priscilla gasped, "She cried the day I brought a
dress over for her to have remade. She was upset
about your grandmother being alone while you were
here in England."

"Grandmother?" He frowned. "Our grandmother
died the year before we came to England." Ackerley
gulped again. "She is my sister and she takes good
care of me and all, but she loses every bit of rational
thought when she starts lamenting about our grandparents. She is furious that our grandfather was killed
during the War of Independence, and our grandmother was badly injured. She has said more than
once that the scales of fortune—"

"The scales of fortune need to be evened." Priscilla grasped Neville's hand. "Quick! We must go back to Mermaid Cottage. Now!"

He did not bother to argue that she should stay here, for she would not remain here while her daughter was in possible peril. Shouting for Wallingford to have two horses saddled, Neville tugged Priscilla after him. The girls had an advantage, and he and Priscilla would have to ride hard. He hoped they still had a chance to stop Martha from whatever crime she planned next.

As they passed the vicarage, Priscilla drew in her horse. She waved to Neville and the constable. "Go and find them! I want to warn the vicar, so he can guard his uncle."

Neville curved his hand on her cheek. "We'll find her, Pris."

She put her hand over his. "I know." Drawing away, she ordered, "Go! Don't waste another minute."

As they rode toward Mermaid Cottage, Priscilla slid off the horse. She was certain she had jarred every bone on the neck-or-nothing ride back to Stonehall-on-Sea. Looping the horse's reins around the porch post, she went to the door and knocked.

No answer.

A frisson of fear shivered down her spine, and she jerked the door open. Her dread became horror when she saw the vicar lying on the floor. She knelt beside him, relieved to see no blood on the stones. She ran her fingers along his skull and winced when she touched a bump that had been raised there. He had been struck as his uncle and the duke had, but not as fiercely.

Someone screamed from upstairs.

Daphne!

Picking up the vicar's umbrella, the only weapon within reach, Priscilla ran up the stairs that her feet knew so well. Another scream came from the right. She ran to the door of the bedchamber where the vicar's uncle had been lying unconscious.

She froze as she stared at a most unbelievable scene. Her daughter was crouching against the wall next to Mr. Kenyon's bed. The old man was propped up on pillows leaning on the headboard. Both of them were staring at Martha who was aiming a pistol at Mr. Kenyon. The old pistol that Priscilla had seen in her room.

"Mama!" cried Daphne, starting to stand.

Martha looked over her shoulder and reaimed the gun at Daphne. "Stay where you are. Both of you."

"Mama!"

Priscilla did not dare to make a motion. "Daphne, obey her. Stay where you are."

Her daughter slid back toward the floor. On the bed, Mr. Kenyon watched in frightened silence.

"Lady Priscilla," Martha said with what sounded like regret, "I am so sorry that you had to intrude. You, of all these accursed English, have been kind to me. I had not wanted to hurt you."

Priscilla edged a single step into the room. If she could distract Martha, even for a second, Daphne might be able to slip out. "Martha, think about what you are going to do."

"I have. I have thought about this moment." Her fingers curled and uncurled along the pistol. "From the day my husband was murdered, I have thought about this moment."

"Your husband? I didn't know you were married."

The tears in Martha's eyes fell along her cheeks, but she did not lower the gun. "My dear husband Thomas—"

"Your husband's name is Thomas?"

"A name that has been given to the eldest son of every generation of his family. He tried to defend me from those marauding redcoats, and they killed him. Right in front of my eyes, they cut his throat. Then they laughed."

As Mr. Kenyon made a choking sound, Priscilla asked, "Redcoats?"

"Those beasts overran our farm." Martha scowled at the old man as she shifted. She stepped on her bag—the bag that had struck Priscilla's wrist. Had Martha had the pistol in there at Lord Wallingford's party? "They thought they could sneak in and do their barbaric work and rush away without anyone being the wiser, but I heard them. I heard them call their leader Meresden. I heard them speak of their village in England as if they were butchering a hog instead of my husband. *They* did not hear my vow to make them rue their savagery." She opened her left hand to reveal the bright button of an officer's military uniform. "And they did not know that I found this and vowed to return it to them when I saw them dead."

Again Mr. Kenyon gasped. He looked beseechingly at Priscilla. She hoped he would not do something foolish now as he must have forty years ago.

Priscilla understood what she should have when Martha had cried about her grandmother's sorrow. Martha had come to England to gain vengeance against those who had killed her grandfather and hurt her grandmother. To even the scales of fortune. Not only that, but Martha now seemed to believe she was her own grandmother.

A door opened below, and she heard someone call her name. Neville! If he came up here, would Martha recall her calf-love for him? Would that bring her back to her senses? Or would she kill him, too? Other male voices rose from the ground floor.

Martha must have heard them through her dementia, because she aimed the gun once more at Mr. Kenyon. Daphne screamed.

"Silence!" shrieked Martha. "Silence, or I will kill you first."

Footfalls pounded up the steps.

"Martha!" Priscilla begged. "Don't be foolish! What happened is long over. Don't start it again."

"My dear Thomas, you are at last revenged." Martha drew back on the hammer.

Priscilla was shoved aside as Mr. Ackerley leaped forward and grasped his sister's arm. "Martha, stop!"

"Not until I have done what I must do to repay these curs for what they did to us." She jerked her arm away.

Priscilla held out her hand to Daphne. As her daughter crept toward her, Mr. Ackerley tried to reach through his sister's madness.

"What they did to our grandparents was to repay *them* for betraying the English soldiers to the American army!" Mr. Ackerley argued.

A hand grabbed Priscilla's arm. She looked back at Neville, then stretched out to catch Daphne's hand as if they were traversing the edge of a precipice. They were—the precipice of Martha's insanity. She clutched Daphne's hand, pulling her toward her as she inched toward the door.

"Our grandparents were Loyalists," Mr. Ackerley continued, "and then they turned their coats when they thought it would be more profitable to be allied with the Patriots."

"No!" Martha screamed. "My husband would never help a British officer." She tugged away and raised the gun.

He jumped toward her again, trying to tear the gun out of her hand. Neville rushed into the room, pulling another gun.

A gun fired.

Priscilla tugged Daphne closer, leaning over her daughter to protect her.

Then, there was silence save for Daphne's soft sobs.

Neville's hand settled on Priscilla's shoulder. She raised her head to see no smoke issuing from his pistol. Then Martha had fired! She glanced toward the bed. Mr. Kenyon was pushing himself up farther to peer over the side of the bed.

She followed his gaze to where Mr. Ackerley was slowly standing. On the floor, Martha lay with the pistol against her chest. Her eyes were closed and her face smooth of anger and madness. Beneath her, blood pooled onto the floor.

# Twenty

Neville sat on the edge of the desk in Priscilla's study. "Why does it always seem so obvious in retrospect?"

"None of us suspected Martha of being capable of such attacks." Priscilla stared at her garden. "But she did have a way to get into my garden, and none of us recall seeing her at the bonfire on the shore."

"When she had the opportunity to steal both sets of church records and attack Kenyon. If she had not ransacked your parlor, she might have had time to kill him, too."

"I agree with Constable Forshaw. She was not interested in who had been born or died. She wanted the registers to discover the names of those men who had joined the company raised in Stonehall-on-Sea and left with the duke to fight in the colonies."

He laughed shortly. "And she got the very opportunity she needed when Wallingford decided to have an assembly, and I was fool enough to invite her to go along to vex your aunt."

"But if you had not invited Martha to Wallingford Manor, we might never have discovered the truth."

"Thanks, Pris, for trying to spare my feelings."

"Your dignity *does* look a bit bruised."

He put his hand on the back of her chair. "When I

got a bruise when I was a lad, my mother used to have a way to make me feel better."

She smiled up at him. "Is that so?"

As he bent toward her, his eyes warming, he said, "Yes, a kiss to . . ."

A knock on the door halted him. She came to her feet and called, "Come in."

Gilbert, his face as serene as always, said, "My lady, His Grace the Duke of Meresden wishes to speak with you and Sir Neville."

She looked at Neville as Gilbert ushered the duke into her study. She greeted the duke, who looked the pattern-card of fashion in his fashionable black coat and brightly embroidered waistcoat.

"Your expression tells me that you did not expect me to call," the duke said bluntly.

"It *is* a surprise, Your Grace," she replied.

He shuffled one foot, looking as guilty as Isaac did when caught in some misdeed. "I have had time to consider the events that have taken place."

"Will you sit?" She motioned toward a chair, then glanced at Mrs. Moore who, from the doorway, was staring wide-eyed at the duke. "Mrs. Moore, would you bring tea please?"

"At this hour?" The housekeeper clamped her mouth closed as the duke looked at her, astonished.

Priscilla smiled. "Now is as good a time as any." The informality of her household was not something she would apologize for, because she liked it as it was.

The duke sat when she did. Again Neville stayed on his feet, and she was grateful to know that he would be ready for whatever had brought the duke here.

"I understand Ackerley has left Stonehall-on-Sea," the duke said.

"Yes. He has been offered a teaching position at Elsworth Academy." Her lips twitched.

Mr. Pritchard had come quickly in response to her summons and had just as swiftly agreed to hire Mr. Ackerley when Neville reminded the headmaster again of how his school would be ruined if his students' parents learned of Mr. Pritchard's sojourn to the public house. Neville vowed to forget the whole event if Mr. Ackerley was offered a position at Elsworth Academy.

"I owe you an apology for not believing your assertions that you were not guilty of my father's murder," the duke said.

"And I owe you the same, Your Grace, for I did suspect you of the crime until I heard of your relationship with Miss Boch."

"*Mrs.* Boch," Neville said softly.

The duke flushed. "I thought I should do more than express my apologies, Lady Priscilla. I have heard that you are considering which school your son will attend."

"Yes."

"I attended Langley Academy, which is not more than a day's ride from Stonehall-on-Sea. If you wish, I would be pleased to offer a recommendation for your son."

"That is kind of you."

"Consider it an apology for comments I have made."

"Comments?"

Color exploded up his face, and she knew he had not intended to reveal that. Although she saw Neville's eyes twinkling and knew he would enjoy making the duke fidget a bit longer—as she would—she smiled and said, "I think it would be for the best for everyone if we learn to forget more easily the wrongs done to us in the past."

The Duke of Meresden nodded in eager agreement

and began to talk with Neville about a new horse he had purchased to begin breeding a line of race horses at Meresden Court.

Priscilla was glad when the duke took his leave.

As she turned to Neville, he said, "You look very pleased with yourself."

"Why not? Langley Academy is the best school for boys in this part of England. Isaac would be close enough to visit home often, and—" She grinned wickedly. "Aunt Cordelia is going to have to eat her words that I am not the best mother for the current Earl of Emberson."

"It's clearly a feast you look forward to serving."

"Most definitely, and I assume you would like to be a witness to that conversation."

He gave her that beguiling, cockeyed smile. "I would, and I suspect I'll be here to see it."

"So you're staying a while longer?"

"I haven't done all I came here to do."

"And what is it you've left unfinished?" she asked.

Stroking her cheek, he said, "I think I'll let you guess for a bit longer, Pris. Do you think your aunt will enjoy tea or brandy more with her meal of crow?"

She put her hand up to her cheek as he winked and went out, calling for her butler. Neville would not tell her what he meant until he was ready. She hoped by that time, she would be ready, too.

# AUTHOR'S NOTE

I hope you have enjoyed the first of Priscilla and Neville's partnerships as sleuths. Their adventures continue in January 2003 with *Grave Intentions*. When Priscilla brings her family back to London for the end of the Season, she does not expect to discover a murderer stalking Bedford Square. But it is only when she and Neville begin to dig into the mystery that they learn that murder is only one of the crimes one desperate person is willing to commit. She is sure they can solve the puzzle if only she could concentrate on the clues instead of how Neville's touch brings feelings she never expected to experience again. . . .

Readers can contact me at:

P.O. Box 575
Rehoboth, MA 02769

or visit my web site at:
www.joannferguson.com.

# More Zebra Regency Romances